PRAISE FOR
BETH KENDRICK'S NOVELS

The Bake-Off

"A warm, winning story about the complications of sisterhood—and the unexpected rewards."   —Sarah Pekkanen, author of *Skipping a Beat*

"Two estranged sisters about as likely to bond as water and oil. A fun book with more twists and turns than a three-layer marble cake."
—Susan Miller, 2000 Pillsbury Bake-Off finalist and winner of
Nabisco's 1999 "Build a Better S'Mores" contest

"Wonderful! Kendrick manages to cook up a tender, touching, and very funny story about the complicated relationship of two sisters torn apart by their own stubbornness and brought back together by love and pastry. With a fresh plot and richly layered characters, *The Bake-Off* is a winner."
—Ellen Meister, author of *The Other Life*

Second Time Around

"Kendrick deftly blends exceptionally clever writing, subtly nuanced characters, and a generous dash of romance into a flawlessly written story about the importance of female friendships and second chances."   —*Chicago Tribune*

"Smart and fun, this is my favorite book this year."
—Jane Porter, author of *She's Gone Country*

"A touching and humorous look at love, loss, and literature."   —*Booklist*

"Extremely engaging . . . [Kendrick's] characters were easy to fall in love with."
—Night Owl Reviews

continued . . .

"Kendrick is an undeniably practiced hand at depicting female bonds."
—*Publishers Weekly*

"A funny, charming story about the power of female friendship, and a must-read for all English majors, past and present."
— Kim Gruenenfelder, author of *Misery Loves Cabernet*

The Pre-nup

"In the exceptionally entertaining and wonderfully original *The Pre-nup*, Kendrick writes with a wicked sense of humor and great wisdom about the power of friendship, the importance of true love, and the very real satisfaction of romantic revenge done right."
—*Chicago Tribune*

"The three female leads all captivate."
—*Romantic Times*

"[A] highly entertaining story."
—Fresh Fiction

"[Kendrick's] heroines are easy to like."
—*Booklist*

"Clever, wise, and wonderful, *The Pre-nup* is Beth Kendrick at her best."
—Jane Porter

"Witty, juicy, and lots of fun! Say 'I do' to *The Pre-nup*."
—Susan Mallery, *New York Times* bestselling author of *The Best of Friends*

"A smart, funny spin on happily-ever-after!"
—Beth Harbison, *New York Times* bestselling
author of *Secrets of a Shoe Addict*

Nearlyweds

"A fun and funny look at marriage, commitment, and figuring out what your next best step is . . . whether it be down the aisle or not."
—Alison Pace, author of *City Dog*

"Very funny." —Carole Matthews, author of *The Chocolate Lovers' Club*

Fashionably Late

"Wickedly clever." —*Booklist*

"Kendrick gives chick lit clichés an adroit turn." —*Publishers Weekly*

"Kendrick's keen sense of humor and pitch-perfect gift for dialogue are excellent accessories to this fun and frothy tale." —*Chicago Tribune*

ALSO BY BETH KENDRICK

Second Time Around

The Pre-nup

Nearlyweds

Fashionably Late

Exes and Ohs

My Favorite Mistake

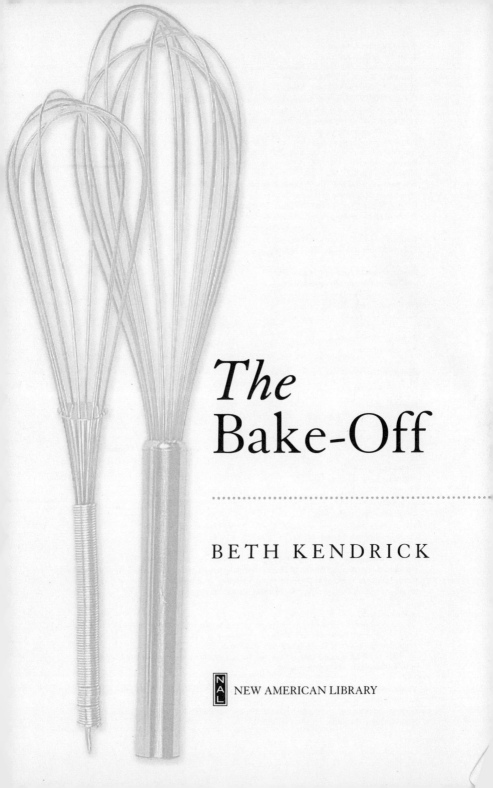

The
Bake-Off

BETH KENDRICK

NEW AMERICAN LIBRARY

NEW AMERICAN LIBRARY
Published by New American Library, a division of
Penguin Group (USA) Inc., 375 Hudson Street,
New York, New York 10014, USA
Penguin Group (Canada), 90 Eglinton Avenue East, Suite 700, Toronto,
Ontario M4P 2Y3, Canada (a division of Pearson Penguin Canada Inc.)
Penguin Books Ltd., 80 Strand, London WC2R 0RL, England
Penguin Ireland, 25 St. Stephen's Green, Dublin 2,
Ireland (a division of Penguin Books Ltd.)
Penguin Group (Australia), 250 Camberwell Road, Camberwell, Victoria 3124,
Australia (a division of Pearson Australia Group Pty. Ltd.)
Penguin Books India Pvt. Ltd., 11 Community Centre, Panchsheel Park,
New Delhi - 110 017, India
Penguin Group (NZ), 67 Apollo Drive, Rosedale, North Shore 0632,
New Zealand (a division of Pearson New Zealand Ltd.)
Penguin Books (South Africa) (Pty.) Ltd., 24 Sturdee Avenue,
Rosebank, Johannesburg 2196, South Africa

Penguin Books Ltd., Registered Offices:
80 Strand, London WC2R 0RL, England

First published by New American Library,
a division of Penguin Group (USA) Inc.

First Printing, May 2011
10   9   8   7   6   5   4   3   2   1

 REGISTERED TRADEMARK—MARCA REGISTRADA

LIBRARY OF CONGRESS CATALOGING-IN-PUBLICATION DATA:
Kendrick, Beth.
   The bake-off/Beth Kendrick.
      p. cm.
   ISBN 978-0-451-23310-3
   1. Sisters—Fiction.   2. Baking—Fiction.   3. Family secrets—Fiction.   4. Domestic
fiction.   I. Title.
   PS3611.E535B35 2011
   813'.6—dc22   2010053454

Set in Granjon
Designed by Spring Hoteling

Printed in the United States of America

PUBLISHER'S NOTE
This is a work of fiction. Names, characters, places, and incidents either are the product of the author's
imagination or are used fictitiously, and any resemblance to actual persons, living or dead, business
establishments, events, or locales is entirely coincidental.
   The publisher does not have any control over and does not assume any responsibility for author
or third-party Web sites or their content.

For Bridget and Joe, my brilliant and beautiful siblings

Secret Sisterhood Szarlotka

ANNOTATED BY AMY BIALEK NICHOLS

SUGGESTED SOUND TRACK: *Beastie Boys' Licensed to Ill, B-52s' Cosmic Thing*

Ingredients:

For the crust

> 2 ½ cups all-purpose flour
>
> ½ cup ultrafine sugar (also known as "baker's sugar")
>
> ¼ teaspoon salt
>
> 14 tablespoons unsalted butter, chilled
>
> 3 egg yolks
>
> 3 tablespoons sour cream

For the apple filling

> 6–7 (3 pounds) large apples—mostly Granny Smith, with one or two Fuji thrown in for variety
>
> 1 tablespoon freshly squeezed lemon juice
>
> ½ cup granulated sugar
>
> 3 tablespoons unsalted butter
>
> 1 teaspoon cinnamon
>
> ¼ teaspoon nutmeg
>
> ⅛ teaspoon allspice

Instructions:

Watch a few hours of the Food Network and/or *Top Chef*. Say to yourself, "How hard can this really be? It's just *pie*."

Have a glass of wine and give yourself a pep talk. Then get to work on the crust.

First, cut the butter into small cubes and store in the refrigerator. The key to light, flaky piecrust is to keep the butter as cold as possible throughout the prep and rolling process. Whenever the dough starts to get warm and difficult to handle, pop it back in the fridge—or even the freezer—for a few minutes.

Using a fork, beat the sour cream into the egg yolks. Blend just enough to combine—it's fine if the mixture is still streaky. Put the egg mixture aside in the fridge for now.

Food processor method

Combine the flour, sugar, and salt in a food processor and pulse a few times to combine the dry ingredients. Add the cold butter and pulse in quick spurts until the mixture reaches the "small pea stage"—that is, there are visible pea-size pieces of coated butter surrounded by tiny, mealy crumbs.

Add the egg-yolk mixture and pulse a few more times to combine the dry and wet ingredients. **Do not overprocess.** The dough should still look mealy and clumpy, but should stick together when you squeeze it in your hand. If the dough does not stick together and instead feels crumbly and dry, try adding another tiny dollop of sour cream.

Stand mixer method

What's that? You say Martha Stewart doesn't live at your house and you don't own a food processor? No problem! Julia Child used to make piecrust with a stand mixer, and if it's good enough for Julia, it's good enough for me.

If you're using a stand mixer, you're going to combine the ingredients in the same order as described above, but you're going to use the flat paddle attachment for your mixer, and you're going to use the very slowest setting on the mixer—"stir." Again, be careful not to overmix—you should aim for about 1–2 minutes to reach the "small pea stage," and maybe another 1–2 minutes after you add the wet ingredients.

Both methods
Once the dough has been mixed, pour it onto a cutting board or sheet of waxed paper and form a large ball. Knead it by pushing down in the center, then pushing in from the sides, about five times. Separate about one-third of the dough from the rest, form the two sections into thick disks, wrap the disks tightly in plastic wrap, and chill in refrigerator for at least 30 minutes.

Resist the temptation to go watch E! for half an hour and instead get started on the apple filling.

Apple filling
Peel, core, and cut up the apples into cubes. Cubes should be about 1 inch square, but there's no need to get all crazy and precise—it's supposed to be rustic.

Place the apple chunks into a large mixing bowl. Drizzle on the lemon juice and mix thoroughly. Go ahead and use your hands—Martha Stewart doesn't live here, remember? Sprinkle on the sugar and mix again.

Melt the 3 tablespoons of butter in a large, deep sauté pan. Add the apple chunks and cook for 15 minutes over medium heat, stirring constantly. The apples should get soft and tender, but not smooshy (that's a technical term). After 15 minutes, take the pan off the burner, sprinkle the cinnamon, nutmeg, and allspice on top of the apple chunks, and stir. Set aside to cool. Now would be a great time to check your e-mail and your favorite celebrity gossip blog.

Putting it all together
Preheat the oven to 400 degrees.

No more stalling—it's time to roll out the crust. Gather your materials: a sturdy rolling pin or dowel, a small bowl of all-purpose flour, a long offset metal spatula, a glass pie plate (about 9 inches in diameter), a cheese grater, and a large cutting board or clean countertop. Resist the urge to break out the premade crust you bought at the grocery store under cover of night, and remember: There's no crying in pie baking.

Retrieve the larger dough disk from the fridge and dust your work surface with flour. Starting from the center of the disk, roll the dough into a circle large enough to cover the entire pie plate and drape over the sides. The rolled dough should be thin enough for you to see a patterned cutting board underneath. Ideally, you want your crust to have visible butter striations. If you can't see them at first, have another glass of wine and check again.

Place the crust into the pie plate. You could try rolling it onto your rolling pin like wrapping paper and then "unwrapping" it into your pie plate. Or you could scrape it up with the offset spatula, fold it in half lengthwise and then into quarters, and unfold it in the pie plate. Trim off any excess dough hanging over the rim of the plate.

Using a slotted spoon, transfer the apple chunks from the sauté pan into the crust. Discard any leftover liquid in the pan—do not pour it into the pie. Use the spoon to press down on the apple chunks and pack them in tightly.

Place the pie on a metal cookie sheet (bonus points if you put a silicone baking mat between the tray and the pie plate). Bake at 400 degrees for 20 minutes. **Note: Baking time varies wildly depending on the eccentricities of your particular oven.**

While the pie is baking, retrieve the remaining ball of dough from the fridge and grate it. Yes, really. Pretend you're preparing a block of mozzarella for pizza topping.

After 20 minutes, remove the pie from the oven and sprinkle a thin layer of grated dough across the top of the apples. See? It really is just like making pizza. Try to cover all the exposed apples, and don't forget the edges. Pop the pie back into the oven and bake for an additional 20–25 minutes.

Try to restrain yourself long enough to avoid scorching your tongue, then grab a fork and dig in. Feign modesty when everyone in your house raves about your culinary genius after they recover from their paroxysms of pastry-induced bliss. Imagine Martha Stewart writhing with envy. Realize that you have now used up everything in your refrigerator and go out for dinner. Your work here is done.

The
Bake-Off

Chapter 1

"Honey, I hope my luck is half as hot as you are," slurred the Hawaiian-shirted frat boy as he studied the pair of cards in front of him on the casino table. "Hit me."

Linnie Bialek kept her expression neutral and her eyes lowered as she flipped over the top card in the deck.

The frat boy woo-hooed and high-fived the guy hunched on the stool next to him. "Hit me again!"

Imbecile.

"Double down," intoned the sidekick. "Double dooooown!"

Frat boy pounded the table. "Yeah, okay. I'll double down."

"I'm sorry, sir, but you no longer have the option to double down; you have more than two cards." Linnie squirmed as the top of her leopard-print bustier dug into the tender skin under her arms. This corset, along with black satin hot pants, fishnet stockings, black patent-leather Mary Jane pumps, and furry cat ears comprised her outfit as a dealer in the "Kitty Korner," the casino's newest marketing ploy: a secluded, cordoned-off area for high rollers who liked a bit of T & A served up along with their complimentary cocktails.

"If I get twenty-one, can I buy you a drink?"

Linnie shook her head. "I'm not allowed to accept drinks from customers."

He stopped hooting and hollering and started to pout. "Are you allowed to smile, at least?"

Linnie tried to force her features into a happy expression. She slapped down the top card with a little extra vigor. "Bust. House wins."

She stepped back from the table and made way for Sasha, the olive-skinned brunette who'd materialized next to her. "That's it; my shift's over. Best of luck to you both."

Linnie brushed off her hands and splayed her fingers so that the tiny bubble "eye in the sky" could ascertain that she hadn't palmed anything during play. Then she slipped past the velvet ropes and into the crowds playing slots.

"Honey!" Hawaiian Shirt howled after her. "Wait! Come back and I'll give you a tip you'll never forget!"

Please. As if she'd ever look twice at a man who hit on seventeen when the dealer was showing a four. There wasn't enough alcohol in the world to excuse that level of dumb-assery.

After working at the blackjack tables for several months, Linnie knew she should be accustomed to reckless bets, but she never ceased to be shocked by how poorly most people understood the natural order of the universe. Many casino games, like craps, black-jack, poker, and baccarat, were not games of chance at all. If you had even a rudimentary grasp of probability and statistics, you could beat the house, provided you were patient and rational in your approach.

But people didn't want a clean, calculated formula for winning. They wanted "luck."

Well, Linnie didn't believe in luck. She believed in logic.

As she strode toward the employee locker room, her heel caught on a loose flap of rug, and she stumbled into a young couple watching the action at a craps table.

"Sorry." She steadied herself, then leaned down to adjust the ankle strap of her shoe.

The male half of the couple did a double take when she straightened up. "Hey. Don't I know you from somewhere?"

"I don't think so." Linnie studied the couple's features, trying to place them. He was short and pudgy, but his charcoal gray suit was obviously expensive, cut to camouflage an imperfect physique. His companion was a willowy redhead clad in a Grecian-inspired white minidress that looked fresh off the rack from one of the Strip's couture shops.

"I know I know you," the guy went on. "What's your name? It's Russian, right? Kind of weird and unpronounceable?"

The longer she stared at him, the more familiar he looked. Linnie lowered her gaze. "I think you have me confused with someone else."

"I'm Sam Janowitz," he said.

She shrugged one shoulder. "Doesn't ring any bells."

Sam snapped his fingers. "I've got it. Science enrichment camp.

Palo Alto, late nineties. You're the girl who whupped all the boys at chess, right?"

"No." *Not anymore.*

"Vaseline! Your name sounds like Vaseline."

"Vasylina," Linnie corrected faintly. She ducked her head so she wouldn't have to watch his expression, which vacillated between disbelief and pity. "And it's Polish, not Russian."

There was a long pause; then he coughed. "So you, gosh, you work here now, huh?" Sam opened and closed his mouth a few times before finally saying, "I went to school for aerospace engineering, but then I sold out and joined up with a hedge fund firm in Manhattan." He fiddled with his cuff links. "I'm out here for a corporate retreat. This is my wife, Mia."

"Nice to meet you." Linnie nodded at the redhead but didn't extend her hand.

Mia gave her a quick once-over, took in the polyester corset and the cleavage, and managed a trace of a smile. "I like your ears. Very frisky."

"We're late for our dinner reservations. We'd better get going." Sam tugged his wife forward and stole one last glance back over his shoulder. "Great seeing you. Good luck with everything."

"You, too." Linnie remained rooted to the carpet.

As Sam turned away, she heard him exclaim to his wife, "That girl is like Doogie Howser trapped in Barbie's body. No exaggeration. She started college when she was fourteen."

Mia sniffed. "Then why is she dressed like a day-shift call girl?"

"Beats me. But I'm telling you, back then, she was Little Miss Priss with an ego the size of a particle accelerator. She told everyone she was going to finish her MD before she was old enough to drink. I wonder what the hell happened to her."

"Don't freak out about the smell. I can explain."

Linnie froze in her apartment doorway, keys in hand. She had been looking forward to curling up in her pajamas and unwinding with an iced coffee and a DVD of the Met's production of *Manon Lescaut*. By herself.

But her roommate, Kyle, was sprawled out across the sofa, peering up at her through shaggy blond bangs with a sheepish smile on his face and a bottle of Febreze in his hand. He looked like a puppy who'd spent the afternoon shredding a box of Kleenex and scattering the wreckage all over the house.

"What happened in here?" She stepped into the living room, surveying the splintered coffee table, crumpled cans of beer, and mysterious new stains on the carpet.

"A bunch of the guys came over. It was my turn to host the VGOs."

"VGOs?"

"Video Game Olympics. We do it every year. My brother, Derek, even drove in from SoCal." Kyle struggled up into a sitting position to get a better look at her new work uniform. "Why are you dressed like a slutty cat?"

She instinctively tried to cover herself from his stare, but between the exposed cleavage, the exposed thighs, and the semi-exposed bottom, she didn't have enough hands. "I started my new job today, remember?"

Kyle let out a whistle of appreciation. "Well, you look *fiiine*. I had no idea you had an ass like that."

She pinned him with a glacial glare. "Don't you ever look at my ass again."

He looked away, muttering, "Someone needs to lighten up."

She stalked across the living room to the apartment's tiny kitchen, perused the nearly empty cupboard shelves, and tossed a bag of artificially flavored butter popcorn in the microwave for dinner. "How long have we known each other? Ten years? Twelve? If I were going to lighten up, it would have happened by now."

Linnie had first met Kyle when she responded to a classified ad for an economics tutor. At sixteen, she'd just dropped out of a top-rated university, and at nineteen, he'd just enrolled in community college. On the surface, the two of them couldn't have been more different. Kyle had enjoyed a brief bout of fame and fortune when he was seven years old, hamming it up in a series of national potato chip commercials. Though he'd never landed another major role after that, his parents had yanked him out of public school to appear at an endless series of casting calls and auditions. He and Linnie had both missed out on a huge, formative piece of their childhoods, and their student-tutor dynamic had evolved into an unlikely camaraderie. Two years ago, after finally being dropped by his Manhattan talent agency, Kyle had relocated to Vegas to take a role in a murder mystery dinner theater, and he'd persuaded Linnie to join him (he'd claimed he valued her companionship, but she suspected he just needed help making rent).

But camaraderie went only so far. While Linnie had been pathetically grateful for any scrap of social acceptance ten years ago, her tolerance for Kyle and his perpetual adolescence had worn thin now that they shared living space. She had applied for the promotion to the Kitty Korner specifically so that she could earn higher tips and afford her own apartment.

Kyle resumed his explanation of the trashed apartment. "So, yeah, a bunch of the guys came over for our Video Game Olympics—it's awesome; the winner gets to wear a yellow jersey like Lance Armstrong—and you earn points by getting the highest scores in the games, but you also get bonus points for drinking."

Linnie handed him a coaster as she sat down on a clean patch of sofa. "I assume 'the guys' will all be chipping in to purchase a new coffee table."

He glanced at the fractured wood as if noticing it for the first time. "Oh. I guess so. Anyway, we decided that since the winner got a yellow jersey, the loser should have to wear a pink one. But I don't have any pink shirts, so Matt said we should check your room."

Linnie lunged off the couch and bolted for her bedroom.

"What did you do?" She froze in her doorway, stricken by the sight of the contents of her closet strewn across the floor.

Next to her, Kyle forced a chuckle. "Turns out you don't have a pink shirt, either. I told Derek to clean up in here before he went home, but I guess he didn't have time to finish."

Linnie knelt down, gathered up an armful of sweatshirts, and was mentally composing the overture to her symphony of vitriol when she noticed the books stacked on her nightstand: a biography of Carl Sagan, *The Joy of Cooking*, and a dog-eared paperback edition of *The Iliad*.

Her breath caught. "Who touched my books?"

Kyle scratched the stubble on his chin. "What books?"

"The Joy of Cooking." She pointed. "It was on the bottom of that pile, and now it's in the middle."

He shrugged. "The guys must've knocked it over, but, like I said, we tried to clean up a little bit. Why are you all emotional? It's not like you ever cook."

The backs of her arms went hot and prickly. "Point A: I'm not emotional. Point B: It's not about the cookbook; it's about what's *inside* the cookbook."

She grabbed the book and flipped through the first few pages to show him how she'd hollowed out the appetizer and main-course chapters with a razor blade to create a hiding place for the only material object that had any real value to her.

Kyle's eyes widened when he spied the rectangular blue velvet box nestled in a berth of black-and-white text. "That's so James Bond. What's in there?"

Linnie skimmed the pads of her fingers across the cool, smooth page and the warm, soft velvet. This cookbook had been a bit of wishful thinking on her grandmother's part. On the morning Linnie started college, Grammy Syl had presented her with two beautifully wrapped packages, along with a note: *Congratulations to my brilliant granddaughter. I hope this gift will provide a connection to your past as you embark on your bright future. P.S. Don't forget to eat. I recommend starting with the hard-boiled eggs and working your way up to the main courses.*

The first gift had been this cookbook.

The second was an antique brooch crafted over a century ago by a master silversmith who'd designed jewelry for Russian royalty.

She pried out the jewelry box and opened the lid, instructing, "You may look, but you may not touch."

But the box was empty.

For a moment, her mind went completely blank.

"Linnie?" Kyle's voice sounded tinny and distant. "Hey, are you okay?"

Her panic returned in full force, along with a sickening sense of vertigo. The room seemed to sway around her, and she braced one hand against the wall for support as she gazed down at the slotted blue velvet padding.

"Maybe it fell out onto the floor," Kyle was saying. "It's probably hiding under a shirt somewhere."

Linnie forced herself to wait until she regained her balance before responding. "My grandmother's brooch is not *hiding*. One of your Neanderthal friends lost it while you were pawing through my personal effects in a blatant violation of my trust."

He edged toward the doorway. "Listen, seriously, I know you're upset, but your voice is all growly and your face isn't moving, and you're kind of scaring me."

She continued to glare at him, and he stammered, "If you kill me, you won't have anyone to help you look." He paused. "What am I looking for, anyway?"

"A one-of-a-kind platinum brooch studded with rare cognac diamonds."

He blinked a few times.

"Silver metal and brown stones." She pointed imperiously at the carpet. "Stop standing around and start searching. Move!"

But a careful excavation of the debris on the bedroom floor yielded nothing. Linnie scoured every centimeter of every article of clothing that had been displaced; Kyle lifted the bed frame and the bureau so she could check beneath them, but all to no avail.

Grammy Syl's brooch had vanished.

"You are going to call every person who was in this apartment last night, we are going to corral them in this room, and I am going to grill them until I get my brooch back."

"Okay, okay. I'll start with Derek. Maybe he put it somewhere for safekeeping when he was cleaning up. Maybe he—" Kyle's expression flickered. "Uh-oh."

"What?"

"Nothing."

She took a single step toward him. "Out with it. Now."

Kyle fidgeted with the belt loops on his baggy cargo shorts. "It's just . . . you know how every family has a screwup?"

Linnie flinched, painfully aware that she herself filled that role in the Bialek clan. "Go on."

"Well, Derek doesn't have the best track record, and he's been having some pretty heavy problems lately with his house and his wife."

"And?" she prompted.

"I'm sure it's just lost. I'm sure it's around here somewhere."

She took off her shoe and imagined wedging it down his throat. "Find a phone and start dialing."

Kyle retreated to the living room while Linnie started yet another inch-by-inch search of the floor and the closet. When he returned, his sheepish smile had been replaced with a dazed expression of dawning horror.

"Derek knows where your brooch is."

Linnie nodded, not trusting herself to speak.

"It's in a pawnshop." Kyle stared at his bare feet. "Someplace out by the Strip called Longbourne Jewelry and Loan."

She nodded again. "So he stole it."

When Kyle started to plead with her, she got a glimpse of the winsome little boy who had sold millions of bags of potato chips with his earnest charm. "He knows he shouldn't have done it, okay? He knows that. And as pissed as you are right now, I'm just as mad. But you have to believe me when I tell you that the guy has, like, an avalanche of financial problems. He lost his job; he's losing his house; his wife just found out she's pregnant."

Linnie pressed her fingers against her temples and inhaled deeply through her nose. "We are going to the pawnshop right now, and we are going to get the brooch back. Where's the claim ticket?"

"Derek's going to send it to me."

"Incorrect. He's going to give it to me when he meets me at the pawnshop."

"He's already on the road to California."

"Tell him to turn around and get back here with his ill-gotten money."

"Well, here's the thing. He went to the bank as soon as it opened. Tomorrow is the first of the month, Linnie. He's out of time. He's been putting off foreclosure for months already."

The pounding of her pulse began to amplify in her ears. "Exactly how much money did he get for the brooch?"

"Thirty-five grand."

She clamped her lips together and bit down so hard she tasted blood. If a pawnshop had paid thirty-five thousand, the actual value of the piece had to be at least twice that amount. Grammy Syl could never find out about this. Linnie had disappointed too many people already.

"Derek says we have thirty days to pay it back, plus a bunch of interest and fees," Kyle was saying. "Grand total should be around forty or forty-five thousand."

"Who is this 'we' you keep referencing?"

"Us—Derek and me." Kyle hunched over, his hands in his pockets. "Try to calm down and get a little perspective. He's got a family to support."

"That doesn't justify stealing. Kyle, what do you suggest I do here? I don't have forty-five thousand dollars. I don't have anywhere near that, and neither do you."

"We'll pay you back, I promise." Kyle lifted his hand in a throwback to the Boy Scout oath. "It might take us ten years, but we'll pay you back."

She shook her head. "Ten years is unacceptable. I have thirty days before the pawnshop can resell it, with interest and penalties accruing by the minute."

"I'll straighten everything out—I promise." Kyle sounded like he was trying to convince himself. "I'm going to land a big role any day now; I can feel it. A TV role, maybe a movie."

Linnie started toward the kitchen. "I'm calling the police."

He raced ahead of her, snatching up the cordless phone by the entryway. "Don't do that. Please. *Please*. There has to be another way to work this out."

"How? The pawnshop's not going to return that piece to me without a police report."

Kyle finally realized she was implacable. His whole body slumped and he dropped the receiver onto the counter with a clatter. "I guess you have to do what you have to do. But tell them I did it, okay?"

Linnie froze, her fingers poised over the phone's keypad. "What?"

"Tell them I was the one who took the jewelry without your permission and pawned it. They can arrest me instead of Derek."

"Absolutely not. Your brother needs to take responsibility for his actions. Why would you—"

"He's got a family and a life and everything, and I don't." Kyle swallowed audibly. "He wouldn't have done this unless he was really at the end of his rope."

Linnie put down the phone, torn between blinding rage and helpless despair. "And you're willing to take the blame for something you didn't even do?"

12

Kyle scuffed the carpet with his toe. "Yeah."

"You can't do that. I won't let you."

"What do you care? You'll still get your jewelry back."

"But letting him take advantage of you like this isn't doing him any favors in the long run. Trust me. It's . . ." Linnie looked away and dug her fingernails into her palms. "It's *wrong*. Not to mention extremely dysfunctional."

"It's not dysfunctional." Kyle stuck out his chin, suddenly defiant. "It's love. It's family."

"You're putting me in an impossible situation here."

"Well, I don't see any other way to get your thing back." Kyle's eyes lit up. "Unless . . ."

Linnie folded her arms. "Unless what?"

"Unless you go gambling."

"No."

"Yes! You could hit the high rollers' table tonight and win fifty grand, easy. I know you could."

She almost laughed at the absurdity of this suggestion. "No, no, a thousand times no. I don't gamble."

"Why not? Just 'cause you're a casino dealer doesn't mean you can't play."

"Being a dealer isn't the issue."

"Then what is the issue?"

She inhaled as deeply as her tightly laced corset would allow. "I just don't. Let's leave it at that."

"Dude, what is the point of having an IQ of a hundred and seventy if you're too wussy to use it when you really need it?"

"It's one eighty," she corrected him.

"You can win. I know you can." He turned on those puppy dog eyes again. "Have a little faith. Give my brother a break. And hey, think about your karma. What goes around comes around, right?"

Linnie's stomach clenched. *That's what I'm afraid of.*

"Texas Hold 'Em, two-hundred-dollar minimum, no limit," the dealer announced when Linnie approached the gaming table. "You want in?"

Linnie hesitated only a fraction of a second before nodding and depositing a stack of black chips on the green felt surface in front of her. She'd just written a check to the casino cashier, and this dismayingly short pile of chips represented the entirety of her savings account, along with a significant cash advance from her credit card.

She'd worn a baggy jacket to cover her body and a baseball cap to obscure her face, but she couldn't hide the fact that her entire body was trembling. High-stakes, cutthroat competitions like this used to send her spirit soaring and her adrenaline surging, but that was before she knew how it felt to fail.

Pure icy panic seeped through her as she sank into her seat. Failure was not an option tonight. She would win, again and again and again.

While she waited for her first batch of cards, she sized up the other players at the table. These six guys looked like expense-account rookies, out for a little male bonding and bragging rights. She surmised from their crisp tailored shirts and European watches that they could afford to lose at two-hundred-dollar-a-hand poker.

She ignored their speculative smiles and devoted her full attention to her cards. Throughout the first few hands, she played very cautiously, hedging her bets and observing her tablemates' styles and skill levels. As her stacks of chips grew taller, she got bolder with her bets and cagier at calling bluffs. Her body stopped shaking and her death grip on her cards relaxed.

Over the next three hours, she doubled her money, then tripled it. Her male opponents had long ago acknowledged her superiority and seemed almost honored to lose to her.

"You're good," said the broad-shouldered Bostonian sporting the gold Rolex. "Are you a professional poker player?"

She stared down at the table, refusing to be distracted. "No. Beginner's luck."

The redhead with a smattering of freckles across his nose and a Patek Philippe on his wrist asked, "Have you ever watched the World Series of Poker on ESPN? You should enter that. Even if you didn't win, you could be the official spokesmodel."

This time, she did get distracted. She slouched deeper into her oversize wool jacket, and before she could come up with a response, a tall, dark Adonis reeking of Scotch and cigar smoke lurched into the empty seat next to her and announced his arrival with a long, guttural belch.

"'Scuse me." He pounded his chest and shot the dealer a cocky grin as he tossed down a fistful of five-hundred-dollar chips.

Linnie wrinkled her nose and inched away.

The other guys glanced at one another and exchanged curt nods. "Last time around for me, guys," the Bostonian announced.

"Yeah," another agreed. "Let's grab breakfast and go crash."

Then Linnie saw the opportunity she'd been waiting for all night: Between her hole cards and the community cards lined up in front of the dealer, she had three tens and two twos. A full house. She could tell from the other players' glum expressions that they posed no threat. The boozehound next to her didn't even try to maintain a straight face. He peeked at his hand and cursed loudly, then let loose with another thundering belch.

She did some quick calculations and concluded that, if she went all in on this hand and convinced the other players to bet high as well, she'd win enough money to buy back Grammy Syl's brooch. Unlike many other high-stakes players, she knew when to quit. She wouldn't get reckless or greedy; she'd cash out immediately and head straight to the pawnshop.

After three rounds of betting, she made her move.

"I'm all in." She pushed her entire stash of chips toward the center of the table.

The members of the yacht club crew pulled back and conceded defeat:

"Guess I'll quit while I'm ahead."

"Me, too. You've cleaned us out."

The interloper to Linnie's left slammed down his glass, spattering drops of amber liquid across the tabletop. "Damn, cutie, how much did you just bet there?"

She adjusted the brim of her baseball cap. "Approximately twelve thousand dollars."

"You got a hand worth twelve grand? For real?" He wiped his mouth on the back of his hand. "This I gotta see. Call!"

She waited while the dealer turned over her cards, then smiled triumphantly. "Full house."

"Well, shit, you got me beat. All I got's a pair of twos. I need another drink, stat."

Linnie stood up to rake in her winnings, but froze when her seatmate's cards were revealed.

The dealer cleared his throat. "Sir, you have four twos."

"Yeah. Two pairs of twos. So?"

"That's four of a kind, sir," the dealer said patiently. "You win."

"Wha'?" The blowhard's bleary-eyed gaze flitted from the cards in front of him to the cards in front of the dealer. "Oh, yeah, I guess you're right. Would you look at that? Four of a kind! Woo! What are the odds?"

"Less than one-fiftieth of one percent!" Linnie cried. "It's statistically impossible."

Players at neighboring tables started to turn around and take notice as her voice got increasingly shrill.

"Things like this do not happen. Not in real life. Nobody actually wins the lottery or gets hit by lightning or gets four of a kind in a poker hand." But even as she said this, Linnie had a flashback to one of her professors reciting the cardinal rule of probability theory: *Statistics don't apply to individual cases.*

"Ma'am," said the dealer, "I'm going to have to ask you to settle down."

Linnie snapped. After hours of holding herself in check, she burst into loud, body-racking sobs.

Five minutes later, she had been hustled outside by a floor manager and banished to the cabstand with a box of tissues. Shivering in the cold night wind, she flipped open her cell phone and reached out to her only remaining source of hope, the woman who always seemed to have an ace up her sleeve.

Grammy Syl answered on the second ring. "Linnie, darling, good morning! I'm so glad to finally hear from you again. How *are* you?"

Linnie opened her mouth to confess everything, but couldn't bear the thought of Grammy's reproach. Her voice dropped to a whisper as she haltingly tried to convey the extent of her plight without revealing that she'd lost the heirloom that had been entrusted to her.

"What's that, darling? I'm afraid you'll have to speak up."

"It's a long story, Grammy, but basically, I need to make money. A lot of money. The sooner the better."

"But why?" Grammy sounded alarmed. "What's happened?"

"I can't tell you."

"Are you in some kind of trouble? Are you sick?"

Linnie closed her eyes, burning with shame. "I can't explain everything right now. But I really need this, Grammy. I'll do anything."

Her grandmother paused. "Anything?"

Linnie gazed up at the casino's flashing neon marquis. "Anything."

"In that case," Grammy said, her voice jubilant, "I have the perfect opportunity for you. Chin up, darling. It's your lucky day."

Chapter 2

"What the heck is 'maceration,' and is it something I shouldn't be doing in front of young children?" Amy Bialek Nichols glanced up from her cookbook with a quizzical frown.

Her husband, Brandon, looked over from the dinner table, where he was refereeing a french-fry fight between their two-year-old twins, Chloe and Ben. "What the heck is *what?*"

"Maceration. I'm trying to make raspberry-lemon tartlets for the day-care bake sale tomorrow. Everyone says if you can read, you can cook, but apparently my vocabulary isn't expansive enough, because I have no clue what these people are talking about." Amy tossed down her wooden spoon in frustration, then winced as her adorable, rosy-cheeked son smeared a handful of ketchup through his silky brown curls as though applying sculpting gel at a salon. "Guess it's bath night tonight."

Chloe immediately attempted her own version of condiment hairstyling, then did her brother one better by using her index finger to rub the bright red sauce around her mouth like lipstick. She blew a noisy kiss to each parent and announced, "Pretty. Like Mama."

Amy had to turn away to hide her grin while Brandon started in with, "We use forks and spoons when we sit at the table, and we don't play with our food."

The entire first floor of their suburban Connecticut home was cluttered with stacks of catalogs, half-empty sippy cups, picture books, mangled stuffed chew toys, and bits of gravel and rock salt that the family had tracked in from the blustery November sleet storm in progress outside. The kitchen had been designed to suit a fashion-forward gourmet, with a six-burner stove and sleek Silestone countertops, but the Nichols house would never be *Better Homes and Gardens* material. Tonight, the dining area smelled like wet dog and greasy fast food, and the braided throw rugs and sage sofa in the adjoining family room were dusted with a light sprinkling of pet hair. Amy had once read a magazine article by an organization expert who'd decreed that most people's homes had "hot zones" where debris tended to accumulate, and that these hot zones must be relentlessly targeted in the ongoing battle for physical and psychological serenity. A messy house meant you were losing the war on chaos.

Chaos: 1, Amy: 0. She had waved the white flag right around the time she found out she was pregnant with twins.

"Why don't you sit down and grab a bite to eat?" Brandon tipped back his chair and snagged a damp dish towel from the countertop. The twins squalled in protest as he began wiping down their faces and hands.

Amy shook her head. "No can do. I've got to get cracking on these tarts if I want to get to bed at a decent hour tonight."

"Where'd you get the recipe, anyway?" Brandon asked. "I didn't realize we actually owned a cookbook."

"The kids and I stopped at the bookstore on the way home today, and I found this in the clearance section up by the cash register. When I saw this recipe, I knew I had to try it. Check it out." She showed him the photo of lemon curd and glazed berries nestled into little golden pastry shells. "Does that not look delectable?"

Brandon cleared his throat. "It does look good. But, honey, it's almost seven thirty."

"What's your point?"

Chloe's and Ben's whimpers escalated into a high-pitched, no-holds-barred brawl over ownership of the last ketchup packet. Mooch, the family's portly old gray schnauzer, darted under the table to gobble up the remnants from the french-fry fight, then began making ominous hacking noises. Brandon looked ready for a beer.

"My point is, this looks like a pretty big project for somebody who got up at five thirty, hit the gym, spent eight hours charting gum pockets and lecturing about flossing, skipped lunch, and hasn't had a moment's peace since she walked through the front door. Chloe, no spitting. Ben, if you pinch, you're going in time-out." Amy's husband joined her at the counter and scanned the recipe text. "This is going to take forever, honey. Look at this: While you're macerating the berries, you're supposed to make a crust from scratch."

Amy shrugged. "How hard can it be to make a piecrust? It's just butter, flour, and water, right? And then you roll it out. Oh crap—do we even have a rolling pin?" She knelt down to rummage through the cabinet. "Didn't we register for one when we got married?"

"We just had our seventh anniversary," Brandon pointed out. "The fact that you haven't used a rolling pin in seven years should tell you something. Why don't I just run to the store, grab a box of brownie mix, and we'll call it a day?"

"No! Last year I showed up with those flat, pathetic chocolate chip cookies made from premade refrigerated cookie dough. I was disgraced and humiliated."

When she reemerged from the depths of the cupboard, Brandon gave her a look. "It's a day-care bake sale. Let's keep this in perspective. Bobby Flay's not going to be there."

"The assistant director threw out the whole batch when she thought I wasn't looking!" Amy covered her eyes at the memory. "She didn't want me to feel bad that no one would cough up a quarter for my 'fail' cookies. I have to redeem myself. At the very least I should make something from scratch. Banana bread, macaroons, something."

"Then make banana bread."

"We don't have any bananas. Besides, I can do this. Just you wait and see." Amy resumed her hunt for a rolling pin and began to hum with a renewed sense of optimism. As she set the oven temperature and located her measuring cups, she started singing softly to herself.

Brandon leaned in to listen. "Are you macerating your raspberries to the Beastie Boys?"

Amy whirled around, pointed her index finger at Chloe, and

belted out, "'No! Sleep! Till Brooklyn!'" She started headbanging, and both toddlers immediately followed suit.

Brandon shrugged and shook his head. "Ever the rocker chick."

Not anymore. Amy smiled ruefully. Ten years ago, she'd been a short-skirted art school grad who'd fancied herself the next Debbie Harry while singing backup for her friends' garage band, the Skinnerists. Though she might not always be the most beautiful girl in the room, she was invariably the life of the party. She'd been aglow from the rush of playing a gig at a university coffeehouse when she first met Brandon, a soft-spoken dental student with a maturity beyond his years who'd been drawn to her spark and boundless energy. "You know how to have *fun*," he'd said to her with an undertone of awe. He'd waited patiently for her to finish working the room, then asked her out and given her plenty of space to carouse and carry on and dance on bar tops until she finally calmed down enough to commit.

Now she had an SUV littered with granola bar wrappers, a ten p.m. bedtime, and a closet full of blue scrubs that she wore to her job as a hygienist in Brandon's dental practice. But contrary to all the clichés about repressed soccer moms languishing in quiet desperation, Amy reveled in her newfound, grown-up identity. She and Brandon balanced each other out. She still broke out her old leather miniskirts and hand-wash-only lingerie on nights when the kids stayed at their grandmother's house. And though she might never be lead-singer material, she had other talents; she could scrape off the plaque around an exposed tooth root with a dexterity that just couldn't be taught.

And who knew? Maybe baking would turn out to be her hidden gift. She grabbed a sack of flour and shook her booty with abandon. "The secret ingredient is sass."

But by the time the twins were bathed and in bed, Amy's singing had given way to a muttered litany of curses. Every single mixing bowl in the kitchen was dirty, the raspberries had disintegrated into a runny red soup, and the sodden, sticky blob meant to be piecrust bore a striking resemblance to mucilage. She couldn't make another batch because she was out of sugar, butter, berries, and eggs. Not to mention patience.

According to the recipe, prep time for these tartlets was forty minutes. She glanced up at the digital clock on the microwave. She'd been at this for nearly two and a half hours, and all she had to show for her efforts was an oncoming tension headache.

Brandon returned downstairs after tucking in Chloe and Ben, clicked on ESPN in the family room, took one look at Amy's expression, then crossed into the kitchen to comfort her. "How can I help you?"

"I think I'm beyond help at this point." She blew out her breath and gazed down at the liquefied berries. "What are the odds that I can pass this off as innovative, cutting-edge cuisine? Raspberry gazpacho?"

Brandon put his arms around her and kissed her temple. "Would you like me to go buy some premade cookie dough?"

She rested her cheek against his soft merino sweater and swallowed her pride. "Yes, please. And a big bottle of wine. I'm starting to remember why we don't have a rolling pin." She snatched up her new cookbook and chucked it toward the recycling bin by the back door. "No wonder that damn thing was in the clearance section."

She had just popped a tray of round, uniform cookie dough slices into the oven and collapsed on the sofa with a glass of merlot when the phone rang. Her grandmother's name flashed across the cordless phone's caller ID display, and Amy snatched up the receiver immediately.

"Is everything okay, Grammy?" she said by way of greeting.

"Splendid, darling." Grammy Syl sounded so upbeat that Amy started to de-stress, too, as if by osmosis. "Why do you ask?"

"It's just that it's so late. I thought you'd be in bed by now."

"Pinochle night," Grammy explained. "I just got home."

Amy smiled. "You senior-center ladies put the *Sex and the City* girls to shame."

"Pish-tosh." Grammy clicked her tongue, but Amy could tell she was flattered. "How are my adorable great-grandchildren?"

Amy glanced over at the ketchup handprints still smeared across the kitchen cabinets. "They're two years old. Need I say more?"

"More important, how are you? You sound a bit run-down. Did you skip dinner tonight?"

"How do you always know these things?" Amy marveled. "Are you psychic?"

"I'm your grandmother. I know all."

In fact, Grammy Syl had been more of a surrogate mother to Amy than a traditional grandmother. While Amy's parents were preoccupied with "handling" her younger sister, Linnie, Amy had spent weeks at a time at Grammy's house. Grammy Syl was the one who helped her shop for homecoming dresses, taught her how to properly apply mascara, and drove her to and from school musical rehearsals (where Amy had spent most of her time painting set pieces and flirting shamelessly with seniors).

"Don't worry about me." Amy tucked her feet up under her on the couch. "I'm okay."

"You're running yourself ragged and you ought to take better care of yourself. Admit it." Grammy's tone brooked no argument.

"Maybe a little," Amy admitted.

"I know just what would put the spring back into your step: a week all by yourself at a five-star hotel, plus lots and lots of money."

Amy closed her eyes and sipped the rich, fruity wine. She fantasized about sleep the way other women fantasized about Clive Owen or the shoe department at Neiman Marcus. "Mmm. Sounds heavenly."

"Then pack your bags, darling, because all that can be yours. All that and more."

Amy's eyes flew open. "I don't get it. You're giving me my inheritance early?"

"Even better, dearest. I'm giving you the opportunity of a lifetime. And all you have to do is hold a mixing bowl and look glamorous. Congratulations!" Grammy crowed. "You're going to be my partner in the Delicious Duet Dessert Championship this year!"

Amy threw back her head and laughed.

The Delicious Duet Dessert Championship was, as the name suggested, a culinary competition focused on promoting wholesome family fun. Teams of two—mothers and daughters, husbands and wives, sisters, best friends, etc.—vied for a major cash prize by entering original recipes. Grammy Syl entered every year, along with her sister Pavla. A few years ago, Syl and Pavla had made it all the way to the semifinals in New York with their Plum Pistachio Macaroon recipe. They hadn't won the grand prize, but they'd received a gilt-edged certificate of participation along with lots of Delicious sugar coupons and some local press. Grammy had framed the certificate and hung it in her living room next to her wedding portrait.

But Great-aunt Pavla died last summer, and Amy had completely forgotten about the annual baking hoopla. Until now.

Grammy was still rattling off her sales pitch. "Since Pavla passed on, God rest her soul, I need a new partner, and so I'm putting your name next to mine on the entry form. Everything has to be postmarked no later than tomorrow. Prepare to bake your way to glory, darling." She paused as Amy choked on her wine. "Why are you laughing?"

"Oh, Grammy. You picked the wrong day to ask me." Amy summarized the tartlet fiasco. "I'm very flattered that you thought of me, but there's no way."

"One little mishap and you're ready to give up? For shame. Baking is in your bloodline," Grammy said loftily. "Don't fret; I'll do the hard work. All you'll need to do smile for the cameras and make the finished product look good. You can act as my food stylist."

Amy's ears pricked up. "Cameras?"

"Oh yes. The winners are going to be showcased in a special feature for the Culinary Channel. It's a very big deal."

Amy had never been on national TV. She'd never even had her name in the newspaper; Linnie had been the undisputed star of the family.

Grammy, sensing weakness, swooped in for the coup de grâce. "And the corporate sponsors put up all the finalists in a swanky hotel in New York. Just imagine: a whole big bed all to yourself. The soft white sheets, the fluffy pillows, nothing to do at night but sleep and sleep . . ."

Amy's resolve wavered. "But don't we have to come up with an original recipe?"

"Already done, darling. I'm submitting my top secret recipe for szarlotka—apple pie with a twist."

"But that's a family secret!" Amy said. "Hence the term 'secret recipe.'"

"Let's face it—I'm not going to be around forever. Family secrets are overrated. Together we can win the whole shebang; I'm sure of it. What do you say? Are you with me?"

"Hang on a second." Amy put down her wineglass and lifted her chin, sniffing the air. It smelled like . . . "Oh *crap*."

"What is it, darling? Is everything all right?"

Amy raced into the kitchen and yanked open the oven door. Dark, acrid clouds of smoke billowed forth. She let out a squeak of despair. "Everything's fine, but I have a code-red cookie situation. I have to go before the smoke detector goes off and wakes the kids."

"Just give me a yes or no."

Amy gazed down at the blackened, deflated blobs on the cookie sheet. "For both our sakes, I'm going to have to say no. I'm so sorry, Grammy, but—"

Grammy didn't miss a beat. "That's all right, dear. I'll just ask Linnie instead."

Amy's eyebrows snapped together. "Come on. That's not going to work on me. I'm not fifteen anymore."

"I'm glad to hear that. It's high time that you and your sister got over that ridiculous rivalry."

"It's not sibling rivalry, Grammy; it's more like guerrilla warfare."

"You haven't seen each other in years."

Amy didn't respond.

"Aren't you ever going to tell me what happened between the two of you?"

"No." Amy's tone was sharper than she'd intended.

"Well, that's your prerogative, I suppose, but it's such a shame. You're sisters."

"Exactly. We're sisters, not friends. We happen to share some DNA through circumstances beyond our control. That doesn't mean I have to feel guilty over not bonding with her."

Grammy sighed and gave up. "Well, have it your way, darling. Go tend to your cookies, and let's see if we can't arrange a family dinner next weekend. I'd better call Linnie before I go to bed."

"Wait." Amy knew she should quit while she was ahead, but couldn't seem to help herself. "Don't ask her yet. Let me think about it."

"I'm going to the post office first thing in the morning," Grammy said.

"I know." Amy flung open the back door and flapped a dish cloth to air out the smoke-filled kitchen. "You promise I don't have to do any actual baking?"

"Perish the thought. You'd only be there for moral support and a smidge of prep work. And press interviews, naturally. You're very photogenic, you know."

"I'm aware that I'm being manipulated."

"Don't be ridiculous; I would never manipulate anyone," Grammy said sweetly. "So shall I sign you up or not?"

Amy took a deep, bracing breath and said, "Okay. I'm in."

A few minutes later, Brandon wandered into the family room, munching a scorched cookie.

"Who was that?" he asked, nodding toward the phone.

"Grammy Syl."

"What'd she have to say?"

"Pour yourself a glass of wine and prepare to have your mind blown." A slow, stunned smile spread across Amy's face. "The time has come to invest in a rolling pin."

The next day at noon, as she drove the four miles from the dental office to the day care to take advantage of the center's drop-in policy and eat lunch with Chloe and Ben, Amy called the florist to make sure that her order had been delivered. Then she took a fortifying gulp of lukewarm coffee and dialed her parents' number.

The phone rang twice before someone picked up, but all Amy could hear was a series of high-pitched, wince-inducing barks.

"Hello?" Amy pulled out of the parking lot and held her phone a few inches away from her head. "Mom? Dad?"

"Hang on." Her mother's voice was barely audible over the barking, which escalated in both frequency and volume.

Two red lights later, the barking stopped and Amy's mother came back on the line, sounding breathless. "Amy? Is that you?"

"It's me."

"Sorry about that. Rhodes just got home from the groomer, and you know how he hates getting his nails clipped. Then a deliveryman rang the doorbell, and that sent him over the edge."

"You got the flowers I sent you?" Amy asked.

"I did, honey. Thank you. You're so sweet to remember that tulips are my favorite."

"That's me." Amy felt a bit wistful. "The good daughter."

She had always been the good daughter in the Bialek family. Even as a baby, she'd been jolly and mellow, sleeping through the night at only six weeks old and greeting strangers with gurgles and a big toothless grin. When she was three and a half, Linnie was born, and everyone remarked on how smoothly Amy made the transition from only child to big sister.

Linnie, on the other hand, had never been easy. She was fussy and high-maintenance from day one, requiring special formula, wailing for hours every evening with colic, refusing to sleep unless the lighting, background noise, and temperature were exactly right. As she progressed from infant to little girl, Linnie demanded ever more of her parents' time and attention. While Amy was the good daughter, Linnie was the gifted one, the wunderkind who needed to be coddled and cultivated like a hothouse orchid.

For the first few years of her life, Linnie had adored Amy, and Amy had relished the role of the magnanimous older sibling. She'd been happy to let Linnie tag along and share her toys.

But then, suddenly, Linnie wasn't tagging along anymore. She started reading by the time she turned two, and was correcting Amy's grade school math homework when she was in preschool. Linnie was an intellectual tour de force, mastering mathematics, science, foreign languages, piano, and even gymnastics. Their parents would meet behind closed doors with educators and counselors about how best to nurture Linnie's burgeoning brilliance while Amy waited out in the hallway, reading Archie comic books and chewing on lollipops.

By the time Amy started high school, she had essentially regained her only-child status, except instead of being the center of attention, she felt more like an afterthought.

"Don't be like that," her mother would say, looking guilty when Amy complained about spending yet another weekend at Grammy's house while her parents drove Linnie to an out-of-state science olympiad. "You know we love you. But Linnie needs us more right now."

"You're lucky." Her father threw one arm around her and squeezed. "You get to hang out with your friends and have fun."

So Amy taught herself to fit in wherever she went. Although she loved to paint and secretly considered herself a budding avant-garde artist, she moved freely through most of the cliques in high school. She hung out with cheerleaders and jocks, the band and theater crowds, student council members and the newspaper staff. She could talk to anyone about anything—except for her own sister, who seemed increasingly closed-off and distant.

On the evening of her sophomore-year homecoming dance, as Amy zipped up her strapless sequined dress and applied her makeup, she tried to chat with Linnie about how she'd been nominated for homecoming court, who else was on the ballot, and which king and queen candidates might win.

Linnie, who used to hang onto her every word and beg Amy for a spritz of perfume, didn't even look up from her textbook. "I believe it was Eleanor Roosevelt who said, 'Great minds discuss ideas. Average minds discuss events. Small minds discuss people.'"

And that had pretty much been the end of their sisterly bonding. Amy went out and had fun; Linnie stayed home and germinated greatness. The long-term plan, everyone agreed, was for Linnie to become a physician and spend her twenties publishing groundbreaking research papers in prestigious medical journals. (Her thirties, presumably, would be devoted to curing cancer and the common cold.)

Linnie had started college at fifteen, right on schedule, then shocked everyone by dropping out after one semester. Desperate to see some return on their financial and emotional investment, their parents had tried everything—threats and bribes and begging—to convince Linnie to give school another shot. But nothing could sway Linnie once she'd made up her mind. As soon as she turned eighteen, Linnie moved out of their childhood home and into a series of increasingly depressing apartments and dead-end jobs. She'd recently started dealing blackjack in Vegas, which surprised Amy, given her sister's vocal dislike of drinking, carousing, and the public in general.

These days, instead of shuttling Linnie from private tutors to piano lessons to chess tournaments, Mom and Dad chauffeured a wiry, bossy Irish terrier named Rhodes from the dog park to the holistic veterinarian to competitive obedience trials. They'd relocated from Connecticut to North Carolina so they could be close to Rhodes's trainer, Shawna. (Or so they claimed. Amy was convinced that after years of her parents' bragging about Linnie to all of their friends, the pointed questions about "Whatever happened to your daughter the doctor?" had shamed them into seclusion.) Purebred Irish terriers were rare and expensive, and Rhodes came pedigreed with an impressive bloodline and a formal AKC name: Blarneystone's Rhodes Scholar.

Fortunately, the rare and expensive Rhodes had now been placated to the point that Amy could finally hear her mother on the other end of the phone line.

"We have an announcement." Mom's voice quavered with anticipation. "Wait till you hear. Pick up the phone, Jim," she hollered. "It's Amy!"

Two seconds later, Amy's father clicked on. "Hi, sweet pea. I'm so glad you called. Did you tell her yet, Linda?"

"Not yet," Mom said. "I wanted to wait for you."

"What's going on?" Amy brightened. "Sounds like good news."

"*Great* news," her father corrected. "Listen, is there any chance you might be able to take a few days of vacation time in May?"

Amy did a quick flip-through of her mental daily planner. "I'm sure we can work something out. What's up? Are you coming up for a visit?"

"Actually, we were hoping you might be able to come down here," her mother said. "Rhodes is going for his UDX."

Amy turned her car into the day-care center parking lot. "UDX?"

"It's the canine equivalent of a PhD." Her father made no effort to conceal his pride. "Only the best and the brightest make it through the testing process."

"And most of the dogs that do pass are herding and working breeds: Border collies, German shepherds," her mother added. "Terriers aren't generally considered good candidates."

"But Rhodes is one in a million," Dad said.

"One in a billion." Her mother laughed. "Moving down here to train with Shawna was absolutely the right decision."

After Rhodes had triumphantly completed his UD title (the canine equivalent of a master's degree) last year, her parents had hosted a family weekend in the little dog's honor, complete with a professional photographer, tearful toasts, and an elaborate bone-shaped cake. Grammy, Amy, and Brandon had all put on their Sunday best and played along. Linnie hadn't even bothered to RSVP.

"Well. That sounds pretty exciting. I'll check with Brandon and get back to you," Amy hedged. "Anyway, Mom, I just called to say—"

"Oh, that's the other line." Her father's voice went tense. "It's Linnie."

"Linnie?" Her mother's entire demeanor changed. "We'd better take it."

"Okay, I'll let you go, but I wanted to say happy birth—"

Click. Dial tone.

The Bake-Off

Amy dropped her phone on the dashboard and sat back in her seat for a moment, staring out her windshield at the heavy gray winter sky.

Two decades later, the sting of coming in second still hadn't worn off.

Chapter 3

"I have good news and bad news." Grammy Syl greeted Amy at the door with a warm smile and a slice of apple szarlotka.

"Oh boy." Amy pivoted on her stack-heeled boot and stepped back into the hallway. "Maybe I'll come back later."

Grammy grabbed her elbow and tugged her inside the condo, or "casita," as it was described in the promotional literature for the Willow Court Senior Living Community. "Don't be silly, dearest. Take off your coat and give me a hug."

Amy obliged, glancing over Grammy's shoulder, on high alert for anything amiss. But the cozy little living room was tidy as usual, full of framed family photos and mismatched antique furniture.

"The suspense is killing me," Amy said when Grammy released her. "Hit me with the bad news and get it over with."

Grammy handed the plate of pie to Amy and toyed with the double strand of lustrous white pearls around her neck. "Good news first: We've officially made it to the semifinals of the Delicious Duet Dessert Championship. I got the certified letter yesterday."

"Already?" Amy exclaimed. "It's only been a few weeks since you entered. Aren't there, like, a zillion entries?"

"At least." Grammy preened. "There's a test kitchen somewhere in California that sorts through all the entries and narrows down the pool to a hundred or so. Then they bake those recipes and select the best fifty."

"Congratulations," Amy said. She leaned in for another hug.

"Congratulations to you, too. You're my co-entrant, after all." Grammy didn't hug her back this time. Instead, she tilted her head and sized up her granddaughter with a cool, appraising stare. "Now I want you to promise me something. You're going to honor your word and go to New York for the finals, right?"

"Are you kidding me?" Amy's eyebrows shot up. "A whole week of room service and sleep? I'm there!"

Grammy folded her arms over her mint green angora cardigan. She looked very formidable for a white-haired old lady who barely topped five foot two in heels. "No matter what crops up at home or at your job? I can count on you?"

Amy sensed treachery and started to backpedal. "Well, I mean, I *want* to go. I plan to. But if Brandon or one of the twins got injured or seriously ill, I'd have to back out."

"Naturally, but barring that—barring a catastrophic emergency—you promise to go to the finals and participate?"

"Ye-es," Amy said. She should have escaped back down the hall while the escaping was good. "Why?"

Grammy nodded, then shifted back into nurturing, maternal mode. "Have a bite of pie, darling, and sign here, here, and here. I'll send this back to the contest officials." Grammy produced a pen and waited until Amy signed and dated the finalist forms. "Now, have I already told you about Ty and Tai?"

"Who?"

"Ty and Tai Tottenham. The husband-and-wife team from Ohio who've been the second-place winners in the bake-off for the last two years. I don't know what it is about Ohio, but that state turns out more than its fair share of finalists. Maybe it's something in the water. Anyway, as for Ty and Tai . . ." Grammy lowered her voice as if preparing to impart juicy gossip. "They're infamous."

Amy couldn't contain a laugh. "Infamous on the bake-off circuit? For what? Using margarine instead of butter? Scandal!"

Grammy pursed her lips. "It's no joke, young lady. Those two want the grand prize, and they'll stop at nothing to win. Rumor has it that last year they got the goods on one of the judges and *blackmailed* their way to the finals."

Amy shoveled in another bite of pie, which tasted as delicious as it smelled. "Are you serious? That's pathetic. I mean, it's just brownies and cupcakes and whatever."

"Just brownies and cupcakes, she says." Grammy Syl shook her head. "You're in for a rude awakening if you think this is a friendly little cookie swap. The Delicious Duet attracts the most talented amateur bakers from all over the country. You need to bring your A game."

"Then it's a good thing I'll have you to be my mentor. When

we get to New York, just point out Ty and Tai, and I'll be sure to steer clear."

"Mmm." Grammy fiddled with her pearls again. "About New York. I won't be going."

Amy froze midchew. "Why not?"

"As it happens, I have a scheduling conflict. I'm going on an Alaskan cruise. I booked the tickets with Harriet Webber ages ago, and it must have slipped my mind."

"But you just made me promise that I wouldn't drop out for anything less than a medical emergency!" Amy exclaimed.

"I *am* sorry, my lamb, but the deposit's nonrefundable and Harriet's counting on me. Her husband died just last year; she needs companionship. Besides . . ." Grammy wrung her hands and let her eyes grow pensive. "I don't know how much longer I'm going to be around. I'd better travel while I still can."

Amy put one hand on her hip. "Are you kidding me with this?"

"We're all going to die someday, and I'd like to see the glaciers before I go."

"Then why did you make me sign all those forms?" Amy made a grab for the contest paperwork, but Grammy was too quick for her. "I can't do this all by myself! Aside from the fact that I can barely boil water, the thing is called the Delicious Duet Dessert Championship. Won't I be disqualified without my partner?"

Grammy beamed. "I've already worked all that out. You'll have a very capable partner."

"Who?" Amy put down her china dessert plate with a clatter. "Your name is already on the entry forms."

Grammy took Amy's elbow again and nudged her toward the

kitchen. "My name, yes, but I may have taken some liberties with the rest of my personal information."

"What are you talking about?"

"Well, you know, we do have a backup Vasylina Bialek."

Amy gasped and dug her heels into the carpet. "Oh no. No, no, no. And did I mention hell no?"

"Don't be so negative. I know you and Linnie haven't had the easiest time of it, but—"

"I see what this is—this is a trap!" Amy flung her purse to the floor. "You never had any intention of going to New York with me. You railroaded me into signing a legal document under false pretenses."

"My goodness." Grammy rewarded this outraged performance with a smattering of applause. "You certainly can emote, darling."

"I know you mean well, Grammy, but there's no way. Linnie and I are like oil and water. Fire and gasoline." Amy glowered as she came up with a more fitting analogy. "The cat and the canary."

"I'm right here," came a familiar voice from the kitchen. "I can hear you."

Amy found herself face-to-face with her younger sister for the first time in years. Linnie was sitting at the table with an untouched piece of pie and an empty glass of milk.

Amy took one look at the beautiful blond bombshell sporting the milk mustache and insisted, "I'm not working with her." She turned toward the window, fuming.

"Hello to you, too," Linnie said dryly.

"You promised," Grammy whispered to Amy.

"No. I promised to do this with *you*. Not her."

"It's okay." Linnie sounded confident and kind of amused, which only fueled Amy's anger. "I don't want to work with her, either."

Grammy grabbed a slotted metal spoon and brandished it like a cutlass. She muttered darkly in Polish for a moment, then switched to English. "Pavla and I never fought like this. You two are sisters; even if you don't like each other, you have to figure out a way to live with each other."

"No, we don't," Amy said.

Grammy Syl spun Amy around and yanked out a chair from the table. "Sit!"

Amy sat.

Grammy pointed the spoon at Amy. "You said you're desperate for a little time away." She turned to Linnie. "You said you're desperate for money. It's time to grow up and get along. Life is too short for all this dysfunctional nonsense. When's the last time you saw each other?"

Amy glanced at Linnie, but her sister had gone into screensaver mode: head bowed, gaze vacant, body motionless.

"Well, let's see." Amy cast her gaze upward, considering. "There was my wedding, of course, and then there was, um . . ."

"When's the last time you spoke on the phone?"

"Ooh, I know this one!" Amy smacked the table as if hitting a game show buzzer. "Christmas."

"Which year?" Grammy challenged.

"I think it was right after I got pregnant. I remember because I had morning sickness, so I had to go throw up about thirty seconds into the conversation."

Grammy nodded. "You two need to reconnect and try again."

Linnie suddenly looked up. "Why?"

Grammy made a horizontal slashing motion with her spoon to indicate that this point was not up for debate.

But Amy persisted. "Yeah, why are you suddenly all worked up about this? It's not like it's anything new."

"You should know by now that my kitchen is not a democracy," Grammy said. "I'm not asking you girls to get along; I am *telling* you. And after all I've done for you over all these years, you can do this one thing for me."

Amy opened her mouth to say no, but discovered she was physically incapable of refusing while Grammy stared her down like this.

"Well?" Grammy prompted.

"I guess," Amy mumbled.

"Good. Now make me proud and win this thing." And with that, Grammy Syl slapped down a yellowing index card bearing their great-grandmother's recipe in fading blue ink and swept out of the kitchen, leaving Amy and Linnie seated at opposite ends of the table.

Several minutes passed, the kitchen so quiet that Amy could hear the wall clock ticking off the seconds.

Linnie tapped her plate with her fork. "Just so you know, I'm not jealous of you."

Amy shoved back her chair and fixed her sister with a death glare. "Don't start. I'm in no mood."

Linnie circled the rim of her drinking glass with one fingertip. "Why so hostile?"

"You know why."

They reverted to the silent staring contest.

Finally, Amy heaved a big sigh. "Why are you desperate for money?"

Linnie sidestepped the question and said, with the air of a teenager in detention, "Look. You don't want to do this. I don't want to do this. But Grammy's right; we don't have to like each other. We just have to figure out how to make"—she picked up the card and squinted at the lopsided text—"szarlotka, whatever that is."

"It's a Polish apple pie," Amy said. "You have a piece of it in front of you right now. Grammy Syl and Auntie Pavla used to make it all the time, remember?"

"Nope."

"I can't believe you don't remember."

"I didn't have a lot of free time to sit around enjoying Grammy's baked goods." Linnie's self-satisfied little smirk vanished. "But I take it you know how to make it?"

"No clue."

Linnie considered this, then shrugged. "Well, how hard can it be? We have step-by-step instructions right here. It's not rocket science. Housewives all over the world do this every day."

"God, you're insufferable."

Linnie blinked at her. "What?"

"'Housewives all over the world,'" Amy repeated. "Like you're so much better than all of us mere mortals."

"Don't be so sensitive. My point is, Polish peasants used to whip this up with no electricity and no running water. If they can figure it out, so can I."

"Ha. That's what you say now." Amy tossed her head. "Hey,

here's an idea: How about I have all the ideas and do all the work, and then, at the last possible second, you sweep in and screw me over and steal all the credit for yourself?"

Linnie blanched, her face going as white as the milk smudging her upper lip.

Amy smote her forehead, her voice still drenched in sarcasm. "Oh, wait, we already did that, didn't we? And look how *that* turned out."

Chapter 4

Linnie had to remind herself to breathe as she wiped her shoes on the welcome mat outside Grammy's front door. The pages of annotated recipes in her hands were damp and curling at the edges from the sweat drenching her palms. The merino wool scarf knotted artfully around her neck started to itch.

After the initial confrontation with Amy two weeks ago, both sisters had agreed to return to Grammy Syl's for a weekend of "baking boot camp," and Linnie hadn't thought much beyond learning to properly crack eggs and roll out paper-thin dough. But returning to the little town of Staunton, Connecticut, reuniting with the people who knew her best, made her feel like more of an outsider than months of being overlooked as just another anonymous pretty face in a Vegas casino.

The scent of fresh coffee wafted out from the apartment, and Linnie could hear muffled laughter and the faint clattering of china teacups against saucers. Amy must already be in the kitchen with Grammy, the two of them chatting and sharing confidences the way they always did.

Linnie had been lying two weeks ago when she'd insisted she wasn't jealous of her older sister. Please. *Of course* she was jealous. Amy had grown up mobbed with friends and besieged by phone calls from boys, and she had frittered away her teenage summers selecting lipstick at the mall and lifeguarding by the lake in a bikini. Amy was cute, not gorgeous. Amy was bright, not brilliant. Amy had been allowed the luxury of flipping through the cable channels on Sunday evenings and saying, "I'm *so bored*, you guys."

Linnie, on the other hand, had never experienced a single minute of boredom in her adolescence. She'd been too busy preparing for the next hurdle on the road to greatness, greatness that she'd been assured she was entitled to achieve because she was, on some fundamental level, better than everyone else.

"You're *gifted*," she heard over and over from her parents and her teachers. She did not have to earn her superiority. Rather, her intellect, like her beauty, had been bestowed by divine favor. She had been chosen. Amy had not.

And to this day, Linnie still burned with envy.

She was jolted out of her reverie as heavy-metal guitar riffs and drumbeats started blasting out of Grammy's apartment and the door flew open.

"Linnie!" Grammy looked disconcerted to find her granddaughter loitering on her doorstep with a furrowed brow and an incipient case of neck hives, but she quickly recovered and commenced hugging and kissing. "Come in, darling. Goodness, I didn't even hear you knock; I was just going to check for the newspaper. I'm so glad you managed to get a few days off work. How was your flight?"

"Fine," Linnie mumbled, staring down at the intricate pattern on the living room rug. "Thanks for sending me the ticket. I promise I'll pay you back."

"Don't give it a second thought. Here, put your suitcase right over here. I'm sorry you had to take a shuttle from the airport, but I finally had to give up driving on the freeway this year. My eyesight isn't what it used to be, and your sister . . . well, you know she has her job and the children to look after. She's always so busy."

"The shuttle van was fine," Linnie said. "I didn't expect Amy to pick me up, believe me. What on earth are you listening to in here? Is that . . . ?"

"Def Leppard!" Grammy Syl clapped her hands together. "'Pour Some Sugar on Me,' I believe the song is called. Amy put together a whole baking playlist on her iPod. Isn't that festive?"

Linnie unbuttoned her coat and grimaced as the vocalist started howling about taking a bottle and shaking it up. "That's one word for it."

"You're just in time. We're getting ready to start the first batch." Grammy led the way down the hall past five decades' worth of Bialek family photos. As they rounded the corner into the kitchen, she squeezed Linnie's hand. "And for heaven's sake, be nice to your sister."

Linnie scratched the ferocious itch at the back of her neck. "I'll be nice to her if she'll be nice to me."

She squared her shoulders, set her chin at a haughty angle, and swept into the kitchen to find Amy lining up ingredients on the countertop and rocking out to the music blasting out of tiny speakers rigged up next to the stove. Amy's thick, wavy auburn hair was slowly escaping its ponytail, and her hazel eyes sparkled as she paused to play a little air guitar. She wore a well-cut green shirt, fitted dark jeans, and a long, stylish gold statement necklace. She looked comfortable and confident in her own skin, the prom queen grown up into the president of the PTA, but without any trace of cliquey cattiness.

Amy had never been a gossip; all these years and she'd never breathed a word about what had really caused the rift between her and Linnie. Her silence protected Linnie, but it also left Linnie alone with the hard, humiliating truth.

For a few moments, neither sister acknowledged the other. Finally, Grammy stepped in between them and exclaimed, "Look, Amy, Linnie's here! All us Bialek girls together again. Isn't this marvelous?"

"I downloaded some songs to inspire us while we work," Amy announced, not making eye contact. "'Pour Some Sugar on Me'; perfect, right? Then 'I Want Candy,' 'Cherry Pie,' 'Appetite for Destruction,' 'She's Crafty . . .'"

Linnie smoothed back her hair and pursed her lips. "Could you please turn it down?"

"What?" Amy yelled.

"Could you please turn it down? I can barely hear myself think."

"Okay, there, Grandma." Amy grinned across the kitchen as she lowered the volume by a few decibels. "No offense, Grammy."

"None taken, dear." Grammy Syl produced a pair of gingham aprons from a drawer next to the oven and handed one to each sister. "Now suit up, darlings. It's time you learned the lost art of making szarlotka. We're going to need plenty of patience, precision, and, most important, teamwork."

"Oh no." Amy groaned. "Here we go."

Grammy Syl ignored this and started rummaging through the pantry. "First, we'll go through our ingredients and set out everything we need so it'll be right here when we need it. Flour, sugar, butter, sour cream, eggs . . . Making perfect piecrust is an art, you know, and timing is everything. The number one mistake new cooks make is overworking the dough."

"I know," Linnie said. "I did some reading on the science of baking on the flight over."

"Suck-up," Amy muttered under her breath.

Linnie "accidentally" whapped her sister with an errant apron string.

Grammy was still peering into the depths of her pantry. "And let's see—we'll need salt."

"Kosher salt is best, right?" Linnie asked.

Grammy looked impressed. "That's right. Very good, Linnie! Now for the apples. Most szarlotka recipes call for Granny Smith, but I like to sneak a Fuji in there, too. It adds a tangy little kick. Plus, let me see, nutmeg, allspice, and—Oh dear." Grammy clapped a hand to her cheek. "I'm almost out of cinnamon."

"I'll run out and buy some more," Linnie volunteered.

"No, no, you stay right here. I'll go." Grammy shook her head with excessive surprise. "How careless of me!"

Amy rolled her eyes and leaned against the counter. "Oh, Grammy. You're so transparent."

"What? It's all gone." Grammy shook the tiny metal canister. "See for yourself."

"Uh-huh. This is like a scene out of *The Parent Trap*. You think that if you lock us up together with enough sugar and spice, we'll magically bond and become BFFs."

Grammy paused for a moment, then smiled. "A grandmother can hope."

"Well, you should spare yourself the trouble, because I can tell you right now that Linnie and I—"

"Are quite capable of being civil to each other for a few hours," Linnie finished, reaching over to turn off the stereo. "We do not have to be BFFs to make a pie. We both have plenty of self-control. We have dignity."

Amy fluttered her eyelashes. "And don't forget the kosher salt. We've got that, too."

Linnie finally snapped. "Oh my God, Amy, why don't you take this whole canister of kosher salt and shove it—"

"Girls!" Grammy Syl pounded on the counter with the solid maple rolling pin. "That is enough! I am going to the grocery store, and when I get back, I expect to see pies baking and child-hood traumas healing. Now, get to it." She stalked out of the apartment, slamming the front door behind her.

The metal measuring spoons rattled from the force of Grammy's exit, and then the kitchen fell silent.

"This isn't going to work out, is it?" Linnie said.

"Probably not." Amy sounded almost cheerful. "Why do you keep scratching your neck?"

Linnie immediately dropped her hands to her sides, then washed them in the sink and tucked her fingers into the pockets of her apron. "Let's start over, okay? I'm sorry. Regardless of our, uh, history, I really want to win this thing. *Really.*"

Amy tilted her head, her gaze suddenly shrewd. "Yeah, I

believe Grammy's exact words were 'desperate for money.' What's going on?"

"Failure is not an option," was all Linnie said by way of explanation. "So we need to do anything and everything we can to blow away the competition in New York. We need to eat, sleep, and breathe szarlotka for the next few weeks. We need to try to get along. I'll do my part, Amy—more than my part. I know I owe you."

Amy's penetrating stare intensified. "You really want to win that badly?"

Linnie nodded, even though she knew that doing so was admitting weakness and providing Amy with the perfect opportunity to deny Linnie what she most wanted. But she didn't have any other options. Her sister was her last resort and her only hope.

"Huh. Interesting." Amy drummed her fingernails on the stovetop. "Well, then, I have some ideas. Like, I was thinking that we should jazz up the recipe name if we can."

Linnie glanced up in surprise. "What does the recipe name have to do with anything?"

"You'd be surprised. The recipe name can make all the difference, according to the online forums I browsed." Amy tucked her hair back behind her ear. "That's right, while you were spending countless hours studying up on salt, I spent five minutes surfing the Internet while the twins tore apart the family room. And word on the Web is, judges like kicky names."

"Really?" Linnie had never even considered this, and the possibility dismayed her. This was exactly the type of curveball that set off a fresh case of neck hives. "Do they have any stats to back up that theory?"

"Don't know. I had to log off before the dog lost an ear. But there was this one chick who'd won three regional cake competitions, and she said judges prefer creative recipe names."

"'One chick'?" Linnie repeated. "Need I remind you, the plural of anecdote is not data."

Amy threw up her palm. "Don't pull that supercilious crap with me. I know I'm right about this. No one knows how to pronounce *szarlotka*, and 'Polish Apple Pie' is a snore. We need to set ourselves apart from all the Caramel Walnut this and Coconut Meringue that."

"You have a suggestion?"

Amy leaned forward, her eyes dancing. "Party Girl Pie."

Linnie struggled to keep a straight face.

"What?" Amy demanded.

"Party Girl Pie sounds like something a sorority house would force pledges to eat during hell week."

"Are you going to come up with any ideas of your own, or are you just going to criticize?"

"A catchy recipe name isn't going to make any difference when we face the judging panel," Linnie insisted. "What's going to win this for us is chemistry, pure and simple." She produced her notes from her back pocket and started pacing the perimeter of the kitchen. "I've spent the last two weeks reviewing the recipe, and I've come up with a few minor refinements that are going to give us a major edge. Like here, for instance: two and a half cups of flour, two-thirds of a cup of sugar—we should be measuring out the dry ingredients by weight, not by volume. Measuring cups are notoriously unreliable."

"But we're allowed to bring our own measuring cups, so let's just bring Grammy's. She's made this hundreds of times, and it's always delicious," Amy said. "I say, if it ain't broke, don't fix it. All we need is hard work and a little luck."

"You're missing my point. If we perfect the methodology, we won't have to work that hard. And PS, I don't believe in luck."

"Did you seriously just say we won't have to work hard to win this?" Amy snorted.

"Grunt work is for suckers." Linnie ducked back into the foyer, dug through her carry-on bag, and returned to the kitchen with a digital food scale, an oven thermometer, and a food science textbook. "Okay, let's go over the major factors that affect crust texture: sugar, which hinders gluten formation; acid, which breaks down existing gluten strands; fat proteins, which can promote gluten formation if not properly coated—"

"Hang on." Amy called for a time-out. "Gluten's like wheat, right?"

"It's a tough, stringy strand of protein that originates in cereal grains, including wheat. Piecrusts need some gluten to hold the dough together, but too much gluten makes the finished product tough and chewy. So you have to be very aware of the protein content of the flour you're using. Also, it's important to give the dough time to chill after you mix it, because that allows the gluten to relax."

Amy's expression was a mix of horror and amusement. "Is there going to be a test on this later?"

"Yeah, and we get a hundred thousand dollars if we pass." Linnie flipped open her textbook. "Now, the eggs help bind everything together and contribute to the dough's structural elasticity while discouraging water absorption." She noticed that Amy's eyes had started to take on a glazed, detached expression. "Hey! Stay with me here. We're just getting started."

Amy rubbed her forehead. "Are you going to act like this for the entire trip?"

"Like what?"

"Like a neurotic, type-A control freak."

"Oh." Linnie considered this for a moment. "Yes."

"Well, I don't want to spend all afternoon solving equations and watching PowerPoint presentations on the molecular properties of gluten. I just want to bake some damn pie."

"But if you understand the scientific principles at work in the process—"

"I don't understand and I don't want to. We're not going to be able to control every aspect of the baking conditions."

"Um, I beg to differ."

"You really don't see that this is ridiculous? Come on. You can't think your way out of this, Linnie. We're going to have to jump in and get our hands dirty. And we're going to make a lot of mistakes along the way, so we'd better get started."

"*You're* being ridiculous," Linnie sputtered. "All the determination in the world doesn't matter if we don't attain the proper chemical ratios and reactions."

"Is that so? Tell you what: Let's each make a batch, right here, right now." Amy rocked back on her heels. "You can go crazy with your Bunsen burner and your Geiger counter and whatever, and I'll be over here playing fast and loose with a measuring cup and a spatula. Whoever makes the better-tasting szarlotka gets to do it her way at the competition in New York. Grammy Syl can judge."

"No deal," Linnie said. "Grammy Syl favors you."

"She does not."

"Does, too!"

"You're just afraid you're going to get schooled by the culinary kamikaze."

"Fine." Linnie rolled up her sleeves. "You're on. But the winner gets to name the recipe, and the loser has to wash all the dishes."

Amy cranked up her iPod. "Let's rock and roll."

"What's going on in here?" When Grammy Syl finally returned more than two hours later, the kitchen was in shambles, the oven was going full blast, and the two sisters hadn't exchanged a single word.

"We're having a pre-bake-off bake-off," Amy said.

"To demonstrate that science beats sloppy technique," Linnie added.

Amy cleared her throat. "To demonstrate that the art of baking transcends a bunch of arbitrary rules and regulations."

Grammy Syl dropped a brown paper grocery sack onto a chair and raised her hands to her face. Linnie was shocked to realize that her grandmother was near tears. "But this is terrible," Grammy cried. "You're supposed to be working together! The whole point of the Delicious Duet Championship is teamwork."

"Sorry, Grammy." Amy shrugged. "Your *Parent Trap* ploy didn't work. And PS, that was the longest grocery run in history. Did you go all the way to Asia and harvest the cinnamon yourself?"

"Don't cry, Grammy." Linnie offered a tissue. "We'll have lots of opportunities for teamwork in New York."

Grammy's lips stopped trembling as she clamped them together in grim resignation. "I give up. You two are hopeless."

"Don't say that until you taste my pie." Amy glanced over her shoulder at Linnie as she pulled a tray out of the oven. "I'm totally going to win."

Amy's words might have been cocky, but Linnie detected a trace of doubt in her voice. They both knew that Linnie always won—if she couldn't win, she wouldn't compete.

When the pastries were baked, Amy and Linnie banished Grammy to the living room as they prepared to present the finished products.

"The judging has to be blind and impartial," Linnie said. "Grammy can't know whose is whose. So you use the plate with the silver rim, and I'll use the one with the blue flowers." She reached into the cabinet, but Amy hip-checked her out of the way.

"I want the one with the blue flowers." Amy grabbed the dish before Linnie could reach it. "Visual presentation matters."

"Fine. You don't have to be a bully about it."

Amy whirled around and stuck her index finger centimeters away from Linnie's nose. "Let's get one thing straight right now. I agreed to participate in this as a favor to Grammy, but you are not calling the shots here. You need to win so much? Then you play by my rules."

"Calm down." Linnie tossed her head and tried to sound blasé. "I cannot believe you're still so mad about something that happened years ago."

"This is not about *some*thing that happened. This is about *everything*." Amy's eyes narrowed. "I don't care how brilliant you are. The days of me giving you special treatment and letting you get away with murder are over."

Linnie glanced over at the slice of tart Amy was plating and did a double take. "You didn't."

"Oh, but I did." Amy had decorated the top layer of her crust with a scrap of dough sculpted into a Greek symbol: π. "Get it? It's a pi crust."

"Wow, that art school tuition was worth every penny."

Amy carried both plates into the living room and set them down upon the lace doilies on the coffee table. Linnie followed with two clean forks, a napkin, and a palate-cleansing glass of water.

"*Bon appétit.*" Amy gestured grandly to the piping hot szarlotka.

"*Smacznego,*" Linnie added. "That's Polish for *bon appétit.*"

"That's right," Grammy said. "Nicely done, Vasylina!" She took a bite of each piece, chewing slowly and deliberately in great concentration.

"So?" Linnie prompted. "Which is better?"

Grammy Syl's gaze shifted from one sister to the other. She cleared her throat. "I couldn't possibly choose."

"Come on!" Amy cried. "Don't be diplomatic."

"Yeah, there's a ton of money riding on this," Linnie said. "We demand brutal honesty."

"Let me taste again." Grammy took another tiny bite from each. "Very well. You want brutal honesty, here it is. There are two kinds of szarlotka, girls, and you were trying to make the other kind."

Linnie furrowed her brow. "What are you saying?"

"She's saying we suck," Amy clarified.

"Don't put words in my mouth, dear heart. All I'm saying is that both of these"—Grammy swallowed again and dabbed her lips with a napkin—"concoctions are lacking a certain something."

"Cinnamon?" Linnie pressed.

"Lemon?" Amy asked.

Grammy sipped her water. "Edibility."

"Fine, so we both suck," Amy said. "But which one sucks *less?*"

"Well." Grammy pointed her fork toward the silver-rimmed plate. "This one has better dough."

"Ha!" Linnie crowed.

"But this one is just beautiful to look at." Grammy indicated the blue-flowered plate. "You girls want to bicker and compete, you should split the work down the middle. One of you should spend the next two weeks perfecting the dough, and the other should work on perfecting the presentation."

"But you have to declare one of us the winner," Linnie said.

Grammy put down her fork and sat back on the sofa. "No."

"Someone has a gun to your head," Amy said.

"Shoot me." Grammy folded her hands primly.

"Someone has a gun to *my* head," Linnie said.

Grammy lifted her gaze heavenward and murmured something in Polish. "Fine." She touched the rim of the silver-lined plate. "This one."

Amy sighed. "Of course."

"But only by one percent." Grammy Syl touched Amy's wrist and tugged her down for a kiss on the cheek. "I'm sorry, darling. Yours *looks* delicious. And that little pi on top—so clever, like something out of a magazine."

Linnie's surge of victory fizzled when she realized that no kiss or warm words of grandmotherly praise were coming her way. She nodded at the bowls, measuring cups, and food processor attachments piled high in the kitchen sink and told Amy, "Enjoy. Oh, and I thought of a name for the recipe."

"What's that?" Grammy asked.

"Secret Sisterhood Szarlotka." Linnie paused. "The secret being, the sisters can't stand each other."

Amy let out a surprised bark of laughter. Linnie laughed,

too, and for an instant she felt a spark of pride that she could still impress her sister.

"See that?" Grammy leaped up from the sofa to hug them both, her eyes going misty again. "You girls are going to be BFFs before this is all over. Mark my words."

Chapter 5

On the morning she left for the Delicious Duet Dessert Championship, Amy woke up to the sensation of something cold and wet squishing against her ankle and the sound of the dog snuffling at the foot of the bed.

She flung her arm over her eyes and groaned. "Did Mooch throw up?"

"No," replied a little voice inches from her face.

Amy's eyes flew open as her nose brushed against her daughter's.

"Hi, Mommy." Chloe grinned and gave her a kiss on the lips.

"Hi, baby." Amy struggled into a sitting position, wedging her elbows underneath her and squinting into the dark. "Did *you* throw up?"

"Uh-uh," Chloe singsonged.

"Did you take off your diaper?"

"Uh-uh."

Amy steeled herself as best she could. "Then what is down there on my foot?"

"Lovey."

Lovey was Chloe's attachment object, a flat pink satin pillow in the shape of an elephant that she'd had in her crib since infancy. As Lovey grew older and stinkier and increasingly ragged, Chloe's love for him only grew.

"Why is Lovey so wet?"

"I sucked on him. I need my cup, Mama. I'm thirsty."

The poor girl must be on the verge of dehydration, if the sodden stuffed animal draped across Amy's ankle was any indication. Chloe had always been a champion drooler.

Amy heard Ben pipe up on Brandon's side of the bed. "I'm hungry."

"So tired," Brandon mumbled. "Five more minutes."

"Get up, Daddy! I want Cheerios."

Brandon burrowed his head into the pillow and lifted up the blanket. "Climb in, buddy."

Both children clambered up and made themselves comfy in the valley of duvet between Brandon and Amy. Mooch took this as his invitation to hop up, as well.

"One big happy family." Amy let out an *oof* as the dog plopped down on her stomach.

"Five more minutes," Brandon croaked. "Please. They can take my car keys and my wallet. I just need five more minutes."

"You better get to stepping—you have to fit a temporary crown at seven thirty," Amy reminded him. "And then—Aigh!"

She yelped as Ben pressed his icy toes into the backs of her knees. "What happened to your socks?"

Instead of answering her, Ben grabbed his sister's hand and started jumping on the bed. Both children shrieked with laughter, the dog barked, and amid the ruckus, the alarm clock started beeping.

Amy and Brandon looked at each other and laughed.

"Why do we bother setting this thing?" Brandon asked as he turned off the alarm. "We haven't made it past five thirty in two and a half years."

"But *someday,*" Amy said in a hushed, reverent tone. "Someday we might oversleep, and when that day comes, we'll be ready." She rolled out of bed, pulled a thick flannel robe over her oversize T-shirt, and launched into a groggy rendition of Journey's "Don't Stop Believing."

"Uh-huh. Right after we finish grooming our unicorn and pruning our money tree in the backyard."

Amy switched on the light and noticed a flurry of dust motes swirling above the comforter. The kids' bouncing had stirred up every allergen in the bedclothes. "Any chance there's a live-in housekeeper out there with the unicorn and the money tree?"

Brandon winced as he stubbed his bare toe on the corner of one of the unzipped suitcases strewn across the floor.

"Sorry about that." Amy kicked the bag aside. "I'm almost done packing. Just have to throw in my toiletries."

Brandon surveyed the array of matching red canvas garment bags, duffels, and valises. "You packed five bags for a week in Manhattan? You *are* planning to come back eventually, right?"

"Yes, but I'm high-maintenance," Amy said. "Actual and factual. I need a complete outfit for every day, plus dress clothes for the evening events, plus coordinating shoes, makeup, jewelry, and handbags for every ensemble, plus workout gear—"

"When are you going to have time to work out?"

"The hotel has a gym. It could happen."

Brandon gave up trying to reason with her. "Tip the bellhop well, 'cause you're probably going to give him permanent back problems."

Amy caught Ben under his arms just as he climbed into the largest suitcase. "No, no, no, Mommy just ironed all these clothes. Go put your slippers on, both of you, and Daddy will make you breakfast." The twins skedaddled, the dog dashing down the hall after them.

Amy crouched down and started to zip up the luggage.

"I still can't believe I got suckered into this with Linnie," she said. "We'll be lucky if we both survive the week. She's such a . . . She just makes me—*Ugh*." She exhaled loudly and shook out her hair. "Sorry, honey. I'm being such a whiny little bitch about this that I'm starting to annoy even myself."

"Hey, don't talk about my wife that way." Brandon wrapped his arms around her, and she rested her head against his chest.

"This is the problem with me and Linnie," she mumbled into his shirt. "I don't like the person I am when I'm around her. I get all petty and negative."

He rubbed her back. "You could still bag the whole trip and stay here."

"I'd bail right now if I thought I could withstand the lifetime of guilt trips from Grammy Syl. She's made it her mission in life to force me and Linnie to become BFFs, and yes, she actually used the term *BFF*." Amy's amusement faded. "The sad thing is, I know she's right—sisters are supposed to share a special bond that

BETH KENDRICK

transcends time and distance and whatever. But I honestly can't imagine ever having anything like that with Linnie. This is terrible to admit, but my relationship with her was why I always said I'd have an only child."

"But aren't you glad we ended up with a twofer on that score?"

"Definitely." Amy pulled out of his embrace and resumed packing. "I miss them already. Give them extra hugs for me while I'm gone."

"Will do. And you know how my mom spoils them when she comes to babysit. They'll probably be in sugar comas by the time you get back next week."

"La, la, la, I can't hear you."

"Don't worry about any of that while you're gone. Enjoy your break and bake your way to riches. How much do you get if you win this thing, anyway?"

"A hundred grand. If I win, we can put my share of the money toward opening your own dental practice."

"It'll be *our* dental practice," Brandon corrected.

"You're sweet, honey, but let's be real. You're Dr. Nichols; I'm just your assistant. No one comes to a dental practice because of the hygienist."

"Don't give me that; all the patients love you, and you know it. I couldn't do this without you." He opened his arms to encompass their house, their family, their lives. "Any of it."

"That's true." Amy brightened. "I am the linchpin, baby. I keep the trains running on time!"

"Yes, you do, and we're all lucky to have you."

"Thank you. Now go toss those blankie-crazed urchins a bagel before I have to crack the whip."

Brandon headed down the stairs, and Amy took a deep breath

as she conducted a quick rundown of her mental checklist. Two hours before she was due to leave for New York, and she still had to shower, get everyone dressed, make sure they had enough dog food, do a frenzied surface cleaning in both bathrooms in anticipation of her mother-in-law's arrival, double-check that all the online bills were paid for the month, drive the twins to day care . . .

Brandon reappeared in the bedroom doorway. "I just gave them the carrot muffins on the breakfast bar and turned on *Sesame Street*. Want to lock the door and, you know, crack the whip?"

"But . . ." *But my shower is my ten minutes of sweet, sane solitude.* Then she looked at her husband, his kind, tired face, and realized that as much as she craved time alone, he craved time together.

She loved that he still looked at her like that, as if she were still the smoldering sex kitten she'd been in her early twenties, rather than an overscheduled mommy in her thirties who sometimes regarded sex as one more item to be checked off the list. He would miss her, she knew, while she was in New York. She would miss him. This knowledge, however, did nothing to shift her mind-set from brisk efficiency into seduction mode.

But Brandon didn't need to know that.

She summoned a saucy grin, grabbed his hand, and tugged him into the bathroom with her. "Grab the soap and let's multitask."

Chapter 6

Linnie hit the snooze button for the third time, then rolled over on her back and stared up at the revolving blades of the ceiling fan. The relentless desert sunlight cast a silhouette of the vertical blinds across the carpet. At this hour of the afternoon, most of her neighbors were at work and the apartment complex was shrouded in total silence. No phones ringing, no TVs blaring, no splashing in the community pool in the courtyard. She could hear the faint, dull thud of her pulse against the pillow.

If I died right now, how long would it be before anyone found the body?

Kyle had packed up his belongings and decamped to his buddy Matt's futon, leaving behind the pawn ticket that Derek had sent. Although Linnie had tried to suppress her anxiety and resentment, their friendship had permanently fractured. She'd asked the landlord to take his name off the lease and change the locks, and now she had the solitude she'd craved. No obligations, no expectations, no friends, and no real purpose in life beyond flipping cards for oversexed men on corporate expense accounts.

As soon as she got out of bed, before she got dressed or even used the bathroom, she picked up the phone and made the call that had become a daily ritual:

"Hi, I'm calling about the antique platinum-and-diamond brooch? Yes, again. Do you still have it?"

Every day she would hold her breath until the pawnshop employee replied, a tad impatiently, that yes, the brooch was still safely in the display case, and if she wanted it she'd better come reclaim it, because they weren't allowed to hold items after the redemption period expired.

"I'll be there," she always said. "Very soon."

But the moment she hung up the phone, her anxiety would return in anticipation of tomorrow's call. What would she do if the stoned-sounding male clerk (or his gum-snapping female counterpart) informed her that "we just sold that piece, actually, but could we interest you in an antique firearm or some collectible crystal stemware?"

She padded into the tiny kitchenette, peeled a banana, and glanced at the digital clock on the microwave. She should leave for work in thirty minutes, and after her shift at the casino, she'd head straight to the airport. No more procrastinating—she had to pack.

She dragged a battered old Samsonite out of the closet and tossed in jeans and T-shirts and wadded-up sweatshirts she'd had for years. Belatedly, she remembered Grammy Syl saying something about cocktail receptions, so she crammed in a dress and a pair of scuffed black sandals.

Cosmetics and jewelry had never held much appeal for her, so she collected the containers of eye shadow, lipstick, and foundation she wore for work, sealed them up in a plastic sandwich bag, and tossed that on top of the pile. Looking into that carry-on was like gazing into a dying planetary nebula: a murky jumble of black and gray. This was the wardrobe of someone who had completely given up.

But somehow, losing Grammy's brooch had swept her back into the world of cutthroat competition, first at the poker table and now at a national baking competition. For the first time in years, she would actually have to *try*.

And odds were, she would fail.

The mere thought of public failure made her throat close up. She couldn't stand to be criticized. She couldn't stand to be judged. Most of all, she couldn't stand to face Amy and, in doing so, face the parts of herself that she least wanted to acknowledge.

But for the next eight hours, all she had to do was tug up her fishnets, wriggle into her corset, and act like the kind of woman who enjoyed wearing leopard-print satin and meeting new people. She had to pretend to be normal. That, she could do.

As she headed out of the employee locker room toward the casino floor, Linnie rolled her shoulders and wedged the knuckles of one hand between the fingers of the other in a warm-up exercise she'd learned years ago from her piano teacher. Dealing cards for hours at a time required just as much dexterity and endurance as mastering scales and arpeggios.

A voice called out as she passed the door of her supervisor's office: "Hey, Linnie, would you step in here for a second? We need a word with you."

Linnie glanced down to ascertain that everything was in place. "What's wrong? Am I late?"

"No, no, you're right on time." Janice, a longtime floor worker with a face like an ex-model's and a voice like a cement mixer, ushered her into the small office filled with cheap corporate furniture and shiny fake plants. Chip, Janice's boss, was squeezed into a Naugahyde armchair behind a laminate desk. He had a clipboard and a somber expression on his face. *Uh-oh.*

"Come on in." Chip beckoned with both hands. "Close the door."

After a moment's hesitation, Linnie did so. The metallic snick of the door latch echoed through the office.

Chip cleared his throat and launched into a speech that had obviously been prepared ahead of time. "We've been noticing a few things over the past few weeks. Both of us."

Linnie's gaze fell on the pile of legal pads, manila envelopes, and pens stacked on the table between her supervisors. *Oh God.* They were documenting and corroborating the details of this conversation.

"You're firing me," she said, bracing one hand against the doorjamb.

"No!" Chip shook his head so vehemently, his glasses fell off. "Absolutely not. We're just making a few minor staffing changes."

Janice pushed back her mountainous blond bangs, opened one of the file folders, and got down to business. "Here's the deal. When we first opened the Kitty Korner two months ago, we thought you'd be a perfect fit. You're a great dealer and a total knockout."

"Ten plus," Chip added helpfully.

....

"But we both feel that there's room for improvement with the way you interact with our VIP guests."

Linnie stiffened. "I'm unfailingly polite."

"I know you are." Janice nodded. "That's part of the problem. The whole point of the Kitty Korner is that it's a little bit secluded; it's a little bit naughty."

"It's a hideaway," Chip threw in.

"Exactly. And when guys come in here, they want a whole fantasy to go along with their gaming. They want you to flirt with them, joke with them."

"I don't flirt." Linnie delivered this pronouncement as though flirting were beneath her, but the truth was that she *couldn't* flirt, even if she wanted to. Giggling and eyelash batting were simply not in her repertoire.

"And nobody's asking you to," Janice said. She and Chip exchanged a glance. "Your comfort and well-being are our first priority. That's why we think you might be happier moving back to the main floor. You can wear your old uniform of black slacks and a white shirt."

Given that Linnie had always felt discomfited flaunting her figure in the Kitty Korner costume, she was surprised at how much this suggestion stung. "So you're saying, in essence, that I'm not hoochie enough for the hoochie room?"

"Oh, hon, no one's saying that." Janice squeezed her hand, looking genuinely distressed. "We just feel that, personality-wise, you may not be the ideal fit here. Since we first opened the area, we've been tracking our customer demographic and behavior. And the guys don't spend as much time at your table as they do at the other girls'. They don't tip you as much."

"But I'm good at my job." Linnie tried not to plead. "I don't make mistakes."

"When it comes to shuffling and dealing, you are absolutely on point," Chip agreed. "But the girls who do well in this room tend to have a little swagger."

"I'll try harder," Linnie vowed. "I'll swagger."

Janice gave her another fortifying hand squeeze. "Swagger's not something you can force. And I don't want you to take any of this the wrong way. You're a good employee, and you're a classic beauty. You just come off as a tiny little bit, uh—"

"Cold," Chip muttered.

"Intimidating." Janice frowned at him. "I know you're scheduled to start a week's vacation tomorrow. Tell you what. Just take tonight off, too."

"Take as long as you need," Chip offered. "There's no rush, no rush at all."

This is where I'm supposed to quit gracefully so they don't have to fire me for being a socially stunted ice queen. But Linnie couldn't do it. She needed this job. This was her only source of income, and now she was in debt.

So she clenched her molars together and thanked them for demoting her with a smile on her face.

"Linnie?" Janice looked alarmed. "You okay?"

"Fine, thank you."

"That's all," Chip said, turning his attention back to his paperwork. "You can go home now."

So she did. She drove her crappy little car back to her crappy little apartment, unlaced her polyester corset and changed into one of her shapeless gray outfits. Then she went to the grocery store, spent the remaining cash in her wallet on butter, sugar, flour, and eggs, and devoted the rest of the night to making piecrusts.

Since she didn't own a food processor, she did it old-school: using a fork to score the cold butter into pea-size spheres. She considered experimenting by adding a few drops of chilled lemon juice, buttermilk, or even vinegar along with the sour cream to help break down the gluten proteins and enhance the buttery flavor, but ultimately she was too afraid and overwhelmed to deviate from Grammy's original recipe. So instead she focused on fine-tuning her rolling technique. She baked the crusts empty, without the apple filling. They turned out even better than she had hoped: flaky, light, rich, and golden brown.

As she broke off a piece of crust and let the delicate layers dissolve in her mouth, Linnie pressed her hands to her face and cried, her tears mingling with the sprinkling of flour dusted across her cheeks. Not because the pastry wasn't perfect, but because it was. She had been speaking the truth when she told her supervisors that she didn't make mistakes. But perfection paralyzed her. Perfection, or the illusion thereof, was what had derailed her life in the first place.

Chapter 7

"You're late." Linnie had an exasperated expression on her face and her watch prominently displayed when Amy pulled up to the airport curb.

"And hello to you, too." Amy tamped down her annoyance and leaned over to open the passenger-side door. "Is that all your luggage?"

Linnie glanced down at the lone carry-on bag. "Yeah. We're only going to be here for a week. Why? How much did you bring?"

Amy jerked her chin toward the backseat. "I'm doing my part to keep the chiropractors of America in business."

While Linnie wedged her black suitcase in amid the pile of overstuffed red bags, Amy reflected that her sister looked and behaved like a 1940s pinup with a mood disorder. From a painter's or photographer's perspective, Linnie really didn't have a bad side. She'd been born with thick, silky hair, perfect bone structure, and tilted coffee brown eyes that gleamed with foxlike cunning and intensity. When she and Linnie were children, strangers would stop the family on the street to ooh and aah over the angelic little blonde.

"What a gorgeous child," cashiers would gush, craning over the counter for a better look at Linnie. Then their gaze would flit over to Amy and their smile would soften. "And you're cute, too, sweetie."

When Linnie climbed into the front seat, Amy opened up the car's center console to display a veritable vending machine's worth of snacks. "Care for some chips? Cookies? Trail mix?"

Linnie refused the offer with a curt head shake. "You know, you were supposed to be here seventeen minutes ago."

"Given the traffic on I-95, seventeen minutes late is practically early." Amy flipped on her turn signal and tore into a bag of Doritos.

"I didn't know what happened to you, if you decided to blow me off or died in a fiery wreck or what," Linnie continued, her whole body tense. "I tried to call you."

"You did?" Amy grabbed her cell phone from the car's cup holder and glanced at the screen, which read: *3 missed calls*. "Oops. Sorry. I guess I didn't hear it ring—I had the stereo on pretty loud."

"Well, being late is really disrespectful, not to mention passive-aggressive. You're effectively conveying the message that your time is more important than mine."

Amy wrapped her fingers around the steering wheel and squeezed. "The only message I'm conveying is that road construction sucks and the Pretenders sound better cranked up to eleven.

There's no psychological power play here. Shit happens, and I'm not even that late. Let's just move on and try to have a good time, okay?"

"Okay." Linnie buckled her seat belt and lapsed into silence for a moment. Then she drew a deep breath, as if she couldn't help herself. "But punctuality is of utmost importance. This competition has a lot of time limits and—" Her lecture ended on a gasp as Amy floored the accelerator. The SUV leaped away from the curb, spun into a sudden, screeching U-turn across four lanes of traffic, and narrowly missed a collision with a rental car shuttle bus.

Linnie clapped her hands over her mouth, then braced herself against the dashboard and cried, "What are you doing?"

"Going home." Amy gunned it for the airport exit. "I quit."

"You can't quit!"

"Sure I can. Watch me." The car screeched to a halt as Amy braked for a yield sign. She turned to her sister with one eyebrow raised. "I'll drop you at the hotel, and then you're on your own. *Smacznego*, baby."

"Slow down!" Linnie cried as Amy merged into traffic. "You're out of control."

"Oh, how I wish that were true," Amy countered. "But actually, I have spent the last few years of my life being completely reasonable and responsible: 'Put on sunscreen, send your mother a birthday card, eat your vegetables, don't forget to floss.' This week is my vacation, and I will not have you badgering me and giving me agita over seventeen stupid minutes."

"But this bake-off is—"

"Exactly that. It's a *bake-off*," Amy said. "Put it in perspective, Linnie: It's just fucking pie."

Linnie slumped back into her seat. "Not to me."

Amy kept one eye on the road and the other on her sister. "Is this about the money? Because I'll write you a check right now if it'll get me out of this. How much do you need? Two thousand? Five?"

"Forty."

Amy choked. "I'm sorry. Could you repeat that? I thought you said you need forty thousand dollars."

Linnie nibbled her lip, calculating internally. "Well, probably more like forty-five once all is said and done."

Amy whistled long and low. "Vasylina Bialek, what did you get yourself into?"

Linnie sighed. "Just come and do this with me, okay? Please. I'll stop badgering you." She paused, then amended that to, "I'll *try* to stop badgering you."

The smart, sensible side of Amy knew this was the time to get tough, cut her losses, and leave Linnie in the rearview mirror. But her sappy, sentimental side had summoned up an absurdly misguided sense of protectiveness. "Fine. *Fine*. But remember, we're supposed to be a team. Cut me a little slack, and I'll do the same for you."

"I don't need slack." Linnie straightened up, straining against her seat belt. "I'm never late."

Amy rolled her eyes. "For anything? Ever? In life?"

"It's one of my rules."

"You sure have a lot of rules."

"What can I say? I respond well to structure."

Amy adjusted the heater vent and bit into a nacho chip. "Do you mind if I turn the Pretenders back on? Or do you have a rule against new-wave music, too?"

"Is it going to be too loud to talk?"

"Yep."

"Then by all means, rock on."

"Good afternoon. Welcome to the Hotel McMillan." A willowy, well-coiffed hotel receptionist smiled expectantly. The little brass pin on the lapel of her maroon blazer identified her as Michelle. "How may I help you today?"

Amy cleared her throat, the sound echoing through the high-ceilinged, marble-tiled lobby. "Hi, I'm with the Delicious Duet Dessert Championship and I have a room reservation through the weekend. Should be under Amy Nichols."

"I've got a reservation, too," Linnie piped up from over Amy's shoulder. "Vasylina Bialek. That's V-A-S-Y-L—"

"Wait your turn," Amy admonished.

Michelle remained perky and attentive, but didn't make any move to enter the information into her computer. She just upped the wattage of her smile and announced, "Well, ladies, I have good news and bad news."

Amy glanced back at her sister. "Uh-oh."

"The bad news is, the hotel has been inadventently overbooked for the duration of the bake-off and we've run out of rooms. But the good news is, we've arranged for our overflow guests to stay a few blocks away at the Hilton. We're going to supply a courtesy shuttle to get you back and forth. Plus, we'll provide you with a hundred-dollar voucher for our hotel restaurant, and—"

"Unacceptable," Linnie said. Her breathing had accelerated, and she was digging her fingernails into the nape of her neck.

"Stop scratching," Amy whispered.

Linnie dropped her hand, but continued hyperventilating. "Staying in this hotel is absolutely imperative," she told the clerk.

"I need to be able to monitor the humidity and air temperature on the mezzanine levels at precise intervals over the next few days and nights. We've got perfect piecrust on the line here."

"Hmm. Let me see what I can do. Give me just one second." Michelle tapped at her keyboard. "Are you two together?"

"No," Amy said, just as Linnie said, "Yes."

"Well, it appears that we do have one last vacancy, up in the South Tower. I'm really not supposed to put Delicious Duet registrants up there, but I suppose, if you don't mind bunking in together—"

"I mind," Amy said.

"It's a suite," the clerk continued. "Normally goes for twenty-two hundred dollars a night."

"We'll take it," Linnie said.

"Hold on a second," Amy interrupted. She addressed the clerk. "Does this suite have two bedrooms?"

"Only one, I'm afraid. And one bed. But it's king-size, with the special linen package we use for our luxury suites: featherbed mattress topper, eiderdown duvet, Egyptian cotton sheets, Belgian chocolates every night with turndown. . . ."

"We'll take it," Amy relented.

"And if you prefer separate sleeping quarters, there is a large sofa in the sitting room," the clerk said.

"Works for me." Amy jerked her thumb toward Linnie. "She'll be on the sofa."

"Very well. You're all set." Michelle handed Amy a small stack of paperwork. "You'll want to use that elevator right over there. Just slip your room key into the slot above the elevator keypad to access the tower floors."

Amy gathered up two of her suitcases, left the rest for the bell-hop, and led the way across the lobby. She assumed that Linnie was right behind her until she heard a muffled thump and a surprised "Oof!"

She turned around to see Linnie struggling to disentangle herself from the long, slender straps of a gym bag carried by a tiny young woman with biceps that would make Madonna jealous.

"Oh gosh, I'm so sorry!" exclaimed the deep-dimpled petite powerhouse, who sported a sassy dark brown shag haircut, tight-fitting workout gear, and diamond stud earrings. "I was gawking up at that huge chandelier, and I didn't even see you. What a klutz! Here, let me help you."

"I'm fine." Linnie pulled away with a frown, her tone positively glacial. Amy shot her a questioning glance.

"Holy cow, are you okay?" A tall, lanky man with wire-rimmed glasses and a wide, earnest face appeared on the other side of Linnie.

"It's my fault," the woman told him, all the while trying to brush off Linnie's coat. "I walked right into her."

"Sugar plum, you have *got* to watch where you're going," the man said. Then he turned back to Linnie. "You sure you're all right?"

"I'm fine." Linnie yanked at her coat lapel and backed away from the couple. Amy felt alternately outraged and embarrassed by her sister's rudeness. Because Linnie had grown up so sheltered and isolated from her peers, the Bialek family overlooked a whole lot of what might tactfully be termed "eccentricity." But there was no excuse for this kind of behavior.

"She's fine." Amy inserted herself between Linnie and the well-meaning couple. "She's just had a very long flight."

"Hey, are you guys here with the Delicious Duet competition?" the man asked.

"Yes, we are." Amy extended her right hand. "I'm Amy Nichols and this is my sister, Linnie Bialek."

"Oh goody!" The little lady clapped her hands. "I'm always so thrilled to meet my fellow bakers."

"I'll say!" The man clasped Amy's hand and gave it a hearty shake. "Pleased to meet you. I'm Ty Tottenham and this is my wife, Tai."

Chapter 8

Linnie saw Amy's smile flicker as Ty and Tai introduced themselves. The change in expression was so fast, anyone else would have missed it, but Linnie caught the nanosecond of pure panic in her sister's eyes.

"Ty and Tai," Amy echoed. "You don't say."

"I know, crazy, right? Obviously we were meant to be." Tai craned her neck to give her husband a quick buss on the cheek, then said, "Hope we'll see you gals around. What room are you staying in, anyway? Maybe we're neighbors."

"We're in a suite up in the South Tower." Amy glanced down at the digits scrawled on the paper jacket for her key card. "Room two-six-two-eight. Ow!" She yelped as Linnie threw a swift elbow jab to her rib cage.

"Lovely to meet you both. We have to go." Linnie strode across the lobby and onto the elevator without a backward glance.

"What the hell is wrong with you? You are *so rude.*" Amy caught the elevator doors just as they were closing and forced them back open. She rubbed her side and winced. "Ow. I think you broke my clavicle."

"Your clavicle's your collarbone," Linnie said. "I hit your asternal ribs. And how could you be so stupid as to tell them our suite number? I can't believe you'd give them ammunition like that. Now we'll have to change rooms."

"We got the last room in the entire hotel," Amy reminded her. "We can't change. Not that there's any reason to."

"Don't be so sure about that." Linnie jammed her key card into the "restricted floors" slot and punched in twenty-six. "I know sharks when I see them."

Amy burst out laughing. "Sharks in L.L.Bean corduroys and Nikes? They were just being friendly, for heaven's sake. They're from *Ohio!*"

"Don't fall for that wide-eyed, aw-shucks facade. What they just pulled in the lobby is a classic two-person pickpocket maneuver: the sandwich." Linnie narrowed her eyes. "The woman bumped me and tried to distract me with her apologies and inquiries about things that are none of her business while her partner started to ransack my coat and bags. She's the stall; he's the pick. I see it all the time on the casino floor."

Amy made a big show of peering into her purse. "Oh, thank heavens, my wallet's still here. Whew, that was a close one."

"How can you be this gullible?" Linnie tapped her foot as the elevator zoomed up. "They don't want our wallets. They want our baking intel!"

"Do you have any idea how insane you sound right now?"

"Who spent five years on the Junior Science Olympiad circuit, you or me? People who spend their lives training for intense competitions don't see the world like you do. They get desperate and irrational. They get vicious." Linnie had to avert her gaze as she finished with, "They stoop to things they never imagined they'd be capable of."

Amy said nothing, so Linnie kept going. "I've met dozens of Ty and Tais. Keep your mouth shut and your guard up or you'll be sorry. Trust me."

At this, Amy grinned. "Whatever would I do without you to protect me from the cold, cruel world?"

"You'd be an appetizer at the Delicious Duet feeding frenzy, that's what," Linnie shot back. "From now on, you're forbidden to talk to any contestants unless I'm standing right there to supervise. That's right, I said *forbidden*."

"So you're not allowed to be late, and I'm not allowed to talk to anyone." Amy ticked off these points on her fingers. "I'm going to have to start writing this down." She swayed on her feet as the elevator car shuddered to a stop.

"What was that?" Linnie demanded, scanning the button panel. "Are we stuck?"

Amy gripped the railing and glanced up at the ceiling. "Evidently."

Linnie immediately shifted into meltdown mode. "What are we going to do? Who should we call? Where's the alarm button?"

"Why don't we just wait a few minutes? I'm sure it'll get going again."

"We're already behind schedule," Linnie exclaimed. "You have no idea how much I have to do this afternoon. I've got to track down the judges and make sure all our equipment arrived and start recon on the baking floor layout and atmospheric conditions."

"And as exciting as that all sounds, there's really nothing we can do to change our situation right now. So let's take a nice deep breath and try to have a pleasant conversation."

Linnie crossed her arms. "I don't do small talk."

She had her finger on the red button depicting the alarm bell when she heard a muted grinding noise and the elevator lurched back into motion.

"See?" Amy released her death grip on the side rail. "Here we go. Just a momentary glitch."

When the elevator finally opened on the twenty-sixth floor, Linnie grabbed her bag and bustled down the hallway, leaving Amy to wrestle with her oversize suitcases and the closing doors.

"No worries," Amy called after her. "I got this." Linnie heard a few muffled bumps and grunts of exertion, and then a deep male voice said, "Let me help you with that."

Amy's voice instantly took on a fluttery, girlish lilt. "Oh, thank you!"

Linnie glanced back over her shoulder to see a tall, dark-haired man hoisting up her sister's luggage. She didn't get a good look at his face, but she deduced that he must be handsome from all of Amy's carrying on.

"Such a gentleman!"

"My pleasure," the man replied. "May I carry these to your room?"

"Oh no, I can take it from here, but thanks again." Amy caught up with Linnie at the door to their room and hissed, "Did you see that guy?"

"Yeah." Linnie shrugged. "So?"

"So he's cute! He's got lots of potential." Wink, wink, nudge, nudge.

Linnie looked down her nose with a stern schoolmarm stare. "Must I remind you that you're married?"

Amy looked shocked for a moment, then laughed. "Oh my God, you're hopeless. Not potential for me—for you. He was so busy checking you out, he practically ran into the wall."

Linnie brushed back her hair. "I didn't notice."

"Of course you didn't. I guess it must be hard to find men who live up to your standards, huh?"

Linnie swiped the key card through the door lock and waited for the tiny lights on the lock to flash green before turning the knob. "What standards?"

"I believe you once told me that any man with an IQ under one fifty might as well be brain-dead," Amy said. "You said you were holding out for Einstein's intellect, James Bond's savoir faire, and Debussy's musical sensibilities."

Linnie thought about the handful of dates she'd had over the last few years: nice, normal men who asked her out with great enthusiasm, only to take her dinner, bring her home early, and never call her again once they realized that the blond hair and buxom body were false advertising and that she was, in fact, more puritan than party girl.

Not that she cared. Much like small talk and tardiness, Linnie didn't do relationships.

She'd tried out a few one-night stands in her early twenties when she wanted to feel more desirable and less lonely, but she found the whole experience—from bar hookup to breakfast—debasing and distasteful.

"I've given up on finding anyone who can actually keep up

with me." She flipped on the light switch, illuminating the suite's interior.

"Dude." Amy dropped her bags, bent her elbow, and jerked down her fist in a gesture of triumph. "Score."

A sumptuous gold brocade sofa and a pair of padded, embroidered French chairs surrounded a limestone-topped coffee table. Floor-to-ceiling silk drapes flocked the huge windows, which were framed with molded wood panels. An original oil painting hung above the fireplace mantel. Silver bowls full of fresh fruit and crystal vases full of fresh flowers completed the atmosphere of quiet elegance. Everything looked authentically antique, exorbitantly expensive, and highly breakable.

"We have our own dining room!" Amy reported, peeking around a corner.

"Where's the thermostat control?" Linnie pulled her coat tighter around her torso. "It's freezing in here."

"Check out this bathroom." Amy's voice echoed off the slabs of white marble. "You could swim laps in this tub."

Linnie zeroed in on the cut-crystal tumbler next to the sink. "Oh my God. Look at this." She pointed out the ring of coral pink lipstick on the rim. "That is *vile*."

But Amy had moved on to the next room. "It's the bed of my dreams," she whispered reverently. "There must be fifteen throw pillows." She ran her hands over the puffy down comforter and the massive hardwood headboard. Her eyes got misty. "And look, there's a white-noise generator right here on the nightstand."

"I just hope it's properly sanitized," Linnie fretted. "Though after seeing that drinking glass, I don't hold out a lot of hope. Bedbugs are absolutely rampant in this city. No one in the hotel industry wants to acknowledge it, but I just watched a PBS documentary on parasites and—"

Amy silenced her with a look. "Stop."

"Stop what?"

"You like rules, right?" Amy kicked off her shoes and flung herself backward onto the bed. "Here's a rule for you: No more complaining."

"But that glass had someone else's *lipstick*—"

Amy turned on the white-noise generator, drowning out Linnie's voice with the sound of waves crashing on the beach.

Linnie stopped protesting when she noticed the time on the digital alarm clock. "The welcome cocktail reception starts at six. I'll go freshen up and leave you to your linen fetish."

When she turned off the faucet after her steamy shower, Linnie heard Amy talking out in the sitting room. She finished toweling off and was reaching for the hotel's hair dryer when she heard Amy utter a word that sounded like "Kyle."

The air-conditioned chill suddenly turned icy against her bare skin. Her limbs broke out in goose pimples.

She cracked open the bathroom door and peeked out toward the sitting room. "Amy? Who are you talking to?"

Amy was nestled into the sofa cushions with her feet propped up on the priceless antique coffee table. She pointed to the cell phone pressed against her ear and made a shushing gesture. "Yes, she has a sister . . ." she said into the phone. "Yes, for real . . . No, I can't imagine why she's never mentioned me."

"Is that my phone?" Linnie demanded.

Amy ignored this and continued her exchange with the caller.

"No, she never mentioned anything about *The Joy of Cooking*. Why do you ask?"

"Is that Kyle?" Linnie charged toward Amy, who pushed off the couch and dashed to the other side of the suite, where she closed the bedroom door in Linnie's face.

Thunk. The dead bolt slid into place. Linnie rattled the knob, then pressed her cheek up against the thick wooden door in a desperate bid to overhear. *"Hang up the phone!"*

"Uh-huh . . . uh-huh . . ." Amy murmured. "Wow, that does sound terrible."

"Hang up!" Linnie shrieked again. She pounded the heel of her hand against the door.

A few seconds later, Amy yanked open the door and stared her sister down with pursed lips and flinty eyes. "That was your old buddy Kyle. Want to guess what he had to say?"

Linnie turned away, suffused with guilt and shame. Then she shook off her self-reproach and went on the offensive. "How dare you answer my phone?"

"It was an honest mistake." Amy strode past her into the sitting room and plunked down the sleek silver phone next to an identical model on the coffee table.

Linie blinked. "We have the exact same phone?"

"And the exact same ringtone, apparently." Amy wrinkled her nose. "'Particle Man,' huh? I never would have figured you for They Might Be Giants. What happened to Debussy?"

Damn. Linnie had meant to update her phone before she left Vegas. "I've basically had 'Particle Man' stuck in my head nonstop since that summer when you played it over and over and over," she said accusingly. "Even the dog probably knew 'Particle Man' word for word. And that other song, what was it?"

" 'Birdhouse in Your Soul.' " Amy brightened. "Ryan Kincaid gave me that CD when we first started dating. Wow. I haven't thought about him in years. Remember Ryan Kincaid?"

Linnie more than remembered Ryan Kincaid; she had *yearned* for him. He had been the star of the varsity soccer team and played the guitar and looked like a cast member of a WB drama, and Linnie had spent that entire summer fantasizing that he would come to his senses, break up with Amy, and realize that Linnie was the only girl he could ever love.

"Ryan who?" she said. "Was he the one who ended up going to Dartmouth?"

"Beats me. But he was a cutie, huh? Good kisser, too." Amy's expression hardened as she returned her focus to Linnie. "Kyle asked if I would pass along a message. He says to tell you that he's 'brutally sorry' and that he got a callback for some regional radio commercial, and just as soon as his voice-over career takes off, he'll pay you back so that you can get Grammy Syl's brooch out of the pawnshop."

Linnie cringed at the disdain in her sister's voice.

"How could you?" Amy demanded.

"I didn't," Linnie sputtered, knowing this would only make matters worse. "Kyle's brother did." She twisted her hands together and summarized the events that led up to her bankruptcy at the high-stakes poker table. "But I'm going to get it back, I swear. As soon as I get the check from winning this competition, I'm going straight to the pawnshop."

Amy stared at her as though she had started speaking in tongues. "We're not going to win."

Linnie stared right back with grim determination. "Oh, yes, we are."

"Okay, now you're scaring me. You're delusional if you really believe . . ." Amy trailed off as suspicion dawned. "Hold on. Does Grammy Syl know about all this?"

"No. Not about the brooch, anyway. She just knows I need money, which is why she let me take her place and—"

"Stop talking." Amy fixed her with a glare of withering scorn. "I can't listen to another word. In fact, I can't even stand to look at you right now. I am going to change into a cocktail dress and get out of here before I do something we'll both regret."

Linnie swallowed and stared out the window. "I'll skip the reception and stay up here tonight. You probably need some time to—"

"Oh, no, you don't. You're not getting out of all the social events just because you pissed me off. You're going to every single luncheon, mixer, and awards ceremony." Amy stormed off, tossing over her shoulder, "You better be on time, too, after all the crap I got for being seventeen minutes late this afternoon."

"I'll be there," Linnie vowed. "Six o'clock sharp. I promise."

Linnie jammed one foot into a pair of sheer black tights and glanced at the clock for a time check: fifteen minutes until she was due at the welcome reception.

The gossamer material snagged on one of her toenails, resulting in a giant, jagged run up the back of one calf. She swore under her breath and dug through her suitcase, knowing as she did so that she hadn't packed extra panty hose.

Well, she'd just have to show up bare-legged, despite the winter weather. She yanked her cheap polyester gray sheath dress over her head, cinched a black patent-leather belt around her waist, raked a brush through her hair, and had just started to dab on makeup when the glass bottle of foundation bobbled in her hand. Light beige liquid splashed across the bodice of her dress as the bottle fell to the bathroom floor, where it shattered and splattered all over the contents of her open suitcase.

The few dressy outfits she'd packed—the evening gown, the stiletto heels, the cashmere cardigan—were now polka-dotted with "porcelain bisque." When she dabbed at the material with a damp washcloth, the stains simply diluted and spread.

Time check: She had twelve minutes to get down to the lobby.

Considering Amy's mood, punctuality took precedence over personal appearance. She gave up on accessories and cosmetics, pulled on a dark gray sweatshirt from a long-ago summer program at MIT, shoved her feet into the pair of black leather flats Amy had left by the bed, and hightailed it to the elevator bank.

She shifted her weight and nibbled the inside of her cheek while she stared at her reflection in the polished brass elevator doors. *Come on, come on, come on. . . .*

Time check: eight minutes.

Screw this. Linnie had worked in a hotel casino long enough to know that there were always shortcuts to avoid the herds of convention-goers all trying to get to the same place at the same time.

She hurried down the hall and around a corner, past the supply closet and the ice machine, until she came upon the small, hidden alcove housing the freight elevator.

The moment she pressed the button, a pair of battered metal doors slid open, revealing a tall, attractive man whose expression of mild surprise mirrored her own.

She stepped aside to let him exit.

He didn't move.

"Are you getting out?" she asked, not bothering to hide her impatience.

"Are you getting on?"

She recognized the voice as belonging to the guy who had helped Amy with her luggage earlier that afternoon.

He was so busy checking you out, he practically ran into the wall.

"Yes," she said.

"Then I'm going back down." He extended his arm to hold the doors open for her. When she raised one eyebrow, he smiled and said, "I'm, uh, testing the elevator."

He didn't have any sort of regional accent, per se, but something about his enunciation hinted at privilege and extensive education, and his navy suit looked understated but expensive.

"'Testing the elevator'? That's the best you can do?" Linnie smoothed back her hair. "Come now. How about the old, 'I forgot something in the lobby'?"

"All right." He smiled, revealing perfect, even white teeth. "I forgot something in the lobby."

She studiously ignored him.

"Are you an MIT alum?" he asked, nodding at the emblem on her sweatshirt.

"Nope."

"What brings you to New York?"

Linnie finally deigned to look him in the eye. "Listen, I understand that you're just being polite, and I'm sure you're a very nice guy, but you're not my type, so let's not ruin this with talking. I'm in a hurry and I'm being stymied by hundreds of baking fanatics."

"Not a fan of baking?"

"That would be an understatement." She turned away again.

The doors rumbled shut and the elevator started its descent with a creaky jerk. Linnie pitched forward, but his hand shot out to cushion her forehead before she hit the metal panel.

She heard his sharp intake of breath as he pulled away.

"Thank you." She watched the floor numbers count down on the digital display above the button panel. She could feel his gaze on her, skimming over her baggy hoodie and polyester skirt, then lingering on her bare legs.

"Stop looking at me."

"You said no talking. You said nothing about looking."

"Well, I'm saying it now: no looking."

"My apologies. You look lovely, if that helps matters at all."

"It doesn't—" The elevator car plummeted. Linnie gasped and squeezed her eyes shut during a few seconds of free fall, before they jerked to a halt.

"Are you all right?"

She opened her eyes, still white-knuckling the handrail. Her whole body trembled from the sudden spurt of terror. "I think so. What was that?"

He appeared completely calm and composed. "I believe that was the elevator malfunctioning. Don't panic; let's give it a minute."

"I don't have a minute!" She pushed the "L" button again and again, to no avail.

"Stay calm."

Time check: four minutes. "I don't have the luxury of staying calm." Linnie shook her head. "This is ridiculous. I've stayed in twenty-dollar youth hostels that were better than this dump. For twenty-two hundred dollars a night, an operational elevator is not too much to ask. I'm going to write corporate a strongly worded letter, and I've got half a mind to sue."

He looked intrigued. "On what grounds?"

"False imprisonment."

"You might have a tough time making that stick."

"Maybe, but they'd probably throw me a hefty settlement just to shut me up." Increasingly agitated, she worked her fingertips into the crack between the elevator doors and pulled with all her might. The doors didn't budge.

She heard him step up directly behind her.

"What are you doing?" he asked.

She gritted her teeth and tried again. "Getting the hell out of here."

He produced his cell phone and started dialing. "I'll call the front desk and ask them to send someone."

Linnie could feel the veins in her forehead pulsing as she struggled with the doors. "Three minutes!"

He froze, his index finger poised above the "send" button. "You're not going to wait for assistance like a rational human being, are you?"

Three of her fingernails broke simultaneously as she clawed at the metal doors. "Argh!"

He sighed, then reached for his black leather briefcase. "Step aside."

"What are you planning to do?"

He popped open the case's gunmetal latches and extracted a small Swiss army knife with a screwdriver attachment. Then he shrugged out of his suit jacket and rolled up the sleeves of his crisp white shirt. Using the slim piece of steel as a fulcrum, he managed to get the doors open wide enough to insert his hands, then slowly widened the gap with a lot of brute force and just a tiny bit of swearing. By the time he finished, his forehead glistened with a slight sheen of sweat.

Through the partial opening, Linnie could see that they were stuck between floors. The thick slab of concrete foundation spanned most of the elevator car's height, and the only way out was the opening at the top, through a four-foot gap that started at her eyebrows.

"Wow. Okay."

"You're welcome."

"Thank you," she muttered. She reached up through the opening, planted her palms on the carpet of the floor above them, and turned to her companion expectantly. "Give me a boost."

He shook his head. "Bad idea. What if the motor starts up again while you're climbing out?"

"What are the odds of that happening?" Linnie scoffed. "I'll be quick."

"Statistics don't apply to individual cases."

She froze. "What did you just say?"

"Citing probability theory isn't going to help you much if you've wriggled only halfway through when the motor decides to start working again. The rational thing to do would be to contact the front desk and wait a few minutes for help."

"No offense, but I didn't ask for your opinion. I take full responsibility for my actions. Now, about that boost . . . ?"

He knelt down, laced his hands together, and positioned himself so that his face was practically smashed into her hip. "This is going to get awkward, isn't it?"

"Only for a second. I took gymnastics for eight years, and I excel at vaulting. Okay, I'm ready." She moved into position, pushing her foot into his palms. He didn't move. She finally looked down and caught him staring at the expanse of thigh exposed by her hiked-up hemline.

She could feel his breath coming warm and fast against her skin, and she must have made an involuntary sound in her throat, because he finally glanced up and their gazes locked.

For once, Linnie wasn't thinking about anything.

The deafening ticking clock in her brain stilled.

He stared up at her as though he could read her thoughts.

Time check: *Who the hell cares?*

She could kiss him right now, do whatever she wanted. He would never know anything about who she was—or who she used to be. This would be an isolated, insulated act of passion with no judgment or repercussions.

Then a lone coherent thought bubbled slowly to the surface: *Now I know what it's like to be stupid.*

Linnie snapped out of her reverie and lurched back into action with graceless urgency.

"Here we go," she said crisply. "Over the wall."

Trying to ignore the pressure of his hands against her calves, her thighs, her backside, she hoisted herself up and scrambled over the edge onto the carpeted floor. One of her shoes tumbled off as she struggled to her feet, but she didn't look back as she raced toward the stairwell.

Time check: fifty seconds.

"Good luck!" called the guy left behind in the elevator.

She didn't waste time or energy replying. He'd served his purpose, so she left him in the dust.

She stumbled on a stairwell landing en route to the lobby, but leaped back to her feet and sped up, impervious to the pain. Then she slammed through the door to the lobby and sprinted across the vast expanse of crystal and marble toward an easel bearing a sign:

DELICIOUS DUET WELCOME RECEPTION

"Hi, there." She skidded to a stop, panting and clutching her side, and hobbled over to the bespectacled event organizer holding a clipboard and a stack of name tags. "Linnie Bialek, present and accounted for."

Chapter 9

"Who is *that*?" The perky, pixieish redhead standing next to Amy interrupted herself halfway through a story about fallen soufflé. Her teammate, a silver-haired matron wearing a pink tweed suit and pearl earrings, followed her gaze and froze, her champagne flute halfway to her lips.

All around them, conversations died, then started up again in whispers and murmurs, swelling into a crescendo of speculation:

"I've never seen her before."

"No kidding. I'd definitely remember her."

"Maybe the sponsors finally broke down and hired a spokes-model this year."

"A spokesmodel from MIT? That poor gal needs a stylist."

Amy didn't have to turn around to know that Linnie had arrived.

Sure enough, when she glanced toward the front of the room, she spotted her sister straggling in just as the clock struck six. Linnie ignored all the whispers and stares, scanning the crowd until she located Amy. She smiled with obvious relief and started toward her.

Amy gave her the warmest welcome she could muster at the moment: "What on earth are you wearing? You look like the Unabomber." She glanced down at Linnie's bare foot, then did a double take. "Hey! That's my shoe."

Linnie nodded. Her hair had tangled around her hoop earrings, and her pale shin sported a big red blotch.

"What happened to the other one?"

"It's a long story; I'll tell you later. But I would like to state for the record that I am here on time."

Keenly aware of their audience, Amy restricted her response to a close-lipped smile, then introduced her new acquaintances. "This is Susan Miller and her stepmother, Joan Whitson. They're making strawberry rhubarb upside-down cake. They grow their own rhubarb in their yards. Isn't that cool?"

Joan and Susan swiveled wordlessly toward Linnie, who shot Amy a filthy look before shaking their hands.

"Delighted to meet you," Susan said to Linnie. "I can't wait to try your Polish apple pie. Amy's told us all about it, and it sounds delicious."

"May I have a word with you?" Linnie hissed, dragging Amy toward a secluded corner by the coat check. "What do you think you're doing, getting all cozy with 'Susan' and 'Joan'?"

"Are you implying those are aliases?" Amy replied with mock solemnity. "Because I'm pretty sure those are their real names. They have badges. Very official."

"You're not allowed to talk to any of the other contestants, remember? They're the enemy."

"Oh my God, give it a rest." Amy slugged back the rest of her punch. "Why does it always have to be you versus the world?"

A burst of microphone feedback reverberated through the room as a gentleman in a gray suit and a striped bow tie called their attention to the front of the room. With his bald pate, bushy white mustache, and short stature, he bore a startling resemblance to the Monopoly mascot in the top hat and tails.

"Good evening, everyone. I'm Snowley Millington, the official contest coordinator, and I'm here to congratulate you and give you a warm welcome to our Delicious Duet Dessert Championship. We had over ten thousand entries this year, and only fifty finalists, so you should be very proud of yourselves." He paused for the audience to applaud themselves before glancing down at his notecards and continuing on. "This year marks the fiftieth anniversary of Delicious sugar, and we have some very exciting surprises in store for our contestants. But first, a few words about the contest rules and regulations."

A tinny, electric version of "Particle Man" blasted through the silence. Amy unzipped her handbag, and Linnie opened hers, too.

"It's mine," Amy murmured. "Same ringtone, remember?"

Brandon's name flashed on her caller ID. She knew he'd be calling during dinnertime only if he was in crisis mode, so she slipped out into the hotel lobby and flipped open the phone.

"Sorry," he said as soon as she said hello. "I know you're in the middle of schmoozing and boozing, but Chloe can't find her Lovey—"

"—and your eardrums are bleeding from the shrieks?"

"Exactly. Where'd you stash the backup?"

"Linen closet in the back hall by the kids' bathroom. Should be on the top shelf tucked under the extra pillows."

"Okay, hang on a second." As Brandon walked over to the closet, Amy could hear her daughter's plaintive wails in the background, and a sharp pang of love pricked her heart.

"Got it," Brandon reported a few seconds later. The wailing subsided. "Thanks, sweetheart. You're a lifesaver. Okay, go back to carousing. Sorry to interrupt."

"No, I'm glad you called." Amy felt simultaneously buoyant with freedom and tethered by homesickness. After she finished saying "I love you" and "bye-bye" to every member of her family, she rejoined the cocktail reception, where Mr. Millington had concluded his remarks and the participants were resuming their conversations. She made her way over to Linnie. "What'd I miss?"

Linnie held up a stack of white paper cocktail napkins, upon which she'd taken meticulous notes. "First they went over all the rules, most of which we already know from the handbook. But they elaborated on what the judges are specifically looking for, so I rated each item on a Likert scale of one to five based on relative importance."

"A what scale?"

Linnie handed over the napkins so Amy could see for herself:

- Each team will be assigned to an oven and prep station tomorrow morning and must use this area for the duration of the competition. NO CHANGES OR SWAPS ALLOWED.

- All fifty teams will compete in a semifinal round on Wednesday; those twenty-five teams with the highest scores will advance to the final round on Friday.
- Each team must prepare three batches of their recipe on the day of competition: one for the judges, one for display/photography, and one for the audience and press to sample.
- Dishes will be scored on each of the following attributes:
  * overall taste and flavor profile (importance: 5 out of 5)
  * texture and consistency (importance: 3 out of 5)
  * prominent and appropriate use of Delicious sugar (importance: 3 out of 5)
  * presentation and visual appeal (importance: 4 out of 5)
- All equipment and ingredients will be supplied by the official "Delicious sugar supply pantry." Each team will be assigned a "runner," who will retrieve from the pantry the ingredients listed on that team's recipe. Contestants are not allowed in the pantry, and inventory is limited. Before you begin baking, please double-check the supplies provided by your runner to ensure that you have sufficient quantities for three batches.
- Food must be served at proper temperature—allow for ample cooling time.
- Entrants may be disqualified if they violate any of the official rules, including:
  * plagiarizing a recipe
  * reusing an original recipe with which they already won a different contest

  * claiming novice status when they are in fact
    culinary professionals (e.g., chef, caterer)
* Judges will remain sequestered throughout competition—
  any attempt to contact or influence judges will result in
  disqualification.

"Hold on, the judges are sequestered?" Amy looked up at Linnie for confirmation. "We're not going to meet them until the day of the competition?"

"We're not going to meet them at all," Linnie corrected. "Their identities are top secret; they don't attend any contest events, and even during the competition, they'll be holed up in a separate area. The bake-off bunker, if you will. Runners bring our food from the competition floor to the bunker. No face time whatsoever."

"But I was planning to dazzle them with my charm and bubbly personality!" Amy exclaimed. "Are you telling me we're going to have to win this on skill alone?"

"I would worry less about chatting up the judges and more about this little rule right here." Linnie pointed to the "no plagiarism" policy.

"Oh, that." Amy shrugged this off. "That's not gonna be a problem. I mean, we have an original recipe."

"But we didn't come up with it." Linnie reddened and glanced away. "It wasn't really our idea."

"Somebody has a guilty conscience?" Amy paused a moment and watched Linnie squirm.

Before Linnie could reply, Susan and Joan flagged them down from across the room. "Amy!" cried Susan. "All the girls are going out to dinner. Come with us!"

"You must!" Joan said. "Everyone's going to love you. There's

BETH KENDRICK

a little Chinese place a few blocks away; supposedly the dim sum is to die for. And then we might head uptown to Serendipity 3 for frozen hot chocolate—a bit touristy, I know, but let's face it: We're tourists."

"Your sister is welcome, too," Susan added as an afterthought.

"Sounds great." Amy nodded. "We're in."

"No, thank you." Linnie slouched into the depths of her sweatshirt. "I'm going to go to bed early."

"Oh, come on," Susan coaxed. "Don't be a stick in the mud."

Linnie whispered to Amy, "May I remind you that we've got orientation tomorrow morning at nine? We are here to work."

"The accusation: being a stick in the mud. The verdict: guilty as charged," Amy whispered back. "I'll be back before sunrise. Enjoy your sudoku and your Sleepytime tea."

"I prefer Tension Tamer, for your information." Linnie shoved her hands into the pockets of her hoodie and marched down the hall.

"Hey, where are you going?" Amy called after her. "The elevators are that way."

"I'm taking a shortcut." Linnie sounded a tad evasive. "Freight elevator."

Amy drifted slowly into consciousness, her limbs stretching out against soft cotton sheets. The hotel suite was silent, save for the hum of the air duct. Judging by the frigid draft blowing across her face, the room's air-conditioning issues had yet to be resolved. She snuggled deeper into the airy down comforter and tried to savor the stillness.

The moment she'd been fantasizing about had finally arrived:

No ravenous toddlers. No digestively disturbed dog. No impetus to leap up, shower, dress, and caffeinate now, now, *now*!

If she so desired, she could lounge around in bed for another half an hour. Read a book. Complete a thought.

Ahhh. Peace. Quiet. Serenity.

God, I'm bored.

She cracked open the door to the sitting area and peered over at the motionless mini–mountain range of blankets on the sofa. Linnie was still fast asleep.

Amy tiptoed toward the couch, perched on the edge of the coffee table, and listened to her sister's slow, steady breathing.

"Psst."

No response from the mountain range.

She leaned closer. Through the shadows, she could see Linnie's eyelids twitching—maybe she was dreaming.

"Hey," Amy whispered.

Nothing.

She leaned closer still, her nose almost touching her sister's, and then—

"Aigh!" Linnie bolted upright, clutching the covers to her chest. "What are you *doing*?"

Amy reared backward to avoid getting bashed in the forehead. "I was checking to see if you were awake."

"I'm awake." Linnie swung her feet to the floor, ready to spring into action. "What's wrong? Are you sick? Is there a fire?"

"No, no. Everything's fine."

"How long have you been sitting there staring at me?"

"Just a few seconds. I—"

Linnie held up her palm. "What time is it?"

"Almost six thirty."

"It's the middle of the night!" Linnie snatched up her feet and burrowed back under the covers.

"What are you talking about?" Amy snorted. "I haven't slept this late in years. Six thirty is positively decadent."

"Some of us work the night shift. I'm used to going to bed at six thirty. Don't make everybody else suffer just because you spawned two children who have profoundly disordered circadian rhythms." Linnie flipped over and nestled back into her pillow.

"Okay, okay, good night." Amy backed off and left her sister alone. For about two minutes. "Hey, I'm thinking about going down to the gym for a little cardio. Want to come?"

Linnie folded up her pillow around her ears and emitted a little growl.

"I see you're still not a morning person." Amy cracked open the curtains a few inches, hoping the sunlight might rouse Linnie. "Aren't you going to ask me about hell-raising with the baking brigade last night?"

"No."

Amy gave up. "You are no fun at all."

"I know." Linnie yawned. "But you know what *is* fun? Going to the gym without me. Do a few push-ups for me; I'll be with you in spirit. Good night."

One hour later, Amy returned feeling refreshed and carrying a shopping bag.

"Are you awake now? I'm back, and I brought bagels."

Linnie stirred under the covers. A few seconds later, her head emerged from within the pillow sandwich. "You're certainly in a good mood this morning."

"Always." Amy dropped to the carpet and started stretching out her hamstrings.

"Does this mean you've gotten past your outburst about the whole brooch thing?"

"No." Amy closed her eyes and inhaled slowly. "But I met a couple of the other contestants down there, and one of them—Jill from Portland—is a yoga instructor, so we ended up doing a few poses and breathing exercises, and I feel much calmer about everything now. More centered. I am not going to let your negativity and self-destructive actions affect me. I choose to stay positive."

"I can't tell you how relieved I am that you've decided not to wallow in the cesspool that is my life." Linnie shivered as she slipped out from underneath her blankets. "It is so cold in here, I can practically see my breath."

"Negativity," Amy trilled.

"I'll be more positive when I can feel my toes again." Linnie picked up her MIT sweatshirt from the carpet and pulled it on. "I called the front desk ten times last night, and they swore they'd have it fixed by tonight."

Amy went from window to window, opening curtains and reveling in the bright morning sunlight. "You did not call them ten times."

"Fine, it was more like fifteen." Linnie reached for the phone on the end table. "And I'm about to go for sixteen."

"A freshly baked bagel will warm you up." Amy opened the bag and headed for the dining room table. "I bought half a dozen. We've got plain, nine-grain, poppy seed, cinnamon-raisin, onion and jalapeño, plus cream cheese and lox. What's your poison?"

Linnie shook her head and paged through the room service menu. "Thanks for the offer, but I'm going to call down and order some egg whites. Maybe steel-cut oatmeal, if they have it. I need to stay physically disciplined if I expect to be mentally disciplined."

"Discipline is overrated. Especially when there's cream cheese involved. Come on." Amy sawed a bagel in half with a plastic knife. "How can you resist?"

Linnie curled up in her chair and tucked her knees under the hem of her sweatshirt. "I'm just not that into food, that's all. If there were a pill I could take once a day that would supply all the necessary vitamins and minerals and meet my calorie requirements, I'd gladly take it."

Amy hesitated, weighing her words. "Let me ask you something, in total seriousness. Do you enjoy *anything*?"

Linnie studied the menu. "Of course."

"What?" Amy folded her arms. "Be specific."

"Well." Linnie had to rack her brain for a moment. "I enjoy being right."

Amy bit into her bagel, then mumbled around a mouthful of crumbs, "I've died and gone to carb heaven. You have to taste this, Linnie. At least have a bite before you commit yourself to a breakfast of bland and blander. Come on."

"Amy—"

"Come on!"

So Linnie leaned in and took a tiny nibble. She chewed, swallowed, and shrugged. "It's fine."

Amy shook her head as she started slathering up a second bagel. "I feel sorry for you. You're, like, dead inside."

"You're just realizing this now?" Linnie sipped from her bottle of water and dialed room service. "Hello? Yes, I'd like to place an order, please. I'll have the oatmeal. Plain. No raisins, no sugar, no cream." She hung up the phone and headed for the bathroom in her shapeless men's plaid pajamas.

"Nice jammies." Amy catcalled after her. "Did you mug a lumberjack?"

Linnie turned around and regarded her sister with a sudden grim intensity that jarred Amy out of her cream-cheese reverie. "The time for mocking is at an end. Finish your bagel and let's get focused. We're about to enter the arena."

Chapter 10

The second she set foot on the hotel's mezzanine level, Linnie was mobbed by her fellow bakers. They grabbed her, they invaded her personal space, and they all had one thing on their minds: Amy.

"Are you Amy Nichols's teammate?" asked a breathless blonde in an argyle sweater.

"You are sooo lucky," gushed a gorgeous black woman with wire-rimmed glasses and a Southern accent.

"That sister of yours is a real firecracker! I've never laughed so hard in my life!"

"I'm hoarse today, and hungover like I haven't been since college. But it was worth it. What's she got planned for tonight?"

They looked at Linnie expectantly, waiting for her to crack a joke and chime in with anecdotes of her wild sisterly exploits, but of course she disappointed on all counts.

"Um, great," she muttered. "I have to go."

She moved to the periphery and tried to avoid any further interactions, but a wan, wired-looking fellow contestant sidled up to her and cleared her throat. "Excuse me? Um, hi, this is my first year to the semifinals, and I was wondering if I could ask you a few questions about how everything works with the runners and the dry-goods supply pantry?"

Linnie shrugged one shoulder. "You can ask, but I probably won't be much help. It's my first time, too."

"Really?" The woman looked surprised. "But you seem to know everyone already; I thought you were part of the in crowd."

"What in crowd?" Linnie said. "You mean like high school? We're adults here; there's no in crowd."

The brunette leveled her gaze. "There's always an in crowd. I heard that the cool clique here calls themselves the Confectionistas. They're very exclusive, too; they don't usually bother with newbies like us."

"The Confectionistas," Linnie echoed, her eyebrows inching higher. "You jest."

"So what's your secret?" the woman persisted, gazing at Linnie with a mixture of pleading and envy.

Linnie turned up her palms and told the truth. "I guess you could say I know someone who knows the secret handshake."

Even as a teenager, Amy had wielded her considerable social power with benevolence. She was friends with *everyone* and she'd try anything once—that went double when it came to dating. Over the years, she'd dabbled with muscle-bound athletes, sensitive poets, and tattooed motorcycle enthusiasts. Linnie had always envisioned Amy marrying a rock star or an international art dealer; it came as a shock to the whole family when she announced she was settling down with a dentist. But once Grammy Syl declared Brandon to be "a fine young man" worthy of her darling grand-daughter, everyone else welcomed him with open arms. Brandon was the kind of guy—sweet, successful, and slavishly devoted—that Linnie secretly wanted for herself, though she would die before admitting it.

When the newly crowned princess of the Confectionistas finally came down from the hotel room (three minutes late, but Linnie decided to let it go), Linnie asked her, "What did you *do* to those women last night?"

Amy rubbed on some Chap Stick and popped a breath mint. "What do you mean?"

"They're all wringing their hands and babbling about you like you're Jon Hamm in boxer shorts."

"Huh." Amy shrugged. "I just took everyone to a karaoke bar in the Village. It was kind of a tame night, to tell you the truth. But two points to you for knowing who Jon Hamm is."

Before they could check in for oven orientation, they had to wend their way through a series of security checkpoints that put airport protocol to shame.

"Please have your contestant badge ready, along with a photo ID," called a green-blazered woman with a headset and clipboard. "And remember that the use of cameras and recording devices is strictly prohibited inside the baking area."

After submitting to having their purses pawed through and their cell phones temporarily confiscated, they were ushered into the official Delicious Duet baking suite. A long expanse of hotel carpeting had been divided into orderly rows of prep stations, each equipped with an oven, a small refrigerator, and a tall, sturdy worktable. All around them, Linnie could hear the whir of stand mixers in motion.

Her heart rate kicked up a notch and her nostrils flared at the scent of vanilla extract. This was it—the culinary Colosseum. They would have today to practice and perfect their technique before the semifinal competition tomorrow, which hopefully would lead to earning one of the twenty-five spots in the final round on Friday.

"Let's see." Amy flipped through the sheaf of papers they'd been handed by the organizers. "We're assigned to station number thirteen. That figures. Remind me to pick up some four-leaf clovers and rabbits' feet."

"Superstition is 'the siren song of unreason,'" Linnie quoted.

"Don't tell me." Amy pretended to rack her brains. "Dr. Seuss? They Might Be Giants?"

"Carl Sagan."

When they arrived at station thirteen, Amy's newfound friends from the cocktail reception were waiting for them.

"You missed a good time last night," Joan told Linnie. "I did my trademark version of 'Total Eclipse of the Heart.' Not a dry eye in the house."

Susan stood next to her stepmother, nibbling her lower lip.

"I have to tell you something, Amy." Her expression grew even more troubled. "You two got assigned to the worst oven on the floor."

Linnie immediately flew into a panic. "What's wrong with it? Is it broken? Is the door latch faulty?" She glanced up toward the ceiling. "Are we under an air vent?"

"Worse." Susan motioned them in, then whispered, "You're right next to Ty and Tai's station."

"And here it's only your first competition." Joan shook her head at the injustice of it all. "I am so, so sorry."

"Ty and Tai Tottenham?" Amy asked. "That married couple from Ohio?"

Joan nodded. "So you've heard of them?"

"Yeah, we met them yesterday afternoon in the lobby." Amy shot a sidelong look over at Linnie.

Susan and Joan exchanged a sidelong look of their own, and then Susan cleared her throat. "You might want to keep your guard up around those two."

"Aha. I knew it." Linnie turned to Amy. "Told you so."

Amy waited for Susan or Joan to elaborate, but when neither did, she prompted, "Well, don't leave us hanging with all these cryptic warnings. Tell us what we're in for."

Joan readjusted the floral-patterned silk scarf draped around her neck. "I hate to say a bad word about anyone, especially anyone on the cooking circuit . . . but they can get a bit overcompetitive."

"Conniving," Susan added, arching one eyebrow for emphasis. "And they're always gunning for the newbies, trying to rattle them so they crumble under pressure. The first year I made it to the semifinals here, they prank-called my hotel room every half hour, all night long. I finally took the phone off the hook, but my nerves were shot and I was a wreck during competition the next morning."

Amy's eyes got huge. "You're sure it was them?"

"I never had any physical proof." Susan glowered. "But I know what I know."

"And it's not just the contestants they terrorize," Joan added. "There have been a lot of rumors over the years about improper contact with the judges. Nothing substantiated, but last year, well, there was quite a kerfuffle."

Linnie wished she had a handy decoder ring so she could translate a soft-spoken ladyism like *kerfuffle* into her native tongue of ruthless virago. "Because they blackmailed some judges?"

Susan coughed. "That's the rumor going around."

"But wait," Amy said. "Nobody even knows who the judges are. So how could Ty and Tai blackmail them?"

"The anonymous-judge rule is brand-new this year," Joan said. "The whole tone of the contest has changed. I've never been warned about getting disqualified at the welcome reception before."

Susan crossed her arms. "Those two give pastry a bad name."

"Shhh! Here they come." Joan and Susan scattered like pigeons in Central Park, leaving Amy and Linnie to fend for themselves.

"Don't worry; just follow my lead. I *invented* overcompetitive," Linnie said. She stood up straighter and slapped on a smile.

"Hey! Great to see you again!" She gave a jaunty wave. "Ty and Tai, right?"

"Right you are." Ty was looking particularly woodsy today in chestnut suede loafers and a chunky knit sweater vest. "Our names are hard to forget, huh?"

"It's so nice to see some familiar faces." Linnie had learned early on in her years at piano recitals and chess tournaments how to handle this brand of cutthroat competitors. "We're new to all this, and it's kind of overwhelming."

Tai, resplendent in a men's white shirt knotted above tight jeans that showcased her glutes of steel, flashed a girlish grin. "Well, if you need any help, just holler. We'd be happy to give you a hand."

"Will do," Linnie said, then murmured to Amy, "Just act clueless while I get down to business."

"Hey," Amy said loudly, fumbling with the mixer. "How do you turn this thing on?"

Linnie had to stifle a laugh. "Let's not overdo it."

She shut out the rest of the world while she got up close and personal with her new best friend for the next few days: her oven.

"Here we go." She ran her fingers along the smooth stainless-steel casing. "Moment of truth."

"What are we hoping for, gas or electric?" Amy asked.

"I can deal with either, really. The bigger issue is going to be achieving and maintaining a true four hundred degrees." Linnie opened the oven door, crouched down, and pulled a tape measure out of her pocket. "All right, first things first. I have to check the internal dimensions. Your job is to record them in this notebook. And don't give me that look—the size of the oven makes a huge difference. Air-circulation issues can drastically affect cooking times."

"Linnie. This is embarassing." Amy sounded like she was back in seventh grade, trying to ditch her kid sister at the mall. "Can't we just break out some butter and start baking? You're the only one in this entire ballroom sticking your head in the oven."

"So all the other contestants are slipshod slackers. What's your point?"

Amy surrendered. "My point is, here's your oven thermometer and hurry up."

"Thanks, partner." Linnie took her time measuring and remeasuring, then positioned the steel-and-glass thermometer in the middle of the oven's center rack and commenced preheating. She brushed her hands together and took inventory of the compact but well-stocked shelves beneath the countertop. "Let's see, we've got bowls, spatulas, whisks, mixing spoons, plastic wrap—and I brought my own rolling pin, naturally." She hefted the fifteen-inch maple dowel that she had bought at a lumber liquidator and custom-engineered for optimum heft, weight, and comfort.

"We should name our oven," Amy said. "She's our sidekick, our trusty companion."

"'She' is an inanimate object."

"Yeah, but she's a lot less likely to turn on us if we treat her right." Amy rubbed the stovetop as if she were petting a Labrador. "How about Beulah?"

"Sounds great. Whatever you say. I'll get started with the crust. You're on apple-peeling duty." When Linnie reemerged from the cabinet, she saw Amy walking away. "Hey, where are you going?"

"I have to run to the ladies' room before we get started."

"Again? Didn't you go before we left the suite?"

"Yeah, but I had, like, a gallon of coffee with my bagels, and my bladder is not the steel drum it was prebabies."

"Too bad," Linnie decreed. "You'll have to hold it. We're on a schedule here."

Amy's eyebrows shot up. "Um, I have news for you: I don't need your permission. If I want a bathroom break, I'm taking one."

"We just got here, and you're quitting already?" Linnie could feel the familiar, itchy heat creeping up her back and into her neck. "This is crunch time, Amy. Are you going to be my partner here, or just more deadweight for me to carry? You have to stop indulging yourself and get tough."

Amy looked at her the way Linnie imagined she would look at a patient with a horrifically botched root canal. "Who *are* you right now?"

"I'm the girl who blew the lid off every standardized IQ test, got accepted to college, and mastered four languages, including Latin, before the age of sixteen."

"And this is your worldview? Bathroom breaks during a practice run constitute a good-versus-evil, life-versus-death dilemma?"

"Yes. There's no such thing as practice—I came to win."

"You're doing that all wrong."

Amy, who had spent the last fifteen minutes hunched over the flour-coated countertop, glanced up at Linnie, making no effort to hide her exasperation. "What now?"

"Don't get snippy," Linnie said. "Let's go through this one more time." She flipped back to the first page of the yellow legal pad she'd filled with instructions and diagrams. "You need to start from the middle of the dough, roll forward, and then roll back. Also, you need to stop rolling over the edges. That makes the sides taper down."

Amy paused for a moment to reshape the marbled yellow dough, which had stretched into a lopsided oval.

Linnie cleared her throat. "And don't handle it too much— you want the mixture to stay cool so it'll be nice and flaky when we bake it. Remember what Grammy said about wanting to see striations of butter?"

Amy made a face. "Grammy Syl has never in her life uttered the phrase 'striations of butter.'"

"Well, I'm uttering it, and you have to listen to me because I'm the dough doyenne."

"If you're the dough doyenne, why am I standing here rolling out crust and getting a lecture?" Amy pushed back from the counter and blew at the stray curl falling over her eyes.

"Because we have to be prepared for any contingency," Linnie said. "What if I break my wrist tomorrow and can't use a rolling pin? What if you get hit by a bus, leaving me to make the apple filling while you languish in a coma?"

"Hey, you two! Care for a sneak preview of our turtle tartlet?" Ty and Tai called over from the neighboring prep station.

"No can do." Linnie didn't even glance up as she used an offset metal spatula to scrape up the crust and drape it into the glass pie plate. "I'm at a critical juncture here."

"How about you?" Ty turned his attention to Amy, coaxing her away from the oversize mixing bowl full of naked apple chunks, sugar, and spices. "Here, have a little nibble."

Like a lamb to the slaughter, Amy abandoned her work, trotted right over to the adjacent prep area, and tried a bite of the pastry Ty proffered.

"Rookie," Linnie muttered.

"Mmm." Amy's eyes widened in appreciation as she sampled the chocolate-caramel confection. "That's really good."

Ty couldn't have looked more offended if she had spit on him.

"It's *excellent*," he corrected, his mouth crimping around the edges.

Amy slunk back with her head hung low and whispered, "Who takes 'really good' as an insult?"

"People who came here to kick ass and take names, that's who." Linnie picked up a pair of scissors and started to trim and flute the edge of the piecrust. "Word to the wise: Avoid future taste tests. The next one'll probably be laced with cyanide."

"Excuse me; can I steal just a second of your time?" A striking woman with glossy black hair and heavy makeup approached their prep station with a microphone and a pair of cameramen in tow. "I'm Jacqueline Aucoin with the Culinary Channel."

"Oh my God, I love your show," Amy exclaimed. "*The Global Gourmet*, right? I watch that all the time on the treadmill at the gym."

"That's me." Jacqueline flashed a dazzling smile. "The network is producing a one-hour special on the Delicious Duet Dessert Championship and I'd love to interview you both."

"We're busy," Linnie said, not bothering to look up from her pie plate.

But Amy preened for the camera and said, "We'd love to help you out, but the truth is, we're both very new to the bake-off scene. You might be better off talking to some of the more established ladies." She pointed over toward Susan and Joan.

"Actually, I'd love to hear your perspectives as newcomers." Jacqueline sandwiched herself between the two sisters. "Are you scared? Excited? Stressed?"

"Excited," Amy said, at the same time Linnie snapped, "Stressed."

The TV host motioned for the camera crew to zoom in on the pie-in-progress. "So tell me, what are you ladies preparing? It smells divine."

"Secret Sisterhood Szarlotka," Amy said. "Basically, a Polish version of apple pie."

"I love the name," Jacqueline said. "Very provocative."

Amy beamed. "Thank you."

"I don't suppose you'd like to let us in on what the secret is?"

"Nope," Linnie replied, her eyes and hands still focused on the task in front of her. As the external pressures racheted up— from the precious seconds ticking away on the official Delicious Duet clock to the television interview being conducted right in her face to the undisguised death glares of Ty and Tai—she found it paradoxically easier to shut out all the distractions and concentrate, with laserlike intensity, on her end goal.

After all these years, she had rediscovered the Zone.

"So what do you two do when you're not taking the baking world by storm?" Jacqueline asked Amy.

Amy gave up all pretense of work and lollygagged over by the minifridge. "I'm a dental hygienist, and my sister here is, um, in casino management."

"And baking is a hobby for both of you?"

"Totally." Amy nodded vigorously. "Nothing helps me un-wind after a long day at the dental office like firing up the food processor and knocking out some lemon-raspberry tarts. I find the whole process very Zen."

The interviewer turned to address Linnie. "And what about you? Would you also describe your baking style as Zen?"

"More like deterministic chaos."

This stopped Jacqueline in her tracks for a moment, but she recovered and segued with, "One more question. How did you two come up with this recipe?"

"Well, that was awkward." Amy fanned her face with Linnie's legal pad as Jacqueline and her production team moved on to a new set of contestants.

"*Awkward* isn't the word," Linnie said. "That was one epic, inarticulate, *incriminating* bout of stammering. Why are you even talking to the press? Media exposure can't help us; it can only hurt us."

"I feel another rule coming on." Amy moved out of the way so that Linnie could slide the szarlotka, carefully arranged on a cookie tray lined with a silicone baking mat, into the meticulously preheated oven.

Linnie checked the readout on the oven thermometer one last time, then closed the door. "No more rules, just a heartfelt request. Try to fly under the radar. I know you don't believe in being low-key, but just for a few days, I'm asking you to try."

Forty-five minutes later, the pie was browned, bubbling, and redolent with a homey blend of apple, cinnamon, and lemon that literally made Linnie's mouth water.

"And now the moment of truth." She sliced into the szarlotka, carved out a sliver, and deposited it on a plain white plate. She handed this to her sister. "Taste, and prepare to admit that my methods are infallible."

Amy took a big bite. Her face contorted and she spit into her hand. "Blech."

"Too hot?"

Amy shook her head, still swiping at her lips with a napkin. "It tastes like we marinated the apples in the Dead Sea."

Linnie didn't bother with the niceties of flatware; she broke off a chunk and popped it into her mouth. Her taste buds exploded at the overwhelming taste of salt. "Blech."

"That is nasty."

Linnie frowned, her mind racing. "I didn't add any extra salt."

"Well, neither did I," Amy insisted. "So what happened?"

Linnie's gaze slid over toward the dynamic duo at the neighboring prep station. "They did something while we were distracted with the film crew."

"Be serious."

"I'm deadly serious."

"When did you become a crazed conspiracy theorist? Let's look at this logically, Linnie—"

"*You're* telling *me* to be logical?"

"That's right. And logically speaking, today's just for practice. Why would they bother?"

"Intimidation tactics," Linnie whispered. "You heard Joan and Susan this morning—they like to psych out the newbies. They're trying to break us down before the big day."

"Elvis is alive," Amy intoned. "The moon landing was a hoax."

Linnie noticed a sudden lull in activity at the next prep station. Ty and Tai were watching them. Waiting for a reaction.

Ty caught her gaze and gave her one of his trademark Mr. Rogers waves.

"Your pie smells delicious," Tai called. "How'd it turn out?"

Linnie took a bite and forced herself to swallow without gagging. "It's *excellent*."

Chapter 11

"This is not over," Linnie warned Amy as they filed out of the baking area amid a throng of other contestants. *"This is not over."*

"It is for today; they're kicking us out." Amy queued up to reclaim her cell phone. "There's a sightseeing tour scheduled for the afternoon for all the contestants. The Empire State Building, Rockefeller Center, the whole nine yards. It's going to be totally kitschy and fun. You going?"

"Tempting as that sounds, I think I'll pass." Linnie rubbed her eyes. "I'm going to head back to the room and take a nap. Somebody woke me up at the crack of dawn, and I need to keep up my endurance if I'm going to properly handle the Tai and Ty situation."

"Want me to bring you back an 'I Heart NY' T-shirt or a Statue of Liberty snow globe?"

"If you'd like to give me a gift, how about letting me skip the ridiculous black-tie ball tonight?"

"Never gonna happen." Amy smiled brightly. "You'll be there with bells on."

"Why do you insist on punishing me? I thought you'd decided you weren't going to allow my negativity and self-destructive choices to affect you anymore."

"Most people don't consider getting dressed up and going to a party with gourmet food and an open bar to be punishment."

"Most people are morons," Linnie muttered.

Amy cupped a hand to her ear. "What's that?"

"I said, have a good time at the Empire State Building." When they reached the lobby, Amy headed for the elevator bank while Linnie kept walking toward the back of the hotel.

"Hold on," Amy commanded before Linnie could make a clean getaway. "I thought you were going up to our room."

"I am." Linnie put on a bored, brusque expression, but Amy caught a glimmer of guile behind the facade. "Shortcut, remember? I'll meet you up there."

The leaky bathroom faucet finally sent Linnie over the edge. She'd closed the curtains, tossed and turned on the sofa, and tried to nap while the steady *drip, drip, drip* from the sink slowly drove her to madness.

Once she'd given up on sleep, she showered and gave herself a lecture on the importance of psychological toughness. Amy was right—she should stop obsessing over every little flaw in her environment and conserve her energy for baking to the very best of her ability. She dried off, slipped into an enormous white bathrobe embroidered with the hotel's logo, and turned on the television to drown out the steady dripping from the sink.

It almost worked.

Drip, drip, drip.

"You can't hear that," she told herself firmly. "You only think you hear it. This is a case of mind over matter, and mind is going to prevail."

Drip, drip, drip.

She picked up the phone, dialed the front desk, and ripped into the hapless employee who answered.

"This is Linnie Bialek, the enraged occupant of room twenty-six twenty-eight. I'm calling to complain about the air-conditioning in my room. Again. Plus, now my bathroom faucet is broken. . . . No, no, no, don't you dare try to fob me off with promises of visits from some phantom maintenance crew. I want to speak with your supervisor. Your supervisor's supervisor's supervisor. I expect a call back immediately. In the meantime, I'll be buying a parka and sending you the bill." She slammed down the receiver, combed out her tangled wet hair, and paced the perimeter of the sitting room, her fury mounting with every passing second.

When she heard a knock at the door, she flung it open, ready to unleash a blistering tirade. But all her frustration short-circuited when she saw who was on her threshold.

"Someone called about a parka?"

Linnie clutched the lapels of her robe together and reminded herself to close her mouth. "It's you."

"It's me." The mystery man from the freight elevator gave her a gracious nod. Although he was impeccably attired in a business suit, he carried a battered toolbox in one hand and a hefty pipe wrench in the other. "I'm Cam McMillan, by the way. I don't think we properly introduced ourselves yesterday. You must be Linnie Bialek, enraged occupant of room twenty-six twenty-eight?"

"I . . . You . . ." Her words came out strangled and shrill. "Cam McMillan. As in McMillan Hotels?"

"You asked for the supervisor's supervisor's supervisor, and here I am. How may I assist you this afternoon, Ms. Bialek?"

When in doubt, she fell back on her customary hauteur to get her through. "This suite is entirely unacceptable."

"So I hear. And I will do everything in my power to make things right." He paused, one corner of his mouth tugging up. "Perhaps by the end of your stay with us, we might even convince you to rescind your 'twenty-dollar youth hostel' comparison."

He was *mocking* her! She straightened her back and strode toward the sitting room in her bare feet. "I stand by that comment. Your ventilation system is atrocious, your room service takes forever, my bathroom sink faucet is dripping nonstop, and worst of all, when we checked in yesterday, there was lipstick on the drinking glasses."

"The lipstick thing is inexcusable, and you have my sincere apologies. I have personally called a plumber and a heating and cooling expert and they'll be here within the hour, but in the meantime, I'll see what I can do about the faucet." He took off his suit jacket and hung it on the back of a chair.

"And another thing." Linnie knew she was being ridiculous, but she couldn't bring herself to back down. "These robes are way too big. Do NBA players typically stay in this suite? Sumo wrestlers? Because I'm five eight, and this thing is swimming on me." She stretched out her arms to prove her point. The cuffs flopped past the tips of her fingers.

"Let me ask you something, Ms. Bialek." Cam walked into the bathroom and crouched down on the tile to examine the faucet. "Is there anything about this hotel that *does* meet with your approval?"

"Well." Linnie crossed her arms and deliberated. "The shower pressure is adequate."

"I can't tell you how relieved I am to hear it." He ducked beneath the sink to examine the drainpipe.

"And the complimentary conditioner works well." She tugged her fingers through her damp hair.

"Truly, I'm humbled by such praise."

"You're going to ruin your suit."

"It'll be worth it if it will raise your opinion of my hotel above 'adequate.'" There was some muffled banging as he went to work with the wrench. "This property used to be the crown jewel of the McMillan family of hotels. It's my job to restore it to its former glory, one enraged occupant at a time."

He reemerged from beneath the counter, got to his feet, and looked her right in the eye.

She tried to hold his gaze but couldn't.

"Give me a chance, Linnie," he said, never breaking eye contact. "It's only my second day on the job."

"You're looking at me again." She shouldn't feel exposed—the bulky bathrobe covered her completely from neck to ankles—and yet she couldn't help tightening the sash around her waist.

In the silence that followed, she realized that the dripping had stopped. She and Cam regarded each other in total stillness for a moment, and then he took a deliberate step toward her.

Her eyes widened and she held her breath, waiting.

"Are you going to kiss me?" she finally prompted.

"No." He gave her that rakish smile again. "You're going to kiss me."

And she shocked herself by doing exactly that. She went up on her tiptoes and brushed her lips against his, once, then again.

Linnie hadn't had her first kiss until she was nearly sixteen, a quick grope with an unshaven college senior in a dark dormitory hallway that reeked of stale beer and sandalwood incense. He didn't know that she was the youngest student on campus. He didn't care that she could do calculus, not to mention abstract algebra and differential geometry. He just grabbed her hand and yanked her out of the milling throng of tipsy undergraduates. "You're hot," he muttered in her ear, then stuck his tongue into her mouth and his hand under her shirt. She'd let him paw at her and waited with an almost clinical detachment for a reaction. Titillation? Revulsion? But she'd felt nothing.

Linnie wasn't sure whether it was due to emotional repression or neurological hardwiring, but while she could appreciate the male physique on an aesthetic level, she rarely experienced raw physical desire.

So her response to Cam took her by surprise. The kiss went on and on, and he urged her back across the sitting room, knocking over a lamp as they tumbled onto the sofa cushions.

She suddenly felt greedy, determined to help herself to everything she'd been missing out on all these years.

The sound of a key in the door sent both of them scrambling into a sitting position.

"I'm home," Amy's voice sang out as she swept into the sitting room.

Chapter 12

"You broke a lamp? I have to admit, I'm impressed. I didn't think you had it in you." Amy put her hands on her hips and surveyed the shattered shards of porcelain strewn across the carpet.

Her sister clutched the fluffy lapels of her robe and retreated to the bedroom. "I am not having this conversation."

Amy stayed right on her heels. "So, who was that guy, anyway?"

"He came to fix the air-conditioning and the faucet."

"Really. I've never met a maintenance man who wears Versace suits and looks like he should be starring on a prime-time soap."

"I never said he was a maintenance man—I said he came to fix the A/C." Linnie switched on the hotel's hair dryer and started waving it around her damp blond locks.

Amy leaned sideways against the doorjamb, grabbed a nail file from her toiletry bag, and worked on her manicure until Linnie turned off the dryer. "Save me the time and trouble of surveilling you and going through all your stuff while you sleep and just tell me who he is."

Linnie sighed, her face bright pink from the heat of the dryer. "You didn't recognize him?"

"Nope. Should I?"

"Of *course*. He helped you with your luggage in the hallway yesterday."

"Forgive me, but I tend not to remember strangers I meet for thirty seconds in hotel hallways."

"His name is Cam, okay? Cam McMillan."

Amy dropped her nail file. "The hotel guy? I've read about him."

Linnie cocked her head, intrigued. "*Wall Street Journal? New York Times?*"

"Celebrity gossip blogs." Amy tried to remember the high-society tidbits she'd skimmed between more salacious posts about Kim Kardashian and Miley Cyrus. "Heir to a gazillion-dollar fortune, jet-setter, dates a lot of models and actresses. Apparently, he also has a thing for girl-genius blackjack dealers."

"He doesn't know I'm a genius or a blackjack dealer, and you're not going to tell him."

"Why not?"

"Because it's none of his business, that's why," Linnie said.

"Half the female population of Manhattan would kill to go out with this guy, and you picked him up so you could use him for steamy, lamp-breaking sex and cast him aside?" Amy joked. Her jaw dropped at Linnie's stricken expression. "Oh my God, you *did*."

"I did not! And besides, you said yourself he was a serial womanizer who throws his money around to compensate for his lack of character."

"So what? He still has feelings," Amy shot back. Her anger was totally out of proportion to the situation at hand, but she couldn't calm down. "Just because you're dead inside doesn't mean everybody else is, too. God, Linnie. You haven't changed at all—you're still a user. You use Grammy; you use me; you use random hotel heirs."

As soon as the words left her mouth, she knew she'd gone too far. She'd just violated the sacrosanct rule of the Bialek family: No one ever called Linnie out on her bullshit.

Linnie sank down onto the couch, looking defeated and overwhelmed in the folds of her robe, and for an instant Amy caught a glimpse of the timid, introspective little girl she'd been before she became a "gifted" and extraordinary stranger.

Amy took a seat next to her. Neither sister spoke; they both stared out the window at the green expanse of Central Park.

When Amy finally broke the silence, her tone had gentled. "I don't understand you. I don't understand why you do the things you do."

"I don't, either." Linnie rested her chin in her hands. "But I'm sorry, Amy. I really am."

Amy had forgiven her long ago for everything that had gone wrong between them. But somehow, forgiveness hadn't been enough. Their relationship had soured and stagnated, but there was no point in making things even worse.

So she stood up and opened the wardrobe, determined to shift her focus to more frivolous and less complicated topics. "Let's just forget it. There's nothing wrong with us that chiffon and a few glasses of champagne won't cure."

"Oh, honey." Amy didn't even try to conceal her pity and dismay when she emerged from the bathroom in a towel turban and a Social Distortion T-shirt that barely covered her butt. "Tell me you're not wearing that."

"What?" Linnie ran her hands over the front of her loose-fitting floor-length black gown and glanced at her reflection in the mirror above the writing desk. "The invitation said black-tie."

"Lucky for you, I'm a pathological overpacker." Amy flipped through the plastic-encased gowns she'd brought. "Try this." She handed Linnie a navy dress with a halter neck and sequins in a chevron pattern. "Or this." A floaty black chiffon number with a cascade of ruffled layers on one side of the skirt. "Or this." A simple, elegant one-shouldered red sheath.

Linnie dismissed them all with a cursory glance. "I don't do sequins. Or chiffon. Or red."

"Are you going to put on makeup, at least? Or do you not do lip gloss, either?"

"I do lip gloss," Linnie assured her. "I brought all the makeup I usually wear for a shift at the casino."

"You are beyond help." Amy threw up her hands, continued into the bedroom, and changed into a hunter green silk gown with a ruched waistline and a full, fluid skirt. She ran a flatiron through her hair and accessorized with ornate, amber-studded gold drop earrings. When she returned to the sitting room, she tried one more time to talk sense into Linnie:

"Will you at least let me fix your hair?"

"No."

"Toenails?"

"Nope."

"Eyeliner?"

"I'll pass."

"At least you're consistent." Amy applied a final coat of mascara, then tossed the tube into her gold leather clutch. "All right, let's get this party started."

"Amy! Over here! We saved you a seat!"

After a long afternoon of sightseeing and scrapping with Linnie, Amy felt drained and subdued, but she pushed aside her fatigue and willed herself into a good mood. She swept into the middle of the crowd, laughing and exclaiming and bringing Linnie along with her.

Linnie's pale face got even paler as the swarm of boisterous women engulfed them. "It's like getting ambushed by the paparazzi."

"Would you calm down and have a drink?"

"I don't drink."

"Have one glass of punch. That's an order." Amy snagged a drink from a passing server and pressed it into Linnie's hand, then commenced the introductions: "Everybody, this is my sister, Linnie. Linnie, this is Melissa and Chantal, and you've already met Joan and Susan, and this is Jill and Bridget and Steph and Dorothy. . . ."

"Hi, Linnie," the bright, bubbly cool girls chorused. "We're the Confectionistas."

By the time everyone sat down for dinner, the Confectionistas had commandeered the ballroom's center table, uncorked the wine, and really started to enjoy themselves. The other attendees ate in small groups around the periphery, but Amy noticed Ty and Tai all by themselves at a table for eight, shunned by their fellow contestants.

Steph was in the middle of a fork-jabbing rant about her sister-in-law. ". . . She thinks just because she studied cooking for two weeks in France that she's the only woman alive who can make a proper palmier."

"Ha." Joan snorted. "Give me a break. I've never understood all the hype about French cooking. Everybody knows the French stole all the best recipes and techniques from the Italians."

Bridget and Jill burst out laughing. "Don't let Chantal hear you say that."

"What?" Chantal, a proud ex-Parisienne who had a charming accent, pried herself away from a debate on whipping meringue with a whisk versus an electric beater. "Who is talking about me?"

Amy took a bite of her halibut, thoroughly enjoying the warmth and camaraderie, when Linnie elbowed her and asked, "So these women hang out together and drink all the time? Like a sorority for competitive bakers?"

Melissa overheard this and teased, "More like a gang."

"The muffin tin Mafia." Steph raised her glass.

"Ooh, that gives me an idea." Amy grabbed the wine bottle for a refill. "Who's up for getting matching commemorative tattoos after dinner?"

Linnie goggled. "Tell me you're kidding."

But the Confectionistas seemed to be seriously considering the suggestion.

"How hilarious would that be? 'Delicious Duet 4-eva' in a big pink heart on my biceps."

"We could all get little rolling pins on our ankles."

"It would almost be worth it, just to see the look on my eighth grader's face."

Linnie looked around the table, obviously mystified. "But don't you guys understand that you're in competition with one another?"

"Well, of course," Susan said. "But it's a friendly competition."

"I really just compete with myself, to tell you the truth," Joan added. "I don't worry about anybody else."

"We're always trying to get better and learn new techniques."

"Screw that." Melissa grinned. "I just want to get out of the house. It's so nice to have this one thing for myself. Every now and then, my husband feels guilty about spending his entire weekend on the golf course, so he'll offer to stay home and help me. But the truth is, I prefer working alone. I love having the house to myself for a few hours."

The other Confectionistas nodded. "Everybody needs a little peace and quiet."

Amy leaned forward and confided, "I love my family, but there are days when an empty house sounds like heaven."

"Not a lot of free time?" Jill asked.

"Not at the moment. I'm working full-time with my husband, fixing up the house, raising the kids."

"How old are your children?"

"I have two-year-old twins. A girl and a boy." Amy punched a few buttons on her phone to display photos.

Bridget craned her head to see the pictures. "Congratulations . . . and condolences. You've got your hands full."

"They're great kids," Amy insisted. "And my husband is a very hands-on dad."

The other women exchanged smiles. "No matter how hands-on the dad is, Mommy is always first on deck. We've all been there."

"I remember those days," Joan said. "Hang in there, honey. Life will open up again in a few more years."

Amy felt her smile falter. "You promise?"

"Promise. In the meantime, you need to cultivate something that's just yours. Even if it's only a tiny little corner of your life."

Chantal concurred. "This is the only way to stay sane."

"You know, when I first got married, I couldn't cook at all," Steph said. "We lived on peanut butter sandwiches and frozen pizza. Then my husband—he was an engineer in the army—got stationed in Papua New Guinea. Needless to say, there were no frozen pizzas or peanut butter for miles. And the kids were going through the picky-eater stage, so they didn't want anything to do with the local dishes. I had to get creative with ingredients from the local markets. Pretty soon, I discovered that I had a real knack for cooking." She raised her voice as a brass band launched into a fox-trot on the other side of the ballroom. "By the time we got back to the States, I was a force to be reckoned with. I got first place in the very first cook-off I entered, won five hundred dollars, and decided to invest it. As I started winning more serious money, I opened my own IRA, contributed to our children's college funds, and diversified my holdings."

Melissa produced a contraband pack of Marlboros from her bag and lit up.

"You're not allowed to smoke in here," Linnie announced.

"Shhhh." Amy shot her a look.

"We're going to get in trouble," Linnie said.

"No offense, sweetie, but you need to loosen up." Jill pushed away from the table and made a beeline for the bar. "I'll fix you one of my supersecret specialty drinks."

"Don't worry," Bridget said. "She's just having a few puffs."

"I only smoke when I'm at competitions." Melissa took one more drag and stubbed out the cigarette on her saucer. "So it doesn't really count." She turned to Amy and changed the subject. "What about you? How did you begin baking?"

Amy didn't even hesitate before launching into the tale she'd been crafting since she'd embarrassed herself in front of the Culinary Channel interviewer. "Well, there was a bake sale at my kids' day-care center, and I was always the mom who brought those presliced cookies from the refrigerated dough."

"*Mon dieu*." Chantal shivered in disgust.

"I know, but I had always been too busy to make something more complicated. But I had to redeem myself, so I found a recipe in a cookbook for lemon-raspberry tartlets and spent a whole night making them."

"And they turned out beautifully?" Joan said.

"No, they were horrible! All clumpy and cloying and nasty. But then I decided, this cookbook author's not the boss of me; I can do better." Amy threw in a sassy little head bob for good measure. "So I read over the recipe again, made a few tweaks and substitutions, and voilà, I was on my way to gourmet glory!"

Linnie gave a strangled cough. "That's quite a story."

"Isn't it?" Amy dug into her dessert. "Why don't you tell them how *you* got started?"

"Oh, I always loved baking." Amy could practically see the wheels turning behind those dark brown eyes as Linnie started lying with breathtaking speed and skill. "My grandmother and I were very close—we still are. We'd spend every weekend together in the kitchen, rolling out dough and talking. She taught me everything she knows about pies and cookies and breads. She always said I was a natural."

The Bake-Off

"And where were you, Amy, while your sister was baking with your grandmother?" Steph asked.

"I was right there with them." Amy tilted her head until it almost touched Linnie's. "Though, of course, I was always a little more advanced. I made a soufflé by myself when I was seven."

"Wow." Oohs and aahs all around.

"I made flan by myself when I was six," Linnie countered.

Amy didn't miss a beat. "I made *pâte à choux* when I was five."

"You two are so lucky." Susan sighed. "Sharing a lifelong interest like that. I wish my sister and I could have the kind of relationship you do."

Chapter 13

"Holy hell." Linnie could barely hear Amy's voice shouting over the blaring saxophone solo. "What did you put in my sister's punch, Jill?"

"Nothing!" Jill was gyrating wildly along with the rest of the Confectionistas on the dance floor. "Hardly anything. Just a little splash of rum. And vodka."

Linnie, trapped in the center of the circle, couldn't seem to keep her eyes focused or her thoughts straight. She jerked her legs roughly in time with the music, bouncing off one woman and careening toward another like she was in a mosh pit.

"Jill!" Amy's customary good cheer had vanished. "She can't handle mixed drinks like that. She's a total lightweight."

"Sorry, but you said she's from Vegas, right? So I assumed—"

"Ungh." Linnie stumbled backward as Melissa shimmied into her.

"I've got you." Amy yanked her out of the fray and over to a table in the corner. "Stay here. Don't move."

Linnie lowered her head onto the tablecloth and rested her eyes for what felt like a second, only to be jolted awake when Amy shook her.

"Drink this." Amy shoved a glass of ice water under her nose.

"Leave me alone." Linnie buried her face in her folded arms. The music from the brass band seemed to fade in and out, as if someone were turning a stereo dial up and down.

"Oh, no, you don't."

Linnie's eyes popped open as Amy flicked droplets of freezing-cold water onto her forehead.

"Do not pass out on me at the black-tie ball. Come on, pull it together."

"I'm fine. I just need a little rest."

"Great idea." Amy bent down and hauled Linnie to her feet. "Let's go back to our room. Hup, two, hup, two."

Linnie's stomach gurgled ominously.

"What was that?" Amy demanded. "Are you going to be sick?"

"No." Linnie took offense at the very suggestion. "What kind of uncouth churl do you take me for?"

Her stomach gurgled again.

"I just hope your billionaire booty call fixed the damn elevators," Amy muttered as they exited the ballroom, which was at the rear of the hotel's ground floor. "The last thing I need is a confined-space puking situation."

"I told you, I'm not going to throw up."

"Maybe I'd believe you if your face wasn't the color of pistachio ice cream."

At the mention of pistachio ice cream, Linnie felt the burn of bile rising in her throat as her abdominal muscles contracted.

"Hey, Amy?"

Amy gazed up the little arrowed plaque affixed to the wall, apparently trying to determine the shortest route to the lobby. "Hmmm?"

"I'm gonna throw up."

"I'm going to look on the bright side here." Amy dabbed the back of Linnie's neck with a tissue while she held back her sister's hair. "At least you're not wearing my new red dress."

Linnie retched again, dispelling the last remnants of her dinner into the dark, damp alley behind the hotel. "See? My wardrobe choices have many hidden advantages." She paused for a moment, then stood up and took a deep breath. Her throat felt raw and her stomach ached, but she no longer felt queasy. "Okay. I'm done."

"Are you sure?" Amy let go of her hair and placed the back of her hand on Linnie's forehead, as if checking for a fever.

There was a momentary lull in traffic on the street adjacent to the alley, and Linnie heard a trickle of water from a drainpipe and a furtive rustling from the trash bins that had to be rodents.

"I'm done." Linnie wiped her lips. "I feel much better. Although the rancid stench from that Dumpster isn't helping matters."

"Then let's get back inside." Amy yanked on the handles of the double doors they'd exited through, but the doors didn't budge. "Crap. We're locked out. We'll have to go around to the main entrance. Just hold your nose and—"

"Amy, wait. Amy!" Linnie ground the tip of her high heel into Amy's toe.

"Ow!"

"Look." Linnie pointed out a patch of graffiti spray-painted on the concrete block wall next to the trash bin: ANARKY.

Amy leaned forward and peered through the shadows. "Yeah? What am I looking at?"

"Anarchy is spelled with a C-H."

"I know that. Everyone knows that. I'm sure it was done intentionally."

"But it's *wrong*." The typo rankled Linnie on an almost physical level, the way a stray hair in her eye or a tiny pebble in her shoe would irritate.

"Who cares?" Amy shuddered as they heard something scurry across the wet asphalt. "Let's get out of here before it turns into something out of *The Secret of NIMH*."

But Linnie stood her ground, fixated on the graffiti. "Do you have mascara in your purse?"

"No," Amy said. But even drunk and disgraced, Linnie remembered seeing her sister slip some cosmetics into her bag as they left the hotel room. So she snatched away Amy's clutch, from which she plucked a tube of maracara.

"Linnie Bialek, you give that back right now, or so help me—"

"I need to borrow this for a minute." Linnie unscrewed the cap, whipped out the wand, and started toward the wall. "I have to fix it. I won't be able to sleep tonight knowing this is out here."

"This is the last time I take you anywhere."

Amy made a grab for the mascara tube. Linnie bobbed, weaved, and toppled into the side of the dented Dumpster. But she managed to regain her footing, blacked out the offending K, and smeared a squiggly CH above the word ANARKY.

"Thief! Vandal!" Amy yelled. "I'm telling Grammy!"

Both sisters froze in place when a blinding flashlight beam spotlighted their silhouettes against the brick wall.

They heard a heavy set of footfalls. Then a gravely masculine voice asked, "I'm Officer Padley, NYPD. What seems to be the problem, ladies?"

"Uh . . ." Linnie looked to Amy.

Amy shook back her hair, which had started to frizz in all the humidity and excitement, and smiled winningly. "Good evening, Officer."

He shone the blinding light directly into Linnie's eyes. "Are you all right, miss?"

Linnie couldn't see his face, but she was acutely aware of the fresh graffiti adorning the wall and the incriminating mascara wand still clutched in her hands.

"Absolutely," Amy said. "Thank you so much for checking on us. My sister and I are guests of the hotel. Just on our way back inside." She put her arm around Linnie's shoulder and prepared to lead the way.

Linnie stumbled over the hem of her gown and emitted a loud, squeaky hiccup. She clapped her palm over her mouth, smearing mascara across her chin in the process.

The officer focused the flashlight beam on her hands.

"Drop the evidence," Amy hissed in her ear. Linnie obliged, tossing the mascara to the asphalt, where it landed in a puddle with a splash.

The policeman studied the lettering, still wet on the brick wall. "This your handiwork?"

"Well." Amy sighed. "Here's the thing. . . ."

"There was a typo." Linnie indicated the wall with a spiraling swoop of her arm. "So I fixed it."

"Don't mind her." Amy made the universal sign for drinky-drinky. "I'll give her some water and pour her into bed."

"I'm fine," Linnie insisted. "And proper spelling is paramount. It's one thing to defile private property, but there's no need to take the English language down with you."

The officer's expression never even flickered. "How much have you ladies had to drink tonight?"

"Barely anything." Linnie punctuated this with another body-racking hiccup.

"I'm totally sober," Amy said, carefully picking up the hem of her ball gown as she made her way across the trash-strewn alley. "And she's only had, like, two glasses of punch. I'll get her inside and under control."

"You're visiting from out of town." This was a statement, not a question. "You should be more careful about where you go and what you do at this time of night. And keep in mind that makeup is not meant to be used to commit misdemeanors."

"Absolutely, Officer. Will do. We apologize, and we appreciate your concern." Amy maintained an expression of grateful humility and tried to hurry Linnie along.

But Linnie refused to be hurried. She dug in her heels and planted her hands on her hips. "It's not a misdemeanor," she informed the officer. "It's *copyediting*."

At this point, the cop's expression shifted just a bit. "Are you waiting for a thank-you?"

"No, but do you have any idea what the crime rate is in this city?"

"Shut up," Amy said into her ear.

But Linnie was on a roll. "I have to assume you have better uses for your time than harassing some harmless tourists."

"I'd stop while I was ahead, if I was you, ma'am." The cop now seemed amused, which Linnie took as encouragement.

She gave him the prissiest smirk in her extensive repertoire. "You mean, 'if I *were* you.'"

Amy sucked in her breath.

The officer pressed the button on his radio receiver and said, "I'm at the McMillan Hotel. I've got criminal damage from a female who appears intoxicated. I'm gonna go ahead and ten-fifteen her."

"What's ten fifteen?" Amy asked.

"Turn around and put your hands on your head, ma'am."

The cop moved fast for a man so bulky. In one fluid motion, he spun Linnie around, captured her wrists, and cuffed her with a rapid-fire succession of metallic clicks.

Amy clasped her hands together and began flat-out begging.

"Oh, please don't arrest her. *Please*, Officer. I know she's obnoxious, but—"

His face was like stone. "She'll go in the holding tank; you can bail her out tomorrow morning."

"She can't spend the night in jail alone. Just look at her."

"I'll be all right." Linnie lifted her chin. "I work in Vegas, remember? I can take care of myself. I'm practically a hood rat."

Amy stopped begging long enough to roll her eyes at her sister. "Define *hood rat*."

Linnie shrugged. "A mouse who wears a sweatshirt?"

"I don't have the time or patience for this, ladies. We're leaving." He escorted Linnie to the sidewalk, opened the door to the cruiser, and helped her into the backseat. "Watch your head, ma'am."

"I'm going with her," Amy insisted, offering up her wrists. "Arrest me, too."

"You're *asking* me to arrest you?"

"Yes, please. You can put me down as her accomplice or whatever."

The officer shrugged. "Have it your way."

Amy winced as the sharp rim of steel handcuffs bit into her skin.

"You have the right to remain silent. . . ."

Chapter 14

"'Hood rat'?" Amy sat down next to Linnie on the cold concrete bench in the precinct's holding cell and grimaced down at the stained cement floor. "What is wrong with you?"

"I had grammar rage." Linnie huddled by the wall. "What's your excuse?"

"Hey, I'm just here to make sure you make it out of here in one piece. I don't want to have to explain to Mom and Dad and Grammy Syl how you died in a prison riot and I wasn't there to protect you."

"I don't need protection."

"Yes, you do."

"Well, I guess you would know." Linnie raised one eyebrow.

"Until they ran your name through the computer system, I had no idea you had a record."

"I don't have a record; I have a prior arrest," Amy clarified. "Big difference. The charges were dropped."

"When did this happen?"

"Art school. It wasn't a big deal. Getting arrested was practically a prerequisite for graduation."

"What was your crime?"

Amy sighed. "What I called an urban interactive installation piece, the police called petty vandalism."

"So you got cuffed for semantics and I got cuffed for spelling. Must be in our blood." Linnie shifted and scowled down at the ink smudges left on the pads of her fingers. "I had no idea that getting arrested was so demeaning. I understand that the fingerprinting, the mug shot, and the background check are standard procedure, but was the full-body pat-down really necessary?"

"You said you were a hood rat—they had to take you at your word."

"I've never been so humiliated." Even clad in a puke-stained polyester dress in a New York City drunk tank, Linnie managed to retain her air of regal refinement, like a Russian princess exiled into poverty.

"Well, the officer who frisked me was really nice." Amy brightened. "In fact, we got to talking about which museums gave you the best bang for your buck around here. She recommends the Frick gallery."

Linnie glowered. "Are you going to invite her to join the Confectionistas for martinis after we get sprung?"

"Maybe. I bet she loves karaoke."

"Speaking of the Confectionistas, are you going to kick Jill out of the clique now?" Linnie grimaced every time she brushed any surface with her hands, as if she could feel the germs accumulating.

Amy shifted position on the bench as her butt started to go numb. "First of all, it's not a clique."

"Don't give me that. You guys have a gang name and you were talking about getting matching tattoos."

"Second of all, while I may be annoyed with Jill for overspiking the punch, you're the grown woman who drank it, mugged me for mascara, and got me arrested. So if I'm kicking anyone out, it's you."

"Fine by me," Linnie said. "I'm too much of an independent thinker to be in a clique, anyway."

"Keep telling yourself that." Amy peered down at the half-moons of grime beneath her fingernails. "Ugh, I'm going to bathe in Purell when we get out of here. And I'm burning everything on my body. This place smells like Satan's sewer."

They heard the dull thunk of the door at the main entrance, followed by an auditory tsunami of high-pitched weeping, whining, and the staccato clicking of stiletto heels against concrete. Amy leaned forward, trying to catch a glimpse of the action through the thick glass embedded with wire mesh that ran along the front wall of their holding cell.

A gaggle of willowy, well-dressed teenagers came into view, each more drunk and distraught than the last.

"What happened to my bag?" moaned a whippet-thin brunette in a shimmering silver minidress. "Ohmigod, you guys, I might have left it back at the club." She addressed the arresting officer with beseeching eyes. "Excuse me; I left my python Gucci clutch at the bar. You have to go back and get it before somebody steals it."

"You can get ask your parents to take you back to that club," the officer drawled. "Right after you explain to them why you were there with fake IDs and a bottle of vodka."

"I'm going to kill Sabrina," vowed a WASPy blonde in artfully ripped skinny jeans. "She swore those IDs would work."

"You guys, it is so bright in here." WASPy blonde number two clasped her palms to her forehead. "I'm seriously going blind right now."

The brunette wrinkled her nose. "What is that *smell*?"

"Ewwww, ohmigod, there's vomit on my shoes from when you hurled in the squad car."

A chorus of squeals. "Eww!"

"These are Balmains, Colette. You owe me nine hundred dollars."

Amy nudged Linnie and muttered, "Now, *that* is a clique."

Linnie looked horrified. "What in *Sweet Valley High* hell is this?"

"Your cellmates," the officer announced as she slid open the metal door and ushered in the teenagers.

"They're going to be in here with us all night?"

The officer nodded. "Judges are pretty backed up right now. They'll probably get to your case in, oh, four or five hours."

"Four or five hours?" Linnie started to panic.

"Don't worry." Amy patted her arm. "We'll go deaf long before then."

"I cannot believe this," Linnie said. "We're spending the night in a New York City precinct and we're stuck with a pack of prep school princesses from Connecticut? Where are all the prostitutes and junkies and sociopaths?"

"You've watched too much *Law and Order*," the officer replied.

"Wait!" Linnie cried as the cop closed the cell door. "What would we have to do to get thrown in solitary confinement?"

"Excuse me? Hello?" One of the girls banged on the glass wall with her impeccably manicured fist. "I have to pee."

"Toilet's in the corner," came the reply.

The teen regarded the small metal toilet in the corner with horror and revulsion. "I'm getting an STD just *looking* at that thing."

"My mom is going to kill me," wailed the Gucci-less brunette.

"Excuse me, could we get some Gatorade, please?" More futile pounding on the front wall. "I can't be hungover tomorrow. I've got an SAT prep class at nine."

"Gatorade doesn't work," said the brunette with a put-upon sigh. "You've got to mix Diet Coke, skim milk, and a bunch of crushed ice and then sip it through a straw. Everybody knows that."

"Am I this annoying when I'm drunk?" Linnie asked.

Amy just smiled. "Don't ask questions you don't want the answers to."

Linnie stood up, stretched her lower back, cleared her throat, and took the floor like a professor launching into a lecture. "Gatorade might help, since your salt and potassium levels are low," she informed her captive audience. "But you could also try plain old orange juice. Freshly squeezed, if possible. The vitamin C increases the rate at which your body breaks down and eliminates alcohol."

The underage drinkers stopped bickering and regarded Linnie with sneers and exaggerated ennui. "Who are you?"

"I'm the Hangover Fairy. Listen and learn, ladies."

Amy raised her hand. "What if orange juice makes you hurl even worse than a Diet Coke–and–milk slushy?"

"You still can't drink orange juice?" Linnie asked.

Amy shook her head. She'd been prone to carsickness in her youth, but whenever the family set out for an early morning drive, their mother would insist that both girls consume a hearty, balanced breakfast—which invariably included orange juice. Which invariably reemerged across the station wagon's backseat and Linnie's lap. "Just the smell of it turns my stomach."

"Try hash browns," Linnie suggested. "Potatoes have a surprising amount of vitamin C."

"Is that really true?" one of the high schoolers asked.

"Yes."

They gazed at her with bleary, makeup-smeared eyes. "Are you, like, an alcoholic?" one of them asked.

"No, but she is a certified genius," Amy said. "Take a good look, girls—this is what happens when Mensa members go bad."

"I work in Las Vegas, so I've had lots of experience dealing with hungover tourists," Linnie explained, glaring at her sister.

"See?" The sun-kissed blonde nudged the brunette. "They are. I told you."

"We're what?" Amy asked.

The girls all giggled, but no one spoke up.

"What, exactly, are we?"

"You know. Escorts."

Amy started laughing and couldn't stop.

"Is that why you're in jail?" the brunette asked, wide-eyed and earnest. "'Cause I know the rules are different in Vegas, but that's not legal here."

"If you're a professional escort, you need to hit the makeup counter at Bergdorf before you go home," said the one with the shredded jeans. "You're wearing the wrong shade of blush for your skin tone. Go to the Chanel counter and ask for Nanette. She'll fix you up. And also, no offense, but your dress looks kind of cheap."

Amy gasped for breath.

"That's because I found it on the clearance rack of T.J.Maxx for eighteen ninety-nine," Linnie informed them with pride.

"Ew." The girls recoiled at the thought of such a garment touching their skin. "After you're done at the Chanel counter, ask Nanette to walk you up to the dress department."

Linnie planted both hands on the door and called out to the officer at the end of the hall, "Move us to a quieter cell. I'm begging you."

"When the judge is ready for you, you'll be the first to know." The officer didn't take a single step in her direction. "But you and your sister can each make a phone call before then."

"Great. Yes. Here we go." She turned to Amy. "Call Brandon."

"No way." Amy shook her head. "My mother-in-law is spending the week at our house. I'm not waking her up in the middle of the night with a call from the drunk tank. She already thinks I'm a bad influence on her precious son." She grinned. "Which, of course, I am."

"Well, then call his cell phone. Be stealthy. Your mother-in-law will never know."

"No." Amy held firm. "He's got to be at the office tomorrow by seven; the man needs his sleep just as much as I do. You're the one getting it on with a swanky hotel scion—why don't you call Mr. Moneybags to bail you out?"

"The man doesn't even know my full name. I'm not calling him from jail."

"Well, you got us in here; you get us out."

Linnie looked at Amy. "Dad?"

Amy shook her head. "Mom?"

Both said in unison, "*No.*"

"Well, that leaves only one other option." Linnie stood up and squared her shoulders. "Let's hope they have cell phone reception in Alaska."

"Linnie, darling!" Grammy picked up the phone on the very first ring. "I'm so glad you called. I've been dying to know how everything's going in New York."

"Well. It's been an interesting couple of days." Linnie cupped her hand over the phone's receiver to muffle the ambient jailhouse noise.

"I can't wait to hear what's going on with you girls. Did you meet Ty and Tai yet?"

"We did. They're thuggish and underhanded, but I can handle them."

"I have every confidence, my dear. And how are you and your sister getting along?"

Linnie mumbled a few platitudes about sisters being different flowers from the same garden.

"You'll have to speak up; I can barely hear a word. My, it sounds like a lively group of contestants this year. Are you at one of the cocktail receptions?"

"Not quite." Linnie screwed up her courage. "That's what I'm calling about—is there any way you could wire me a thousand dollars? Like, immediately?"

"You need money? Again? What's going on?"

Linnie gnawed the inside of her cheek. Amy definitely should have made this call. She could handle people so much better. "Don't worry, Grammy; it's no big deal; we just—"

"Don't try to fob me off with that nonsense." Grammy's voice went steely and stern. "Last month you called me and asked for forty thousand dollars, and now you need more? What on earth am I supposed to think?"

"Well, when you put it that way, I admit it does sound shady. But I swear to you—"

"Cut the bullshit, Vasylina, and answer me right now."

Linnie sucked in a breath. She'd never, ever heard Grammy Syl swear.

"Are you buying drugs?" her grandmother demanded.

"What? No! How could you even think that about me?"

"Look at the evidence: You're so thin and pasty; you don't return my calls; you always seem so jittery."

Linnie went to massage her temple, then stopped herself as she considered the exotic variety of surfaces and substances she'd handled in the last few hours. "I'm antisocial; I'm not a crackhead."

"I was thinking heroin, actually."

"Grammy, be serious. I don't even drink alcohol, let alone shoot heroin."

"Well, something's going on," Grammy said. "Out with it. Have you developed a gambling addiction? Do you have a mob enforcer threatening to cut off your fingers?"

Linnie slumped back against the peeling plaster wall. "Amy and I need to post bail."

Grammy gasped. "You're in *prison?*"

"No, no, no. Prison is for convicted criminals. We're just spending a few hours in the holding tank due to an unfortunate misunderstanding."

"Oh Lord." Grammy sounded defeated. "What did Amy do this time?"

"Nothing." Linnie closed her eyes. "It was me." She delivered a bullet-point summary of the evening's adventures, concluding with, "And you know how I feel about phonetic spelling."

Grammy digested this information for a few seconds in silence, then said, "Well, you had to act out sometime, I suppose. You did miss most of your adolescence. But this all sounds very worrisome. Do you need me to come to Manhattan? I can be there by morning."

"You can?" Linnie frowned. "Aren't you in Alaska right now?"

Grammy paused again. "I'm still here in Connecticut, actually. Slight change of plans."

"But I thought you and Harriet—"

"Don't concern yourself about me; I'll explain everything later. Right now, let's worry about you."

"There's nothing to worry about," Linnie assured her. "We just need you to post bail. We'll pay you back as soon as we get out of here, and then we'll never speak of this again. It'll be like the whole thing never happened."

"That's what I'm afraid of." Grammy clicked her tongue. "Your sister's there with you?"

"Yes. She didn't technically do anything wrong, but she made the arresting officer take her in, too, to make sure I didn't fall in with the wrong crowd."

"That's my Amy. Such a trouper." Grammy sounded aglow

with pride. "You know, I can't think of a better way for you girls to reconnect than spending some time together behind bars."

"Grammy!" Linnie's eyes flew open. "You can't do this to me. We have a national baking championship to win, remember?"

"Bonding takes precedence over baking."

"You're just going to leave us in here to rot?" A note of hysteria crept into Linnie's voice.

"Don't fret, my lamb. I'll come down and arrange for your release. Eventually."

"This isn't funny. We're dying in here. The stench alone is going to give me permanent neurological damage."

"Kiss, kiss, darling. Talk soon!"

"Grammy, please. If you've ever loved me . . ." Linnie trailed off, remembering Amy's warning about not asking questions she didn't want to hear the answers to. "If you've ever loved *Amy*, you'll wire money right now."

"Let me ask you something." There was a clinking noise on Grammy's end of the line, and Linnie imagined her stirring a mug of hot tea. "Do *you* love Amy?"

"What does that have to do with anything?"

"Don't be evasive. Do you love Amy?"

Linnie frowned. "Is this a trick question?"

"Why must you be so prickly?" Grammy Syl sighed. "Of course you love her. She's your sister."

"Okay, fine. I love her. Can I have my bail money now?"

"After you tell Amy that you love her."

"Fine." Linnie threw up her hands. "You win."

"I'm delighted to hear it. Now go share with Amy what you just shared with me."

"And you'll post bail as soon as you can?"

Grammy's laugh was sprightly and warm. "When have I ever let you down?"

"Hey." Linnie flung herself down next to Amy on the slab of concrete in the holding cell. "I love you."

Amy tipped back her head in disgust. "Oh my God, are you still drunk?"

"No, Grammy strong-armed me into saying that. She agreed to bail us out, but first she made me promise we'd spend the rest of the night bonding."

"The old lady plays hardball." Amy straightened up as a thought occurred. "Do I have to say I love you, too?"

Linnie plucked at the folds of her baggy black dress. "Do you?"

Amy grinned. "If it gets us bailed out of here, I do."

"That's what I said, too." They both snickered. "But you want to hear something weird? She's not in Alaska. She's at home."

"In Connecticut?" Amy finally looked Linnie in the face. "Why?"

"I asked her, but she got cagey and changed the subject. She sounded fine, but I can't imagine why she would cancel that trip. Her friend Harriet was counting on her to go, remember?"

"She probably just said that to coerce us to go to New York together," Amy said. "Maybe the whole cruise was a ruse to begin with."

"Maybe. Under all that cashmere and pearls beats the heart of a ruthless mastermind." Linnie glanced over at the teenagers, who had huddled together and dozed off to sleep on the bench on the opposite wall. "So. You, uh, feel like bonding?"

"Sure."

Linnie opened her mouth, then closed it again, then repeated the motion a few more times while trying to dredge up an appropriate topic of conversation.

"I never knew that about potatoes and vitamin C," Amy finally said. "Now I won't feel so bad when the twins are eating Tater Tots for dinner."

"I had fun tonight." Linnie had to force out the words, stilted and self-conscious. "Hanging out with the Confectionistas. I mean, I know they're really your friends—"

"They're *our* friends," Amy said firmly. "We're a team. A Delicious Duet."

"Well, in any event, I've never really had a lot of girlfriends."

"Most of your friends are male?"

"Nope." Linnie shrugged. "I just don't have friends."

"Sure you do. What about Kyle?"

"He was my roommate, not my friend. Big difference."

"Well, you don't need a lot of friends—that's one area where quality is way more important than quantity. I mean, sure, I hang out with people from my book club and playgroup and the office, but I don't share all the nitty-gritty details of my life with them. I know it sounds cheesy, but I think Brandon's my best friend."

Linnie nodded. "That's because you have the perfect life."

"Are you kidding me? I'm a dental hygienist. People loathe and fear me. I have one patient who has to take Ativan before he can even sit down in my chair."

"Well, I make my living degrading myself for tips as Blackjack Barbie," Linnie countered.

"You're only Blackjack Barbie because you're slumming it intellectually." Amy waved her hand dismissively. "But if you wanted to, you could be curing cancer. Let's face it: You got the brains, the beauty, the good genes, the good name—"

"Objection. By no stretch of the imagination is Vasylina a good name. It's impossible to spell and impossible to pronounce."

"Yeah, but you're named after Grammy Syl. It has history and significance. 'Amy' is so ordinary. Do you know how many Amys there were in my graduating class? Four. I had to go through high school as Amy B."

"I would have killed to be Amy B.," Linnie said. "When I was little, I told Mom that I was going to change my name to Jennifer Sarah Smith as soon as I came of age."

Amy laughed. "What'd she say to that?"

"She said that once I grew up, everyone would just call me 'Doctor,' so it wouldn't matter."

"Figures. Mom always had big plans for you. I think she gave up on me around adolescence." Amy's lips twisted into a wistful moue. "Marrying a dentist was the most I could aspire to, in her eyes. Success by association."

Linnie wanted to argue this point, but they both knew that the two of them had grown up with very different sets of parental expectations. "So you didn't cure cancer," she said instead. "So what? I'd say you've done all right for yourself."

"I've done all right," Amy agreed. "But sometimes, I'd like to be really great at something. Look at the Confectionistas—all of them are 'normal' moms with 'normal' lives, but they have this one talent, this one part of their lives that's only theirs, and they really kick ass. It makes me wish I were really a baker and not just a fraud. Doesn't everyone want to be exceptional?"

"No," Linnie said flatly.

"You only say that because you already had your chance."

"Yeah, and look what happened." Linnie pulled her knees up to her chest, wrapping her arms around her legs. "I used to think that if I was smart enough and careful enough, I could map out my whole life and sidestep all the stupid mistakes that trip people up: falling in love with the wrong person, committing yourself to the wrong career path, all that stuff. I honestly believed that everything bad in life could be avoided, and when I was on my deathbed, I would look back at my life and see a perfectly executed master plan where everything had meaning and purpose." She paused. "I no longer believe that."

"Dude. Why are you wasting all your time thinking about your deathbed? You're only twenty-eight—you could still finish college, go to med school or whatever. You're exceptional. It's not fair, but it's the truth."

"Let me ask you something. Have you read the latest experimental research on intelligence?"

"Can't say that I have."

"Well, it turns out that the traditional view of IQ testing might be all wrong. Early performance on standardized intelligence tests doesn't reliably predict performance in adulthood. Lots of higher-level processing functions don't even come online until adolescence. In fact, most truly gifted individuals are late bloomers, cognitively speaking. So it doesn't mean anything that I qualified as a genius when I was four or six or eight." Linnie raked her fingers through her hair. "By now I could be, you know, normal."

Amy started laughing again, so loudly that she woke up the snoozing trio of teenagers. "Linnie, I promise you that you'll never, ever have to worry about being normal."

"Don't you dare make fun of me."

"I have to, a little bit. This is ridiculous. You started college at fifteen."

"But I dropped out at sixteen." Linnie couldn't stop herself or even slow down as she blurted out her darkest, deepest doubts. "For all we know, you've been the smart sister for the past twenty years."

Amy gave up trying to reason with her. "One thing we know for sure: I'm definitely the *sane* sister."

"At least Mom and Dad have Rhodes now." Linnie finally cracked a smile. "It's a sorry state of affairs when the overachiever in the family is the dog."

Amy wriggled around on the bench, trying to get comfortable. "Grammy Syl better spring us in time to make it to the semifinals. What time are we supposed to be there?"

"Noon."

"Well, I guess we should try to get some sleep. If we lean back against each other, we won't have to get our heads in the mud, à la *Forrest Gump*."

They arranged themselves back-to-back, the curves of their necks and shoulder blades nestling in against one another. The warmth of their bodies lulled and relaxed them both, and though Linnie had thought sleep would be impossible in such circumstances, she felt herself drifting off.

As her eyes fluttered shut, she murmured, "Your sunny disposition must be rubbing off on me."

Amy yawned. "How so?"

"I was just thinking, it's a lot warmer here in jail than in our five-star hotel suite."

"See? There you go. The glass is half full."

"And no lipstick on the rim."

Amy reached back and patted her sister's side. "Night, Linnie."

"Night, Amy."

"Hey, do you think we're actually going to make it past the semifinals?"

"Bet on it."

Chapter 15

"Ugh. I could really go for some orange juice and hash browns right about now." Amy shaded her eyes from the harsh morning sunlight as she and Linnie straggled into the hotel lobby. "You know, if orange juice didn't make me throw up."

"I've got some vitamin C tablets in my bag upstairs," Linnie said. "I never travel without them. I'm like a one-woman Linus Pauling fan club."

"There you are." Susan spotted them from across the hall at the coffee cart and rushed over. "Amy, Linnie, where have you been? The semifinals start in half an hour."

Joan was hot on her heels. Her mouth formed a cartoonish O while she took in their state of postparty disarray. "What happened to you girls last night? You look like death warmed over. Is everything okay?"

"Fine, fine. We were just doing a little late-night sightseeing. We wanted to get a taste of the *real* New York." Amy tossed her head and tried to look as if she weren't blanketed in grime, grease, and germs. "What'd we miss?"

"Lots of media interviews, for one thing," Joan said. "That nice lady from the Culinary Channel came by to talk to us. She wanted to interview you, too. Here, she left her card so you can call her producers and arrange a time to meet."

"Gee, thanks. We'll get right on that." Linnie accepted the card and tossed it into a nearby trash can.

Amy maintained her perky demeanor. "We'd love to stay and chat, but I really should freshen up a bit before we start baking."

They kept their heads down as they scurried past the check-in counter and concierge desk.

"We are so lucky the cop didn't show to testify at the arraignment this morning," Amy muttered as they stepped into the elevator. "What the hell were you thinking, insisting on representing yourself?"

"I know what I'm doing." Linnie inserted her suite key into the access slot. "I've read a few law textbooks. I would have wiped the floor with opposing counsel."

"The scary thing is, I believe you." Amy leaned against the brass side panel. "I'm going to die if I don't get some coffee. Let's hurry up and get dressed so we can grab a latte before the competition."

"Forget coffee. Have you looked in a mirror? We both need a shower, a change of clothes, and probably a professional delousing."

"I can't face another piecrust without caffeine. I seriously—"

The elevator jerked to a halt.

"No," Amy breathed.

"No!" Linnie slammed the heel of her hand into the keypad. "No, no, no! Not again!"

"Don't freak out," Amy said.

Too late. "We'll never break out of here; this isn't like the freight elevator. This one's up to code! We're stuck here. We're going to miss the semifinals and lose a hundred grand because this stupid, worthless piece of—"

Amy backed up a few steps, whirled around like a ninja in three-inch heels, and whipped her forearm against the key plate.

The elevator started up again.

Neither sister uttered a syllable until the doors dinged open on the twenty-sixth floor.

"How did you do that?" Linnie asked.

Amy shrugged. "You can solve differential equations and represent yourself in a court of law; I can pound on things until they come unstuck. We all have our God-given talents."

"I'm starting to get into the Zone," Amy announced as they arrived back at the lobby after rushing through showers that removed only the first layer of filth, then changing into jeans and sneakers. "How about you?"

"The Zone is my permanent address," Linnie said.

"And check it out—we still have fifteen minutes to get coffee."

"You're forgetting about the search-and-seizure security line."

"Okay, we have five minutes to get coffee."

Linnie's stomach growled. "I need a snack, too. Doing hard time is hungry work."

"Good luck finding steel-cut oatmeal and egg whites before game time."

"I'd eat doughnuts and bacon at this point."

"Wow, you *are* desperate."

While Amy queued up at the coffee stand, Linnie darted into the lobby café and purchased a bagful of muffins and croissants. She emerged from the restaurant to find Amy loitering by the cream and sugar, a steaming cup of java forgotten behind her while she chatted up yet another random stranger.

Linnie quickened her step and prepared to roll out her famous "time is money" spiel when she caught sight of Tai. Right behind Amy. Slipping something into her drink.

Linnie raced over and whispered in Amy's ear, "Hey."

"Hi." Amy held out a hand to introduce her companion. "This is Denise. She's from—"

Linnie didn't even glance at the new acquaintance before she yanked her sister aside. "Whatever you do, don't drink your coffee."

Amy picked up her latte and held it protectively to her chest. "Why not?"

"I'll tell you in a minute, but right now, it's imperative that you do exactly as I say. Remember when we first met Tai and Ty and they tried to pull that sandwich maneuver on me?"

"How could I forget?"

"Well, we're turning the tables on them." Linnie jerked her chin in the direction of Tai, who was sidling around the corner and out of view. "She's our mark; you're the stall; I'm the pick."

Amy furrowed her brow. "What?"

"Go smack Tai like you smacked the elevator." Linnie shooed her sister along with her hands. *"Move."*

Amy moved. She grabbed a wad of napkins, chased Tai around the corner, and "accidentally" crashed into her, splashing coffee all over Tai's puffy pink parka in the process.

"I'm so sorry." Amy brushed at the coat with both hands. "Are you all right? God, I am out of control today! Must be nerves about the semifinals. Do you get nervous at these things?"

Tai threw up both hands in a futile attempt to ward off Amy's onslaught. "Um . . ."

"Here, let me see." Amy broke out the napkins and started swiping at the down-filled sleeves. "Did I burn you?"

"No, no, I'm fine." Tai tried to escape, but Amy had her backed up against a large marble fountain. Linnie materialized behind Tai and slipped her fingers into her purse.

"Are you sure?" Amy got even more zealous with her pat-down. "Ever since I heard about that crazy McDonald's lawsuit, I freak out every time I spill coffee."

"It's fine," Tai murmured.

Linnie's hand closed around an object that felt like the shape of the vial she'd seen in Tai's hands.

"You'll have to send me the dry-cleaning bill," Amy said. "I absolutely insist."

"Aha!" Linnie plucked the small white plastic dropper out of Tai's purse and waved it around like a weapon. "What's this?"

Tai's face drained of color and a small muscle under her eye started twitching. "I . . . I . . ."

"What seems to be the problem here?" Ty suddenly materialized at his wife's side. His demeanor was unflappable, but he was slightly out of breath from his haste.

"The problem," Linnie spat out, "is that your wife here just tried to poison my sister!" She uncapped the tiny squeeze bottle and sniffed the contents. "She poured this into Amy's latte. I saw the whole thing."

"I think there's been a mistake." Ty stepped in between the

two women. As usual, he was all decked out in pleated khakis and a raglan sweater. "Those are just eyedrops."

Linnie raised her fist in triumph. "Exactly!"

"Why would I put eyedrops in somebody's drink?" Tai finally regained the power of speech, though her whole body was visibly trembling.

"Don't play innocent with me. Everybody knows the rumor about saline eyedrops and digestion."

"I don't," Amy piped up.

"It's supposed to give you cramps and diarrhea," Linnie said. "Incapacitate you for the next few hours so we crash and burn in the semifinals."

"Huh." Amy nodded. "I never heard that."

"But there's a problem with that little rumor—namely, it's a load of crap. The active ingredient in these eyedrops is tetrahydrozoline hydrochloride, which, yes, can cause nausea and abdominal cramps. However, it can also cause plummeting blood pressure, seizures, tremors, and neurological disruptions resulting in coma or death." Linnie ticked off these complications on her fingers. *"Death."*

"I—I had no idea." Tai's purse handles slid off her shoulders and down to her elbow as her trembling intensified. She glanced at her husband, whose jovial demeanor had soured.

"You went through my wife's purse without her permission and now you're accusing her of trying to harm a fellow contestant?" Ty asked.

Linnie nodded. "Damn straight."

He took off his glasses and started cleaning the lenses with a handkerchief. "I have to say, I'm disappointed and more than a little hurt."

He tucked his glasses into his sweater pocket. "I understand this is your first major competition. I understand you may be buckling a little under the pressure. But this—this kind of slanderous, unfounded accusation—is going too far. My wife has eyedrops in her purse because we've been on a plane and are staying in a hotel with very dry air. Her eyes are irritated. That's it. So let's not be looking for drama, shall we, ladies?"

If there was one thing Linnie couldn't stand, it was being patronized. *She* would do the patronizing around here, thank you very much. "Don't you take that tone with me. I know all about you and your reputation. You're just lucky she didn't drink that. She could be passed out on the floor right now, spasming and coughing up blood and gasping for breath."

"That's right," Amy threw in. "You got *told.*"

Ty threw her a look that was half pity and half disgust. "May I please have my wife's eyedrops back?"

"Not a chance." Linnie crammed the vial into her back pocket. "I'm saving it for evidence."

"I see. Well, if that's the way you're going to be . . ." Ty's frown lines deepened. "You'll be in our thoughts and prayers." The Tottenhams hustled off, Tai risking one last worried look back over her shoulder.

Linnie watched their retreat with narrowed eyes. "I'm telling."

Amy looked dubious. "Telling who?"

"The contest administrators. The media. Grammy Syl."

"But we can't prove anything. It's going to be their word against ours."

"We have proof! Where's your coffee?"

"All over Tai's parka. And I don't think she's going to hand that over without a court order."

"So they're just going to get away with this?" Linnie fumed. "That's not fair!"

"News flash: Life isn't fair."

"She could have killed you!"

"But she didn't. She wasn't trying to off me; she was just trying to give me the runs. And she failed so miserably that I'm kind of embarrassed for her."

"You and your bleeding heart. The question we should be asking ourselves is: Why us? Is it because we're new? Is it because we're popular? Is it because they've heard something about how incredible Grammy Syl's—I mean, *our* recipe is and they know we're the team to beat?"

Amy shrugged. "What is the sound of one hand clapping? If eyedrops are deadly, why do they sell them over the counter? Life's full of questions. But there's only one that really matters right now: Are you ready to make the best piecrust of your life?"

Chapter 16

"Relax." Amy had to raise her voice so that her sister could hear her over the roar of food processors and the metallic clatter of whisks against bowls. Thirty minutes into the semifinals, the air in the ballroom was thick with powdered sugar and adrenaline. Although the physical environment was exactly the same as in the practice round, the ambience had changed entirely. Green-blazered officials roamed up and down the aisles, and there was an almost palpable current of anticipation flowing between the prep stations. "Making crust is supposed to be Zen, remember?"

"I *am* relaxed," Linnie snapped. A droplet of sweat trickled down her nose and plopped onto the chilled marble pastry slab she was using to roll out her dough.

"Here, let me help you." Amy gently removed Linnie's fingers from their death grip on the maple dowel and replaced them with her own. She flattened the dough with firm, steady strokes, all the while humming under her breath.

Linnie stood back for a moment, tying and retying the strings on her Delicious Duet–mandated green-striped apron. "What's up with you? You have a crazed glint in your eye."

Amy looked up with a grin. "I never thought I'd say this, but I'm in my element right now. The time limits, the intensity . . . it makes me feel alive."

"Well, something definitely clicked with you," Linnie said as she started to peel the apples. "Your rolling technique is flawless."

"Yeah, I'm actually kind of flattered that Tai tried to poison me. I've never been so good at something that someone else would feel the need to *kill* me to put me out of commission. Talk about high praise."

Linnie winced as she peeled the first layer of her thumb off. "Seek help."

"I'm starting to see why you kept entering all those science fairs and essay contests and chess tournaments when we were growing up. Pressure is kind of awesome when you're at the top of your game." Amy paused, took a good look at Linnie's face, and put down the rolling pin. "What's up with the flop sweat? I thought you said the Zone was your permanent address?"

"I lied." Linnie swiped at the back of her neck. "I think I'm going to pass out. I'm serious. You need to talk to Brandon tonight and tell him to phone in an antianxiety prescription for me. Valium, Xanax, Ativan, whatever. I need it."

"Don't psych yourself out." Amy resumed work on the crust. "Repeat after me: We got this."

Linnie mumbled something unintelligible.

"I can't hear you!"

"We got this," Linine said, but it came out more of a question than a pronouncement.

Amy shook her head. "I hear you, but I don't believe you."

"We got this!" Linnie yelled, just as all the nearby teams turned off their food processors.

"That's more like it." Amy nodded. She gave a friendly wave to the onlookers. "Now peel those apples. Peel like you've never peeled before."

Linnie had to laugh. "If only that weren't so close to the truth." She sliced her thumb again, slapped on a Band-Aid, and demanded a labor shake-up.

Amy was happy to relinquish crust duties, and the sisters worked side by side until Linnie grabbed the paring knife from Amy. "Whoa. What do you think you're doing?"

"Cutting each apple into thirty-six chunks." Amy referred to the annotated legal pad. "That was your edict. Says so right here."

"That was only half of my edict. Yes, we need thirty-six chunks per apple, but even more important is that each chunk be of uniform size."

"I'm doing it this way on purpose." Amy grabbed back the paring knife. "I want some to be thicker than others so there's a little crisp in every bite. Szarlotka is supposed to look rustic and homemade."

" 'Homemade' is just another word for sloppy," Linnie argued. "I don't like inconsistency."

"I know, I know. You're an excellent driver. You worry about your duties, Rain Man, and let me worry about mine."

Amy braced herself for a fight, but Linnie backed down and went back to draping the dough into the pie plate.

When the pie was assembled and ready to bake, Amy sprinkled a thin layer of grated pie dough across the top to give the finished product a textured, confettilike effect, then stepped back to assess the result. "Does it look okay?"

"It looks like the cover of *Bon Appétit*," Linnie said. "I hope it tastes okay."

Amy licked the spoon they'd used to scoop the apple filling into the pie plate. "It tastes like we swiped it off Martha Stewart's windowsill." She placed the pie plate on the silicone mat atop the baking tray. "What now?"

Linnie slid the baking tray into the oven, set the Delicious Duet automated kitchen timer, and clicked her thumb on the stopwatch she carried for backup. "Now we wait."

"Why does judging take so long?" Two hours later, Linnie wiped down their prep station for the umpteenth time and started fraying the threads on the edge of the fluffy greenlogoed dish towel. "Are they cleansing their palates with an entire gallon of milk between each piece of pie?"

"They have fifty entries to taste and discuss," Amy pointed out. "Stop scrubbing the same section of counter over and over. You're making me nervous."

"What if something's gone wrong?" Linnie's dish towel was quickly unraveling. "What if our runner dropped the szarlotka on the way to the judges' room? That kid looked like he had bad knees and the grip of a newborn."

" 'That kid' probably has ten years' worth of experience working in Manhattan's finest restaurants." Amy popped a leftover apple peel into her mouth and chewed, hardly tasting the browned and shriveled fruit skin. "I'm sure everything's fine. I'd tell you to

have a drink and relax, but I don't want to end up arrested again."
Amy sniffed the air, then motioned Linnie closer. "Come here. We
both still reek of booze and bodily fluid." She grabbed the bottle of
vanilla extract and shook a few drops into her palm.

"What are you doing?"

"Freshening us up." Amy dabbed the sweet-smelling liquid on
the pulse points behind her ears and wrists, then did the same to
Linnie. "It'll have to do until we can go back upstairs and shower
again. Plus, men love the scent of vanilla extract."

"Says who?"

"Some women's magazine we had in the waiting room of the
dental office. But in my personal experience, it's true. You should
try wearing some to work—you might see a significant increase
in tips."

"I'll keep that in mind." Linnie checked the clock again.
"Argh. The suspense is killing me."

The big double doors at the ballroom's main entrance swung
wide, and a supercharged silence settled over the room as an elderly
gentleman in a three-piece suit and a green Delicious Duet necktie
walked through.

"Moment of truth." Amy wrapped her fingers around one end
of Linnie's dish towel. Linnie held tight to her end until the cloth
was stretched taut between them.

The contest coordinator stepped up onto the dais, which was
draped in green-and-white bunting, then cleared his throat once
more before speaking. "Will contestant Vas"—he frowned down
at the name printed on the index card in his hand and tried again—
"Vasylina Bialek please step forward?"

"Oh my God," Amy squeaked. "What's going on?"

"People are *looking* at me," Linnie whispered back. "Hide me."

Amy's mind raced. "That guy is the one who went over all the contest rules on the first day. Snowley What's-his-face. Do you think he knows something?"

Linnie's big brown eyes filled with panic. "What could he know?"

"Uh, let's see: That our recipe isn't ours? That you were recently jailed for criminal mischief? Shall I go on?" Amy waited for Linnie to come through with her usual snooty self-assurance, but her sister just kept staring at her with those terrified, Bambi-in-the-forest-fire eyes.

"Vasylina Bialek?" Snowley What's-his-face's voice boomed through the hall once more.

"Let's go." Amy raised her hand and called out, "That's us." She took Linnie's elbow and guided her toward the front of the room.

"What are you doing?" Linnie asked.

"I'm coming with you, obviously. If you're in trouble, so am I."

This show of allegiance seemed to jolt Linnie back to her senses. "Listen to me very carefully. If they try to interview us separately, do not waver. Admit nothing, Amy."

"I'll admit nothing."

"You swear? Don't forget what game theory says about the prisoner's dilemma and the Pareto-suboptimal solution."

"I have no idea what you're talking about, but they'll never break me," Amy assured her.

Amy greeted Snowley with a big smile and a hearty handshake. "Hi. I'm Amy Nichols and this is Vasylina Bialek. We're team number thirteen."

The official frowned down at his paperwork. "I'm to understand that you two are sisters?"

"Yes, sir, righty-o." Amy's tone was so cheery, she was setting her own teeth on edge.

"And you have prepared the apple szarlotka this afternoon?"

"That's correct."

"I see." The contest coordinator put on a pair of spectacles and peered closely at Linnie's face. "Ms. Bialek, do you mind if I ask how old you are?"

Linnie cast a confused, sidelong glance over at Amy before replying, "I'm twenty-eight."

"I see." Snowley nodded to the assistant two steps behind him, who scribbled something on her clipboard. "Ms. Bialek, would you mind stepping into the next room for a moment? We'd like to have a word with you in private."

Amy started to offer to accompany her, but Linnie cut her off with a quick shake of her head.

"I can handle this," she muttered. "Just remember what I said about game theory."

With her posture resolute and her head held high, Linnie went with the officials into a small conference room at the end of the exhibition hall. Amy trailed after them until the door closed.

Then all she could do was wait.

And fidget.

And pace.

Finally, after what seemed like hours, Linnie emerged by herself and closed the door behind her. Her perfect posture had devolved into a slouch, with her hair hiding most of her face from Amy's view.

"Well? What happened?" It was all Amy could do to restrain herself from grabbing Linnie by her apron strings and shaking her. "Are we busted? Are we facing disqualification and public humiliation?"

Linnie remained determinedly detached. "We're going to the finals."

Amy's hands dropped to her sides. "What?"

"The finals. We're in."

"But why . . . ? How . . . ? What . . . ?"

Linnie strode toward the exit. "Let's go. Everyone's staring."

"Hello?!" Amy chased after her. "I asked you a question."

"I heard you." Linnie blew through the double doors, rounded the corner, and buttonhooked into a secluded little alcove, where the sound of their voices was nearly drowned out by the gurgle of the lobby's fountain.

"So why won't you answer me?"

"Because." Long, gusty sigh. "It's stupid."

"I know you did not just *sigh* at me. Sell that supercilious crap somewhere else," Amy warned. "You either start talking right now, or I'll—"

Linnie crossed her arms and looked up at the ceiling. "They asked me if I wanted to do some media promotion for Delicious sugar."

"Media promotion? Like what? Interviews?" Amy envisioned hours of the same question on an endless, repeating loop: *How did you come up with this recipe?*

"No, more like print work."

Amy could see an angry pink blotch appearing at the hollow of her sister's throat. "You mean modeling?" she pressed.

"I don't know." Linnie blinked up at the emergency fire sprinklers. "I guess."

"Well, what exactly did they say in there?"

The Bake-Off

"Just that they're trying to update their corporate image and they want to produce some ads featuring contestants who are young and fresh. 'The new face of the Delicious Duet Dessert Championship' or whatever." Linnie shrugged one shoulder. "I told you, it's stupid." As an afterthought, she added, "Oh, and they said you could do it, too. Since you're the other half of my duo."

"I see." Amy's voice was high and tight.

Linnie finally looked her in the face. "What?"

"Nothing."

"You're mad."

"Of course I'm not." Amy turned away. "Why would I be mad?"

"I don't know, but you look like you're about to go on a bloody rampage with an apple corer."

Amy pressed the heel of her palm to her forehead and tried to articulate her frustration. "I'm not angry, Linnie. I'm just sick of being the runner-up. When there are two sisters, one is supposed to be pretty, and the other one's supposed to be smart. Smart *or* pretty. You don't get to be both. Everybody knows that."

"You're pretty," Linnie said.

"I'm cute. *You* got stopped in the airport when you were twelve by a modeling scout."

"Oh yeah." Linnie nibbled her lower lip. "I forgot about that."

"Well, I remember. Vividly. You ripped up the poor woman's business card right in her face and went off on a rant about how the modeling industry dehumanizes young girls and undermines the fundamental tenets of feminism."

"I stand by my rant." Linnie lifted her fist to indicate power to the people. "So let me get this straight: You'd actually want to be the face of Betty Crocker two-point-oh?"

"Who wouldn't?"

"Me." Linnie slouched even further into the depths of her striped apron. "But, I mean, if you want to . . ."

"Well, they're going to pay us, right?" Amy tried a different tack. "I thought you agreed to all this because you need money."

"I need at least forty grand. They're only offering to pay 'union scale,' whatever that is." She paused. "But it's up to you."

Amy, who had been mentally composing a list of debate club–style points of persuasion, felt almost disappointed by this easy acquiescence. "Really?"

Linnie nodded. "It's the least I can do. I still owe you for what happened in high school."

"Consider your debt repaid." Amy did a little dance of joy, punctuated by uncoordinated attempts at vogueing. "Sashay, Shante."

"They said we should be at the photographer's studio at nine sharp tomorrow morning," Linnie said as the sisters got off the momentarily glitch-free elevator and headed for their hotel room.

"Excellent." Amy rubbed her palms together. "I plan to enjoy every moment of my fifteen minutes of fame, even though I only got it by default. But I'm starting to wonder: Did we make it to the finals because our szarlotka was good or because they had us in mind for the advertising gig?"

"Who cares?" Linnie said. "As long as the grand prize check clears."

"I care. I want to win because I was the best baker, not because my partner happens to be a hot blonde. Hey, what's this?" Amy picked up a small oblong box propped against the outside of the suite door, glanced at the card, then passed it on to her sister. "Here you go, blondie; I believe this is for you."

Linnie lifted up the lid and pulled out a soft wool Fair Isle scarf in shades of cream, brown, and green. Then she opened the accompanying note scrawled on a folded piece of hotel stationery.

"Lemme see." Amy knew it was none of her business, but she couldn't resist peeking over Linnie's shoulder to read along:

I'm in the penthouse and would love to see you. Hope this keeps you warm until then. —Cam

"Oh my God." Linnie opened the door and hurried inside as if pursued by a pack of model scouts.

"Boy Toy wants you baaad," Amy singsonged as she took off her shoes and turned on the coffee brewer in the kitchenette. "You should show up at his door tonight wearing that scarf and nothing else."

"Don't be vulgar," Linnie called from the sitting room. "So he sent me a scarf. It's the least he can do, considering the air-conditioning is still stuck on subzero. He probably didn't even buy this himself. I'm sure he sent one of his minions out to get it."

"And the minion just happened to pick out the one that matches your eyes exactly? Hey, maybe he's got a knitting fetish. This could be totally hot. You could buy a few skeins of yarn and get crazy."

Linnie was not amused. "While you sit here entertaining your depraved fantasies, I'll be in the shower for the next hour trying to scald off the stink, thank you very much."

There was a knock at the door. Both of them raced to get there first.

"Butt out of my business," Linnie said, jostling Amy out of the way.

"No way. I have to see what else this guy's got up his sleeve." Amy jockeyed for position. "Maybe he sent up champagne, or exotic French truffles, or something sparkly from Tiffany."

They threw open the door to find themselves staring into a very familiar but totally unexpected face.

"Well." Grammy Syl heaved a powder pink overnight bag over the threshold. "I'm relieved to see you girls made it out of the correctional system in one piece."

Chapter 17

"Grammy Syl!" Linnie cried. "What are you doing here?"

Their grandmother held out her arms for a big, Estée Lauder–scented group hug, kissed each sister on the cheek, and then resumed chastising them.

"I'm here to restore law and order." She took off her fur-trimmed wool coat and handed it to Amy, along with her suitcase. "Clearly, you two hoodlums need a chaperone."

Amy pointed at Linnie. "She's the hoodlum. Hood rat, actually."

"I'm a martyr to the cause of proper spelling." Linnie regarded her grandmother with suspicion. "How did you find out our room number, anyway? Did you bribe someone at the front desk?"

"It was a gift, dear heart, not a bribe. And you know people are powerless to resist my chocolate-chip cookies." Grammy cocked her head and studied Amy's face for a moment. "You aren't getting enough sleep," she announced. The she turned to Linnie and arched one eyebrow. "And *you* are falling in love."

Linnie choked. "I am not!"

"She so is." Amy hung up the coat and took Grammy's arm to lead her into the suite. "He's a smooth-talking hotel magnate who's plying her with knitwear."

Grammy surveyed the sitting room, clucking with disapproval at the open suitcases spilling clothes and shoes across the floor. "My word. This place looks like a refugee camp. Aren't you embarrassed to live like this?"

Amy immediately started making the bed while Linnie picked up the sitting room. Her breath caught when she realized she'd left the claim ticket for the brooch in plain sight on the end table after her daily phone call to the pawnshop, but with a deftness honed by years of dealing cards, she managed to palm it and tuck it into her sleeve.

Fortunately, Grammy had turned her attention to other matters. She unzipped her overnight case, extracted a stack of folded sweaters, and placed them in an empty dresser drawer.

"What are you doing?" Linnie blurted out.

"Unpacking." Grammy added a nightgown and velour robe to the drawer.

Amy and Linnie exchanged a look, and then Amy said, "You know, we are so thrilled you're here—"

"Thrilled," Linnie emphasized.

"—but you're right about the sorry state of this suite. It's a sty, and you shouldn't be subjected to our filth. You'd be much more comfortable in your own room. Let me call downstairs and ask if—"

"I already checked; they're booked solid. Don't fret about me." Grammy hummed and plumped the pillows on the bed Amy had hastily made. "I'll be quite comfortable on the sofa."

"Absolutely not, Grammy," Amy said. "You're sleeping in the bed. I'll take the sofa."

"Then where will your sister sleep?"

"She can crash on the floor. There's an extra blanket in the closet."

"Thanks," Linnie said.

"You girls are too good to me." Grammy shivered a bit as a blast of cold air blew out of the vent.

"Sorry about the cold." Linnie retrieved her MIT hoodie from the closet and offered it to Grammy. "The A/C guy claimed he fixed it yesterday."

"In his defense, he did fix it, but it broke again four hours later." Amy sat down on the sofa and patted the cushion next to her. "Speaking of cold, why aren't you in Alaska right now?"

Grammy made no move to sit down. She peered at Amy, imperious in her cabled turtleneck and pearls. "I'll be asking the questions here, my lamb."

"Is there something wrong?" Linnie asked.

"Yeah, what's going on?" Amy stood back up. "We demand answers."

"Don't be impudent."

"You can't stonewall us forever."

Grammy patted her carefully styled white hair and smiled.

"We'll just see about that, won't we? So, tell me everything. How were the semifinals? When do you hear the results?"

"Oh, we heard already," Linnie said. "It's official: We made it to the finals."

"You did?!" Grammy Syl registered pure shock for a moment, then clapped her hands in elation. "I can't believe—I mean, I knew you could do it! Oh, I'm so proud of you both."

"But we're not sure if it's because our pie was good or because they want to pimp out Linnie." Amy provided a quick summary of the advertising gig they'd booked.

"Modeling! My goodness! Oh, there's no telling how far you two could go if only you'd work together and stay out of trouble. Tell you what: We'll go to the grocery store later and have a few more practice sessions to make sure you're ready for Friday. But right now, I'm a bit knackered from the trip and a catnap sounds divine. So if you don't mind, I think I'll lie down for a bit."

"Sounds good," Amy said. "I'm always up for a nap."

"I'll see you two later," Linnie announced with what she hoped would pass for casual nonchalance. "I'm just going to run out and grab lunch."

Amy jerked her thumb toward the desk. "Room service menu's right over there."

"No, I'm craving a hot pretzel."

Amy did a double take. "What?"

"Yep." Linnie never wavered in her composure. "And I saw a street vendor selling them over by the park. I'll be back in a little while."

Amy looked skeptical, but all she said was, "Uh-huh."

"Good night." Linnie gave Grammy a kiss. "Give me a call if you need anything."

The Bake-Off

"Night-night," Amy called as she started closing the curtains and turning off the lights in the bedroom. "Spelled N-I-T-E."

Thirty minutes later, Linnie crept back into the darkened hotel room, taking care to close the door silently. The bedroom door was shut, and Amy didn't stir from her slumber on the sitting room sofa.

Linnie barely breathed as she tiptoed across the room and removed the plain brown paper bag from inside her sweatshirt. Slowly, slooowly, so as not to rustle the wrapping, she slid the bag's contents into the exterior pocket of her suitcase.

With no warning, Amy sprang from the couch like a puma. Linnie put up a valiant struggle, but Amy wrestled the object out of her fingers.

"Aha! What have we here?" Amy snapped on the newly replaced table lamp and read the DVD's title aloud: "*Naughty Nympho Call Girls 4*." She blinked a few times in rapid succession. "Well. This is a new and unexpected side of you."

"Lower your voice," Linnie hissed, dragging Amy into the dining room. "Do not wake up Grammy."

Amy followed, too stunned to argue.

Linnie sat down at the sleek varnished table and covered her face in shame. "I need help. Please."

"Oh God." Amy plunked down across from her, sounding queasy. "Now what? You have some seedy porn addiction?"

"No. I've never watched porn before in my life, but I have to do something drastic." She lowered her voice to a funereal whisper as she confessed, "I'm bad in bed."

Amy started banging her head against the table.

"Stop it!" Linnie shot her hand in between Amy's skull and the wood to muffle the thumping sound. "What are you doing?"

"I'm trying to give myself amnesia so I can forget the last two minutes of my life."

"I'm desperate, Amy. This attractive, worldly man gives me his room number and tells me to come on up, and I can't. . . . I mean, I just don't think . . . I have no idea what I'm doing."

"Okay. Let's just take a deep breath and step back here. It's not like you've never had sex before." Amy's eyes widened as a thought occurred. "Right?"

"Of course I've had sex. But not steamy, seduce-a-stranger-in-his-hotel-room-with-my-irresistible-wiles kind of sex."

"What kind of sex are you having, then?"

"Bad sex." Linnie drooped in despair. "Boring sex. That's why I'm freaking out. I need a tutorial before I go see Cam tonight, and it's not like I can just order up a porno on pay-per-view and charge it to the room."

"Why not?"

"Because! What if Cam—"

"—scrutinizes your room account like a crazed stalker?" Amy finished for her. "He'll assume you're a hot-blooded vixen, that's what."

Linnie started picking at the table's edge with her thumbnail. "I was going to wait until you and Grammy went out to dinner and pretend to be sick so I could stay here and watch this. But would you please spare me the indignity and just give me a few pointers? Please?"

"I have to tell you, I'm weirded out by this whole conversation. And anyway, how do you know that I'm any better than you?"

Linnie snorted. "False modesty doesn't become you. You could teach a master class on men, and we both know it."

"You must really like this guy. I mean, you wouldn't even put on lipstick for a cocktail party, and now you're sneaking out and buying X-rated movies so you can fine-tune your wiles?" Amy poured herself a mug of coffee from the glass carafe warming on the brewer. "Look. There's no big secret to being good in bed—although ditching the flannel lumberjack pj's would probably be a good start. Most guys are just looking for enthusiasm."

"Enthusiasm," Linnie repeated.

"Yeah. Whatever it is you're doing, if you get into it and act like you're having the best time ever, he'll automatically consider you good in bed. You don't have to be a Cirque du Soleil acrobat or a porn star. All you have to do is enjoy yourself."

"Well, there goes that idea." Linnie swung her feet under her chair and brooded. "How did I get myself into this mess?"

"You met a hottie in the freight elevator and went for it. Nothing wrong with that. You want him; he obviously wants you. Stop overthinking everything and just go for it."

"But that's not who I am."

"You seemed pretty into it when I caught you making out on the sofa yesterday."

"That was different; I didn't have any time to think about it beforehand." Linnie pushed the DVD case across the table. "This is pointless. I quit."

"Well, you'll never qualify as a naughty nympho with that attitude. I mean, if I can get freaky in the backseat of an SUV with all my cellulite and twin skin, you should be able to make Cam McMillan your sex slave, no problem."

Linnie paused. "I'm probably going to regret this, but I have to ask: What's twin skin?"

"It's the special souvenir nature leaves on your stomach after nine months of carrying multiples. Picture saggy elephant skin that's been mauled by a mountain lion." Amy popped open the DVD case. "So are we going to watch this or what? Grammy Syl's not going to sleep forever, you know."

Linnie shoved her chair back from the table. "I'm not watching that with you!"

"Fine, I'll watch it on my own. Don't hoard all the high-class-hooker tips for yourself. I've been married for seven years; my bedroom routine could use a little spicing up."

"Brandon doesn't strike me as the spicy type."

"You'd be surprised." Amy winked. "The buttoned-up, repressed guys are always the kinkiest."

"We're both going to be scarred for life by the end of this afternoon."

"Probably." Amy sounded cheerful. "Now fire up the DVD player and let's broaden our intellectual horizons."

Chapter 18

"Damn," Amy murmured later that afternoon as they rolled out pie dough under Grammy's tutelage. "That's one thing to cross off my life list. Who knew porn would be so, well, pornographic?"

"My sensibilities may never recover." Linnie still looked a little shell-shocked. Only four minutes into the DVD, she had turned off the TV and announced she'd seen enough. "And if I'm expected to contort myself and carry on like a strumpet with men who look like cast rejects from *Jersey Shore*, then I'm going to be bad in bed forever."

"Stop ruining this for yourself. I promise you, guys care more about your attitude than technical proficiency. Nobody's sitting there with a scorecard, judging you."

"Now, remember what I said about overmixing." Grammy

sprinkled a light coating of flour across the top of the priceless antique table. "If you insist on using the food processor, go easy on the 'pulse' button. And once you've mixed in all your liquid ingredients, it's too late to add more flour."

Amy tried to look earnest and attentive, succeeded for about thirty seconds, then nudged Linnie again. "The real question is, What are you going to wear? The MIT sweatshirt with nothing under it? A Fair Isle negligee?"

"Girls." Grammy Syl rapped her wooden spoon against the table. "Stop that whispering and pay attention. I don't want to have to tell you again."

Amy dropped her head and resumed work on her szarlotka crust, which had taken on the pale, uniform texture of manila card stock. Not a butter striation in sight. "Yes, ma'am."

"What are you two being so secretive about, anyway?" Grammy demanded. "I hope for your sake you're not conspiring against me."

"You know we'd never do that, Grammy," Amy said.

"Never," Linnie added. Then she turned back to Amy and said out of the side of her mouth, "By the way, I'm totally going to call her doctor later and make sure everything's okay."

"Good idea. I can help you get around those pesky HIPAA regulations if you want."

"How?"

"I've got my Grammy Syl impersonation down to an art form. How do you think I got away with Senior Skip Day in high school?"

Grammy exclaimed something in Polish, scraped up her piecrust-in-progress, and tossed it in the trash. "That's it. If you two aren't going to pay attention, I'm not going to waste my breath."

"We're sorry!" Amy said. "We're listening."

But Grammy had taken off her apron. "We could all use a

break." She assessed Linnie's striated, symmetrical circle of dough with approval. "Very nice, darling. That looks perfect."

"If it's not perfect, it's pointless. That's my motto," Linnie said. But she didn't sound at all pleased about this.

Grammy stepped into the powder room to wash her hands, and when she emerged, the customary snap had returned to her blue eyes. "Let's go out and have dinner someplace nice to celebrate your victory at the semifinals. Anywhere you want. What'll it be?"

"The Confectionistas texted me and said they're going to some world-famous steakhouse in Brooklyn tonight," Amy said. "We're more than welcome to join them."

"Sounds delightful. I only brought a simple skirt, but I can dress it up with accessories," Grammy said. "Linnie, my love, did you happen to bring my grandmother's brooch? Any chance you'd let me borrow it for the evening?"

Amy froze, but Linnie didn't hesitate. "Gosh, Grammy, I didn't pack it. I was afraid to take it on the plane."

The furrows above Grammy's mouth deepened. "You left it somewhere secure, I hope?"

"Of course. It's in my safety-deposit box." Linnie made lying look so easy and natural. She didn't sweat or fidget; her gaze never wavered.

Grammy smiled fondly at her granddaughter. "It means so much to me to know that you have it, that you can pass it on to your own daughters one day."

"Well." Linnie finally faltered a bit. "I might never get married."

"You will," Grammy said with absolute authority. "I know these things."

"Really?" Amy asked. "What else do you know? Are we going to win on Friday? Is there anything juicy in my future?"

"I'm not a carnival psychic, darling. Just because I know things doesn't mean that I'm under any obligation to tell you." She traded her small pearl studs for a bigger set and winked at them. "But as for the finals on Friday . . . Let's just say I've got a good feeling."

"Ladies, may I take your orders?" The lanky young server seemed slightly overwhelmed by the crowd of brightly dressed women talking and laughing at the private table tucked away in the back room of the masculine, dimly lit steakhouse. Though the main dining room retained a hushed atmosphere of refinement, the Confectionistas brought the party with them wherever they went. Everyone finished remarking over the menu offerings, and requests came tumbling out on top of one another:

"I'll have the sirloin medallion, please."

"How are the seared scallops? Be honest."

"We'd like to get a round of martinis for the whole table, please. Actually, could you just bring us a pitcher or would that be too déclassé?"

"Linnie," Grammy piped up. "Would you care to share the lobster with me?"

"I'd love to," Linnie replied.

The waiter made the rounds patiently, answering every question and accommodating every special order, until he arrived at Amy.

"And for you, madam?"

Amy nibbled her lower lip. "I'll have the garden salad. Dressing on the side."

"What?" Steph cried. "Honey, you're on vacation!"

"This is the best steakhouse in the known universe," Susan said. "Indulge a little."

In the face of all this peer pressure, Amy relented and asked for filet mignon, but when her dinner arrived, she left her meat and martini untouched, restricting herself to leafy greens and a few mushrooms.

"What's up with you?" Linnie asked after swallowing a mouthful of butter-drenched lobster.

"I can't eat anything," Amy explained. "I have to try to lose some weight before the photo shoot tomorrow morning."

Linnie did her patented Stare of Disdain. "I have so many things to say about that, but I'm not even going to start."

Melissa leaned over from across the table and yelled at them, "Ladies, your grandmother rocks."

Grammy beamed.

"*Mais oui!* She's like the grande dame of the Confectionistas," Chantal agreed.

"Really, Mrs. Bialek," Joan said, "it is so great that you spent all those years baking with your granddaughters."

Grammy shot a look over at Amy. "Pardon?"

"Oh, yes." Amy slung her arm around Grammy. "I told them all about how we learned to bake, and the *pâte à choux* I made when I was five."

"I see. Well, they get all their baking talent from me," Grammy boasted. "And my girls have always been close. That's how Linnie got her nickname, you know."

"How?" Bridget asked, swilling her second martini.

"Yeah," Linnie said. "How?"

"When Linnie was a baby, Amy couldn't pronounce Vasylina. So she started calling you 'Linnie,' and it stuck." Grammy smiled at the memory. "She would correct people anytime they called you anything else."

"I didn't know that," said Amy.

"Neither did I," said Linnie.

"Well, it's the truth. Your father wanted to call her Syl or Sylvie, but you wouldn't hear of it." Grammy said this in such a way that Amy believed her, even though all three of them knew everything else was wishful thinking and outright lies. "You took her under your wing as soon as she was born, and she's been there ever since. Now. Who wants dessert?"

"Oh my God," Linnie said as the group poured out of the steakhouse and into a waiting group of cabs. "Is Grammy *drunk*?"

"Heavens no, Vasylina," Grammy admonished, stumbling a bit as the heel of her boot caught on a crack in the sidewalk. "I only had the tiniest nip of sherry."

"She's sloshed," Amy confirmed. "You must have inherited your lightweight tendencies from her, too, along with all that baking talent." She herself hadn't touched a drop, and started shivering as soon as the icy winter winds smacked her in the face.

She waved good-bye to the departing Confectionistas, and put a steadying arm around her grandmother. "Hey, Grammy, there's a coffee shop right over there. Let's run in and get a cup of cocoa to warm us up. Linnie, you want anything?"

Linnie looked offended. "Am I not invited to Starbucks?"

Amy used her other arm to steer her sister in the direction of the neon-lit lingerie shop on the corner. "You need to pick up a few things."

"Who wants to go for a carriage ride in Central Park after this?" asked Grammy. "Or, ooh, we could go ice-skating!"

"She is not mixing sherry and skating," Linnie declared. "I forbid it."

"Let me worry about her," Amy said. "Now skedaddle, and don't come back until you've found something that's going to inspire that guy to break another lamp."

"Wait till you see what I got," Linnie said after they'd returned to the hotel suite and tucked Grammy into bed with a bottle of Gatorade and strict instructions to alert them if she needed anything else. "It's utterly racy and scandalous."

Amy snuggled under the comforter and stretched out her legs—the sitting room sofa had turned out to be surprisingly comfortable. "Let's see."

Linnie tossed over the shopping bag. Amy peeled back the layers of floral-scented tissue paper to reveal a very modest set of boy shorts and a bra in a blue-and-green tartan pattern. She managed to bite her tongue, but her eyes must have betrayed her, because Linnie instantly demanded, "What's wrong?"

"Nothing. It's, uh, it's very you."

"Don't give me that." Linnie bristled. "Why are you laughing?"

"I'm not." Amy couldn't hide her smile. "It's just that you said 'racy and scandalous,' so I was expecting a little more La Perla and a little less Brooks Brothers."

"Well, I like it and I'm the one wearing it." Linnie flounced over to the bathroom, changed out of her clothes and into her new undergarments, yanked a sweatshirt and jeans on top of that, raked a comb through her hair, and settled into her makeshift nest of pillows and quilts on the floor with the poise and posture of a visiting dignitary. "And you'd better not thrash around and keep me up all night."

"I won't thrash if you won't speak in tongues," Amy said.

"How dare you? I do not speak in tongues in my sleep."

"Latin. Ancient Greek. Whatever, it's creepy."

"All right, girls," Grammy called from the bedroom. "Lights-out."

"She sounds so tired," Amy said. "Do you think she's okay?"

"It's probably just the sherry wearing off." But Linnie sounded doubtful.

"Sleep," Grammy barked. "Now."

Without another word of protest, Amy reached over and turned off the light.

The room was completely dark, except for the red smoke-detector light on the ceiling. A few minutes later, Amy heard the sound she would forever associate with breaking curfew on Friday nights: the soft rumble of Grammy's snoring.

"Okay." She reached down and poked Linnie's shoulder. "The coast is clear. Be back before sunrise, and remember: Have fun."

Chapter 19

When Linnie arrived at the door to Cam McMillan's penthouse suite, she had two uncomfortable realizations:

1. The sales tag was still attached to her underpants and digging into her hip.
2. She had no idea what she was going to say when he opened the door.

She reached under the waistband of her jeans, ripped off the tag, and stuffed it into her pocket. One problem solved, one to go. She cast her mind back to the afternoon's X-rated tutorial and decided that words probably weren't necessary. She'd simply grab him, kiss him, and rip off his clothes.

Just as soon as she scrounged up the courage to knock.

She shifted her weight from foot to foot, staring at the tiny round peephole in the door. *Okay, on the count of three.*

One ... two ... two and a half ... two and six-elevenths ...

This was ridiculous. He probably wasn't even in there right now. And if by some remote chance he was, it was so rude to show up unannounced, although technically he had invited her, but—

"Linnie." The door opened, revealing Cam in a starched white undershirt and belted khakis. Judging by his surprised expression, he hadn't known she was out here. "What a pleasant surprise. If you'll give me a second, I'll get dressed and—"

"No need." She wet her lips with her tongue and stepped over the threshold into a high-ceilinged apartment that made their luxury suite look like a shabby dorm room. "I'm here to seduce you."

He froze for a moment, waiting, and when it became clear that she had nothing else to add, he nodded. "I'll consider myself on notice."

She tossed back her hair and tried again. "No, I mean right now."

"You'll want to close the door then."

She complied, but startled when the door slammed shut behind her.

"Okay." He braced himself, settling into a slight crouch in anticipation of her tackle. "Fire when ready."

Linnie remained rooted to the carpet, her arms folded tightly across her chest. Her gaze bounced from the gleaming hardwood floors to the grand piano across the room to the view of the park and the glittering skyline outside the window, everywhere except for him.

"You all right?" He'd gone from sounding amused to concerned.

"I'm fine." She took a deep breath and wiped her palms on her jeans. "I'm just showing up at your door unannounced, some might say rudely—"

He reached over and grazed her wrist with his fingers. "I'm delighted to see you, and may I say you look lovely."

"No, you may not." She shook her head, exasperated. "You're not supposed to say I look lovely. You're not supposed to say *anything* because you're too busy being mauled by me."

He opened up his arms, indicating his total cooperation. "By all means, maul away."

"Damn it!" She stamped her foot, the sound echoing through the cavernous space. "This is supposed to be steamy and spontaneous."

"If I may make a suggestion—"

"Argh! Stop being so gentlemanly! Stop saying 'may'! You're ruining the mood."

"Okay, then," he drawled, giving her a slow and scorching once-over with those gleaming dark eyes. "Take off your shirt, woman."

She started laughing. "I want a do-over."

"Good idea." He stepped around her, opened the door, and escorted her back out into the hallway. "Let's try again. I'll be checking my BlackBerry in here, totally unsuspecting."

"All right. Okay." She inhaled, exhaled, and gave herself a little shake. "Oh, and you might want to move any breakables out of reach and take off your watch, because it looks expensive and I don't want to accidentally damage it."

He raised one eyebrow. "*I'm* ruining the mood?"

"Can you please just play along?"

"Linnie, look at me. Do I look like I care if you break my watch? I hope you do. I hope we trash this hotel room like rock stars on a three-day bender."

Her hand fluttered to her throat. "Oh my."

"Bye now. See you in a minute." He shut the door in her face.

She stared blindly ahead, trying to catch her breath and sort through the sudden whirl of thoughts and urges.

Cam cracked the door open again and prompted, "This is the part where you're supposed to knock on the door and attack me like a pack of ravening wolves."

"Hang on." She braced her palm on the doorframe. "I just need a minute."

The door opened wider. "It's easy. Here, I'll give you your cue: *knock, knock.*"

"I can't." Linnie hung her head and conceded defeat.

"You can!" He caught her hand and pulled her back into the penthouse.

"No, I can't. I realize you don't know me, but this is the way I am." She sighed, disgusted with herself. The luxurious apartment was lit solely by the moonlight pouring in through the tall windows and balcony doors. If she couldn't seduce a guy here, she was hopeless. "I'm not spontaneous. I'm not sensual. I wasn't even hoochie enough to stay in the hoochie room in the casino."

There was a long, confused pause. "What?"

"Never mind. I need a drink." She leaned back against the wall. "Do you have any wine?"

He kept his hand clasped around hers. "You don't need a glass of wine. Getting buzzed is the easy way out." He pulled her against his chest. "Seduce me. Not because you're drunk, not because you have something to prove, but just because you can."

"I can't." She tucked her head beneath his chin to hide her face. Now that she had a better view into the living room, she noticed a gilt-trimmed chess set on one of the decorative tables by the bookshelf. "I can beat the pants off you in chess but I can't seduce you. Sorry."

He pulled back and peered down at her. "You play chess? Really?"

"Absolutely." Linnie nodded. "I hate to brag, but I'm virtually unbeatable."

"What if I told you that I was the captain of my prep school's chess team?"

She smiled at the mixture of pride and embarrassment in his voice as he confessed this. "I'm sure you're a very skilled player, but trust me, I can beat you."

"You're sure?"

"Very." She slipped off her shoes and allowed him to lead her across the woven Persian rug toward the chess set.

He pushed aside a pair of heavy club chairs and set down the game board on a patch of rug bathed in luminous white moonlight. Then he toyed with the tiny metal zipper pull on her sweatshirt. "Care to make it interesting?"

"Checkmate." Linnie used her index finger to slide her queen along the board until it came to rest next to her pawn and Cam's now-unguarded king. He'd fallen right into her trap of taking her knight with his rook. "You can't escape."

Cam blew out his breath as he recognized her strategy too late. "I can't believe I didn't see that coming. In my defense, it's been years since I've played, and you're very distracting."

At this point, Cam had lost his belt, his watch, his pants, and his shirt—everything except his boxers, which turned out to be green tartan, in a pattern remarkably similar to Linnie's bra and boy shorts. Linnie, at a distinct wardrobe disadvantage due to her lack of layers and accessories, was also down to underwear only.

He'd surprised her with his skill, and, though she'd never admit it, there had been a moment or two when she'd actually worried she might lose the game.

"I'm enjoying the view, at least." He gazed across the chess-board. "How did you know I have a thing for plaid?"

A few hours ago, Linnie would have turned away from him or covered herself with her hands. But tonight, for the first time in memory, she felt beautiful.

"How did you know *I* had a thing for plaid?" she countered, smiling up at him as he moved to sit next to her. His fingers threaded through her long hair, and she rolled onto her stomach to afford him better access.

"Your hair is very unusual back here." He traced two spirals on the back of her head. "Do you have two crowns instead of one?"

"Mm-hmm. It's called a double whorl." Linnie rubbed her curled toes against his bare calf. "It's rare, but it happens. Some geneticists think Einstein had a double whorl. That may be why he had such an unruly hairstyle."

"You and Einstein, huh?" His hands moved from her hair to her shoulders and back. "No wonder you trounced me in chess. You must be brilliant."

"Not really," she said. "I never finished college."

"I did, but it took me a few tries. I was too busy partying to crack a book. Is that what happened to you?"

She sighed and shifted position. The short woolen bristles of the rug chafed against her skin. "Not exactly. You know, now that we've played chess *en déshabillé*, I really should ask your name," Linnie said. "I assume Cam is a nickname?"

"It is."

"Cameron?" she ventured.

He shook his head. "Guess again."

"Camden?"

"Claudius. My mother has a thing for Roman history. She wanted something regal."

"How on earth do you get Cam out of Claudius?"

He resumed his roving massage. "My middle name is Augustus. Yeah. Take it up with my parents. My initials are C. A. M. By the time I started kindergarten, I figured out I'd be better off as Cam than Claudius."

"I have a weird name, too." She stopped swinging her foot as his fingers dipped just beneath the waistband of her boy shorts. "Linnie's short for Vasylina. It's Polish. My sister, Amy, started calling me Linnie when we were both little. You remember Amy—she's the horrified bystander who interrupted us on the sofa the other day."

"Oh, I remember," he assured her. "Are you close to her?"

"No. We had a falling-out a long time ago; it was my fault." Linnie surprised herself with her own casual candor. She'd never confessed this aloud to anyone before. "I—I stole something from her." She expected to be suffused with shame, but instead she was flooded with relief. It felt so freeing to let this secret out, to confront the person she truly was instead of the image she tried so hard to project.

"Boyfriend?"

Linnie had to laugh. "No. God, no. Her boyfriends were slavishly devoted to her. What I did was much worse than stealing her boyfriend. I stole her ideas. I stole her creations." She stopped, waiting for him to react.

"I'm not following."

"I cheated," Linnie said, splaying her fingers across the intricate pattern woven into the carpet. "I cheated my way into college. When I applied, I was fourteen, and even though my SAT and AP scores were off the charts, the dean of admissions expressed some concerns that I wasn't emotionally prepared. I believe the phrase she used was 'adding too much steam to a pressure cooker.' She told my parents that I needed to demonstrate to the admissions committee that I was a well-rounded, creative individual. Which I wasn't. But my parents and my teachers kept urging me to put something together, and my whole identity was wrapped up in being gifted and extraordinary, so I sent in my sister's art portfolio as my own."

He didn't say anything, and she felt a perverse surge of satisfaction that she'd shocked him, that she'd shown him how much less appealing her interior was than her exterior.

"Amy is the creative one. She has an instinct and a vision that I will never have. She was getting ready to apply to college, too, and had spent months putting together a collection of her best work. These were paintings she had done all through high school, and I knew they were good. Her art was the one thing that really made her stand out, and I took credit for it so that I could impress everyone."

"And she ratted you out, and the college asked you to leave?"

"No, the college never found out." She had spent months in a state of unrelenting anxiety, always certain that she was on the verge of being discovered and disgraced, but the accusations never came. The suspense of waiting had been far worse than any administrative punishment. Once she had broken down and begged Amy to retaliate, scream at her, or at least acknowledge how much Linnie's betrayal had hurt her, but Amy had simply looked at her with expressionless eyes, said, "I guess you needed it more," and then stopped speaking to her entirely.

"The only people who knew were me, my sister, and my parents," Linnie continued, "and we never said a word about it, even to one another. Amy packed those pieces away and never looked at them again, as far as I know. Everything changed after that."

She waited and waited through another long pause, and then finally, Cam said, "You applied to college when you were *fourteen*?"

"Were you not listening to the rest of that story? What kind of person does that to her own sister? Go ahead and say it," she challenged. "Don't hold back."

"I'm not going to judge you."

"Why not?"

"Because, as you yourself pointed out, I don't know you."

"Well, I would never forgive someone who did that to me—who took my ideas and passed them off as her own. I thought I deserved to get everything I wanted just because I was 'special.' I was going to be a doctor. Not because I wanted to help people, but because I excelled at science and that's what my parents wanted for me. But it turned out that the dean of admissions was right about me. I had a breakdown the day after finals."

"You panicked and flunked the exams?" Cam asked.

"No, I aced them all." Now the shame and humiliation started to resurface. "I wanted to flunk out so I could have an excuse to leave, but I was incapable of throwing a test. My ego wouldn't allow it. So instead I just moved back home at Christmas and never went back to campus. My parents were mortified, especially my mom. You should have seen her face when her friends asked why I wasn't at college anymore. And would you like to know what I do now? I deal blackjack in a Vegas casino."

"You can keep going with this all night, and I'm still not going to judge you."

"I just want you to know who you're dealing with: A cheater. A quitter. A failure."

"Did you cheat at chess?" He kissed the instep of her foot. "Because it might assuage my ego if you did."

"This is never going to go anywhere, you know," she said. "I'm due to fly back to Nevada in three days."

"As it happens, McMillan Hotels is currently developing a new resort in Vegas." His lips moved to the sensitive skin behind her knee. "I can arrange to fly there frequently for business. We could see each other—go out, stay in."

After all this talk about the past, Linnie had no interest in planning for the future. She just wanted to jump him and not have to map out eighteen thousand contingency plans.

Holy crap, I'm doing it. I'm having fun.

In one fast, fluid move, she flipped over and straddled him.

"Let's just enjoy the moment, shall we? You in your plaid under-wear, me in mine."

He grabbed her hips and pressed up against her. "You know what's even better than wearing plaid underwear?"

"What's that?"

"Not wearing plaid underwear."

Chapter 20

"Did you get any sleep last night?" Amy asked Linnie as they sat in a pair of canvas folding chairs, trying not to move while the makeup artist worked her magic.

"About an hour." Linnie stifled a yawn with the back of her hand.

"That would explain these dark circles." Ori, the shoot's makeup artist and wardrobe stylist, dabbed on concealer beneath Linnie's eyes. In an effort to help both sisters appear fresh faced and natural, she'd stuck to neutral tones like brown and bronze, with only a light dusting of blush and a bit of lip gloss. "Close your eyes for a second—I'm going to glue on a few false eyelashes."

"Getting glam takes forever," Linnie said.

The alarm had gone off at seven, which to Amy had felt like

the equivalent of sleeping in till noon. Her sister, however, had refused to stir until Amy flicked some cold water onto her toes.

Amy dug her phone out of her bag and snapped a photo of their reflections in the mirror. They both had pink Velcro rollers in their hair and voluminous black smocks draped across their shoulders.

"Brandon and the kids will love this. We look like Grammy Syl before she 'puts her face on.'"

"Don't knock the old-school rollers," Ori said. "They give your hair just the right amount of volume." She stepped back to assess her work, gave Linnie's forehead one more swipe with the powder brush, and nodded in satisfaction. "If you need to go to the restroom, go now. Once you put on your outfit for the shoot, you can't sit down or lean against anything. The clothes photograph best without creases or stains."

"Got it." Amy got to her feet. "Any other tips?"

"Just relax and be yourself. No one expects you to act like a professional model."

"Yeah, but I still want to *look* like one." If only she'd had time to watch all those seasons of *America's Next Top Model* that her TiVo had recorded and deleted over the years. "Give me some hints. 'Smile with your eyes' and all that."

Ori started packing up her supplies. "I always tell people to stick out their chin a little bit. The camera doesn't register depth, so that helps your jawline look more defined and your neck look smoother. Also, try to look down before each photograph, and then look up just in time for the shot. That makes your eyes look fresher."

"Ooh, thanks. I'm totally going to do that for our next family portrait." She nudged Linnie. "Are you getting all this?"

No answer. Linnie had slumped down in her chair, her artfully bronzed eyelids at half-mast.

"Linnie! Wake up."

"Huh?" Linnie's head snapped up. "I'm awake, I'm awake."

"I'll go ask the photographer's assistant to make some fresh coffee," Ori said. "Any other questions before we get started?"

"Yeah, what do we get to wear?" Amy asked, with visions of Gucci and Hermès dancing in her head.

"Button-down shirts and A-line skirts." The stylist laughed at Amy's evident disappointment. "You're supposed to look wholesome. I do have some fashion-forward jewelry, though."

"Sign me up."

"We'll get started as soon as the food stylist arrives to make sure the baked goods look as beautiful as you two."

Amy waited until the makeup artist was out of earshot, then resumed the interrogation of Linnie she had started in the cab on the way from the hotel to the photographer's studio.

"So what exactly did you and Moneybags end up doing last night?"

"Don't call him that. He has a name." Linnie paused. "Claudius."

"Shut up. I thought his name was Cam?"

"C. A. M. are his initials. So he goes by Cam because his full name is—"

"Wow. Claudius and Vasylina. You two are quite the couple."

"We're not a couple," Linnie corrected her. "We're, um, fellow chess enthusiasts. And by the way, I'll have you know that some people consider plaid lingerie the height of provocative sophistication."

"Are you sure you're not a couple? Because you sound like a perfect match."

"Please. We barely know each other."

"Yeah, but if you took the time to *get* to know each other—"

"Everything would be messy and complicated," Linnie finished. "I need to keep things simple and self-contained. My libido may be in the freight elevator, but my focus is one hundred percent on this competition."

Marc, the photographer, strode into the dressing area, distributed cups of coffee to all, and announced, "Well, ladies, I just got a call from our food stylist. She's stuck in traffic in the tunnel, and it sounds like it's gonna be a while, so we're going to go ahead and get started without her."

"It'll be fine," Ori said. "This shoot's mostly with fruit and the premade pies, and you can always Photoshop later."

"What about the next duo, though?" Marc rubbed his chin. "With those sticky caramel tart thingies? That's going to be a mess."

"Amy can do it," Linnie piped up. "She's got a gift for the presentation aspect of baking. She went to art school, you know."

Amy was so shocked to hear Linnie describe her as gifted that she started stammering. "Oh, well, I'll do my best, but I'm not a food stylist by any means."

Ori dismissed this with a shrug. "You're not a model, either, but here you are."

"Yeah. Don't be so negative," Linnie said in a pitch-perfect imitation of Amy.

Amy's mental wheels started whirring again and she turned to the photographer. "Wait a second. You said the duo you're shooting after us is making caramel tarts?"

The photographer nodded and squinted down at his light meter. "Mm-hmm. Some husband-and-wife team. They have the same name. Chris and Kris?"

"Ty and Tai," Amy told them.

"Yeah, that sounds right," Ori said. "You know them?"

"You could say that." Amy froze with her coffee cup halfway to her lips, suddenly paranoid about eyedrops and slow death. "They're not here already, are they?"

"Nope. Why?"

"No reason." She took a tiny sip of the dark roast and glanced over at Linnie. "I just like to keep up with our competition."

"This is so uncomfortable." Linnie squirmed and fidgeted in her black-white-and-green floral-patterned skirt. "It doesn't fit."

"Yes, it does." Amy emerged from behind her dressing screen decked out in white jeans and a ruffled pink blazer. "You're just not used to wearing anything other than XXL sweatshirts or skin-tight corsets." She had done a double take when Linnie returned from the changing room. Gone was the surly, slouchy fashion victim. In addition to the skirt, Ori had outfitted her in kitten-heel mules, a fitted green blouse, and dangly purple sapphire earrings. "You look like a Talbots catalog."

Linnie made a face. "I look like you, and it's freaking me out."

"Just go with it," Amy advised. "Pretend you *are* me. Smile. Be friendly."

Linnie summoned up a pained, stiff-lipped grin.

"Okay, now you look like a serial killer."

Ori arrived to retouch their hair and makeup, then sent them out for test shots in front of the white screen.

"We're going to do a few warm-up shots first," said Marc. "Adjust the lighting and angles. Just try to look natural."

Amy did her best to utilize Ori's tips, but while she was

blinking her eyes and jutting out her chin, Linnie started to look even more psychotic.

"Hey. Relax."

"I am relaxed," Linnie gritted out between clenched teeth.

"Wait, wait, wait." Marc beckoned to Ori, then pointed to Linnie's shirt collar. "Can we do something for her neck?"

Linnie's hands flew to her throat. "What's wrong with my neck?"

Amy winced at the sight of the angry red splotches. "It looks like you got attacked by a swarm of hornets."

"Do you have sensitivities to skin-care products?" Ori asked. "Maybe you're having a reaction to the foundation I used."

"No, no, don't worry," Amy said. "I've got this under control." She put her hand on Linnie's forearm. *"Relax."*

"You know what might help?" Ori suggested. "Close your eyes for second and think about the happiest moment of your life."

Amy knew this was directed at Linnie, but she closed her eyes, too, and did a quick flip through her memory's greatest hits: holding Ben and Chloe for the first time, backpacking through Europe with her friends the summer she turned twenty, kissing Brandon in the dental school parking garage until his car windows fogged up, watching a black-and-white movie marathon with Grammy Syl when she was bedridden with mono in high school. . . .

She felt her lips curve slightly in a peaceful smile, then opened her eyes and glanced at her sister, who remained wide eyed and strained.

"I can't think of anything," Linnie said, her voice pinched with desperation.

And when Amy opened her mouth to suggest sublimely joyful moments in Linnie's life, she came up blank. Though her sister's formative years had been bursting with accolades and accomplishments, Linnie had never seemed very *happy* about any of them. Everything she did had been considered merely another step on the way to something greater. "Think about . . . think about, uh . . . naked chess games in the freight elevator?"

Linnie's whole face lit up.

"Perfect!" The photographer started snapping away. "Stay exactly where you are."

"That's it, baby." Amy started to growl like a tiger, clawing with her hands. "Work it! Own it! You're so money and you don't even know it!"

Linnie started to laugh. "Can I please have her escorted off the premises?"

The camera kept clicking; then the assistants brought out a sturdy wooden table laden with pies and produce.

"Okay, one of you grab the green apple, and one of you take the red one, and—"

"Hold on." Amy plucked the apple from Linnie's hand. "The Red Delicious isn't quite right."

"Oh, is that the wrong kind to use in baking?" Marc asked.

"Beats me," Amy admitted before she remembered she was supposed to be the expert. "But it's kind of discolored." She held it up to display the yellow spots on the skin.

"Can you turn it to show the other side?"

But the other side was also pale and splotchy.

Amy dashed over to Ori. "Do you have any dark red lipsticks?" She selected a glossy maroon shade and applied it liberally to the apple. "There. That looks better."

"That really does look better." The photographer seemed impressed; Ori, mourning the loss of a perfectly good lipstick, was less so.

"I told you," Linnie said. "She's an artist. It's not easy always being right, but it's my cross to bear."

After an hour of posing and smiling, the photographer declared the shoot at an end. "I've got what I need. Thanks, guys, you did great."

Linnie started back toward the dressing area, and Amy noticed how differently her sister carried herself in the cute, colorful clothes. She looked almost cheerful.

"Hey." Marc waved her over. "Thanks for all your help today. That thing with the apple and the lipstick was great."

"Thanks. I'm a former wannabe artist who never passes up the chance to multitask with my makeup. I never really thought about table food as art until I started baking, but it's fun to tart up tarts, so to speak."

"Well, if you're interested, I team up pretty frequently with a few food stylists, and they're always looking for reliable assistants. The pay's pitiful, and you'd have to come into the city for shoots, but you'd be learning from the best. We've done everything from print ads for potato chips to a Thanksgiving buffet for a feature film scene." He handed her his business card, and Amy pressed it between both palms, feeling like she'd just been given the key to another restricted-access suite in the sky.

By the time Amy returned to the dressing area, Linnie had already changed back into her uniform of dull and drab, but her confident demeanor remained.

She sat down on one of the wobbly wooden stools behind the bamboo screen and indicated that Amy should do the same. "I have to tell you something."

"Oh no." Amy covered her head, bracing for impact. "What now?"

"No, it's nothing bad; it's just . . . I've never properly apologized. About the art thing. From high school."

"Ah." Amy paused, very reluctant to start poking and prodding this particular scar. "Well, that was a long time ago. I'm over it."

Linnie shook her head. Under the glaring overhead lights, Amy could see the faint, tense lines around her sister's mouth and eyes. "No, you're not."

"Of course I am." Amy forced a little laugh. "I mean, it's not like I was going to be the next Damian White or anything." After she'd found out what Linnie had done, she'd moved on with surprising ease, as if she'd never had any rights to her own work in the first place. She'd accepted that the Bialek family had been allotted a finite amount of talent and intelligence, and Linnie had dibs on the entire supply. "I had a little rage at the time; I'm not going to lie. Okay, a lot of rage. But I didn't have the pressure you did. And I didn't have your potential. Seriously, we don't need to rehash everything right now."

"But we do, because nothing's been the same since then." Linnie stared at her hands. "You weren't my sister anymore."

Amy had gone from feeling drained to overwhelmed in a matter of seconds. "It wasn't just that one incident, though. A lot of things had been building up for a long time."

"I wish I could have gone to Europe with you in college," Linnie said softly. "I wish I could have been the maid of honor at your wedding. I wish you would have come to see me when I moved to Las Vegas."

"None of that stuff is because of what you did, Linnie. It's because of who I am." Amy moved from the stool to the floor, where she rested her back against the cool plaster of the wall and tried to explain. "I just got so tired of always being forced into competition with you and losing. You needed Mom, you needed Dad, you needed my art, and after while, I was done. I couldn't stand to give up one more thing for you."

Linnie looked so little and lost perched up on her rickety stool. "Well, you can take consolation in the fact that your life turned out a hundred times better than mine."

"Why would that make me feel better? I never wished bad things for you. You were always so different, even when we were little, and I don't begrudge you that. I just wanted to be special, too."

Linnie relocated to the dusty tile floor next to Amy, and they sat side by side without speaking for a few moments.

"I've never even met my niece and nephew," Linnie said.

"You never asked to meet them," Amy pointed out. "I thought for sure that you would visit when they were born, or fly out to Mom and Dad's house for one of our weekend reunions, but you didn't. You've never sent them a birthday card or a Christmas present."

"I know. There's no excuse. I let my whole life crash and burn, and then I was so concerned with what everyone else might think that I kept letting it get worse. But I'm trying to be a better person now."

"You are a good person," Amy said with the authority only an older sister could invoke. "You may have made some questionable judgment calls over the years, but hey, who hasn't? I mean, do you remember some of the guys I dated back in the day? Making the choice to be with a nice, normal guy like Brandon was probably the smartest thing I ever did."

Linnie frowned. "So you're saying you settled for him?"

"Not at all." Amy shook her head. "I didn't *settle* for my life; I strove for it. I made a deliberate decision to stop dating dark, 'complicated' guys and instead to be happy with a really sweet guy who loves me." Amy touched her wedding band. "Our marriage is peace, punctuated by passion. If that's your definition of 'settling,' then that's sad."

Linnie dusted off her hands as if this clinched everything. "I knew it—you *are* the smart sister."

They were starting to get to their feet when the studio door opened and a pair of voices, one male and one female, filled the small, echoing alcove.

Amy pushed away from the wall to peek out from behind the screen and announce their presence when Linnie raised her index finger to her lips.

"We're late." The male spoke softly, but there was no mistaking the cold anger in his tone.

"Only by two minutes." The female sounded flustered and breathless. "They said ten o'clock and it's—"

"After ten o'clock. This is completely unprofessional, Tai, and it's all your fault."

Chapter 21

Linnie tugged Amy back down to the floor, and the two of them instinctively huddled closer together. The photographer and his assistant had run across the hall to retrieve some more equipment, and Ori had stepped out to make a phone call, so the Tottenhams assumed the room was empty.

For a guy who looked like the mild-mannered, goofy host of a PBS morning kids' show, Ty sure had a surly side. He launched into a cutting little lecture on the importance of punctuality, at the end of which Tai responded meekly, "I'm sorry, honey. I'm just still freaked out about yesterday."

"You mean the semifinals?"

"No, before that." There was a rustling sound—they were

taking off their coats. "At the coffee stand. We could have killed that woman."

Ty snorted. "Don't tell me you bought into that hysteria. That insufferable blond know-it-all was just trying to bully you, and apparently she succeeded."

Linnie went rigid, and Amy clamped a restraining hand down on her shoulder.

"But she said that people have died from that," Tai said.

"Oh, for God's sake. Saline eyedrops aren't going to hurt anyone. Use your head, Tai—it's salt and water."

"But she said the active ingredient—"

"'She said, she said,'" Ty mimicked, and Linnie could imagine his face twisted into a grimace. "She can't prove anything. But you know what? If you feel so guilty, you should confess. Be my guest."

"I never said—"

"No, Tai, I mean it. If honesty is so important to you, step right up and tell Mr. Millington to disqualify us. Bring me down with you. Hey, I deserve it, right? According to you, I'm an attempted murderer."

"Stop it." Tai sounded exhausted now. She knew how this conversation was going to end, clearly.

"You're the one who put the drops in her drink. You. Not me."

"I know."

"And while we're on the subject of integrity," Ty continued, "let's not kid ourselves about those two sisters: There is something off about them."

Linnie's ears strained to keep eavesdropping over the thundering rush of her pulse.

"They seem nice."

The Bake-Off

"Who cares if they're *nice?*" Linnie winced at the derision in his tone. "A hundred grand is on the line and you're worried about who's nice? Those two are rank amateurs who don't know a croque monsieur from a croquembouche. They stand around all day bickering about oven temperature, but they can't even roll out a piecrust properly. They don't belong in this competition, and I am not the only one who's noticed. We both need to keep a close eye on room twenty-six twenty-eight and find out what they're hiding."

Amy looked like she was mid–heart attack. Linnie gave her a little shake to get her to start breathing again. She kept waiting for their bodies to betray them with a sneeze, a hiccup, a twitch, but they both maintained total silence, and Ty just kept on yammering.

"So get with the program," he finished. "I mean it. If we lose again this year, it's on you."

"Second place is hardly losing," Tai said.

"Yes, it is. Second place is first loser." He wasn't yelling, wasn't even raising his voice, but his bitterness came through loud and clear. "Second place might be good enough for you, but not for me. We had it in the bag last year, we had everything lined up and locked down with the judges, and you *still* managed to screw it up. You owe me a hundred thousand dollars, as far as I'm concerned."

Tai mumbled something in response but Linnie couldn't make out the words. She was too busy replaying Ty's invective in her head.

Second place is first loser. In those five angry words, he had summed up Linnie's lifetime motto, the subliminal message that had been running through her brain on a continuous loop for the last twenty years. There was first place, and then there was failure. No middle ground. When her internal voice said this, it sounded reasonable, even noble. But to hear someone else say it aloud . . . well, he sounded like a draconian, abusive asshole.

"Just hold it together for twenty-four more hours," Ty said. "I've told you a million times, I've got this all figured out. I ran a statistical model on the winning dishes for the past twenty years, and the judges gravitate to chocolate and caramel. Stop arguing and start working with me, and we'll be fine."

"But—"

"What did I *just say?*" He sighed as if showing superhuman patience and restraint. "We're a good team, but you need to trust me. Do you trust me?"

"Yes." Tai's voice had flattened into a monotone.

"Good." There was a quick smacking sound as they exchanged a kiss. "Now let's get this photo shoot over with."

The second their footsteps retreated into the adjacent room, Amy and Linnie grabbed their clothes and bags and escaped out the studio door. Linnie purposely let the door slam behind them.

"Why did you do that?" Amy asked as they changed into their street clothes in a restroom in the bookstore on the building's ground floor. "Now they're going to know somebody heard them."

"Good. I want them to know. Let them wonder who heard what. Let them lose a little sleep over it."

Amy collected the outfits they'd worn for the shoot and folded them neatly. "We have to return these to Ori, you know."

"I can't believe that half-wit ran the stats to find commonalities in all the winning recipes." Linnie was a little peeved she hadn't thought of it herself. "Who would've guessed he could operate a calculator, let alone a computer program?"

"Those two are so weird. At first I thought they were Ozzie

and Harriet, then I thought they were Bonnie and Clyde, and now it's like they're, uh . . ." Amy groped for an appropriate cultural reference. "Heidi and Spencer?"

"Who?"

"Never mind."

When they got back to the hotel suite, Grammy was perched on the sofa in her customary cashmere and pearls, flipping through the latest issue of *Food & Wine* magazine. "How was the photo shoot? My goodness, you two look lovely."

She picked up the mug of herbal tea resting on a coaster on the end table. "Linnie, I just got off the phone with Cam. He'd like you to call him back at your earliest convenience."

"What is up with everybody intercepting all my phone calls?" Linnie demanded, working herself up into an indignant lather. "I have a right to privacy, you know."

"He seems like a very well-mannered young man," Grammy Syl said. "So hospitable and attentive."

"He's handsome, too," Amy added helpfully. "Plus, he's loaded and apparently quite a good kisser."

"I approve," Grammy announced.

"Gee, I'm so glad. Now, can you both please leave me alone?"

"Hey." Amy unwrapped her scarf and peeled off her jacket. "It's not freezing cold in here anymore."

Linnie flexed her fingers, waiting for the icy tingling to set in. But nothing happened. In fact, standing here in her sweater and coat, she was actually a little too warm.

"Oh yes, there was a tiny glitch with the air-conditioning, but I got it fixed." Grammy picked up the room service menu and started perusing the brunch specials.

"How did you do that?" Linnie asked. "Did you have to call in an exorcist? A meteorologist?"

"Don't be silly, lamb. I just asked your boyfriend to send up another maintenance crew, and when they had trouble, I called Hal from the senior center. Hal used to work for NASA—he can fix anything. Or, at least, he could before the arthritis set in. Anyway, I put Hal on the phone with the repairmen and he talked them through it. They had it fixed in a trice. Cam offered to hire him as a consultant."

"You're a superhero," Amy said. "Admit it. As soon as we leave, you bust out your cape and a unitard and fight for justice and the American way."

"Don't be ridiculous, darling." Grammy winked. "I wouldn't be caught dead in a unitard."

"Hang on." Linnie's attention had been snagged earlier in the conversation. "How long were you and Cam on the phone, anyway?"

"Oh, just a few minutes."

"Uh-huh. And by the way, he's not my boyfriend."

"I know." Grammy crossed her ankles. "That's how you young girls do things today, always playing the field. Though, if I may offer a word of advice—"

"You may not."

"Mind your tongue, Vasylina. There's no need to get snippy."

"Yeah, lay off Grammy Syl," Amy chimed in. "She's had a long day fighting crime."

"Now, then." Grammy picked up the phone again. "Who wants pancakes?"

"I do, I do." Amy bounced on the sofa cushion. "Make mine blueberry, please!"

"I'll just have oatmeal," Linnie said.

"Nonsense." Grammy started dialing. "You'll have Belgian waffles and you'll enjoy them. And please don't forget to return Cam's call. I gave him my word."

Linnie surrendered and slipped into the bedroom. She flipped open her phone, then realized she didn't have Cam's cell number. So she stuck her head back into the sitting room, where Amy was recounting her triumphant foray into food styling.

"Hey, Grammy? Did Mr. Manners happen to leave his personal contact information?"

"You know, dearest, I don't believe he did. Just call down to the front desk, and they'll connect you."

"They're not going to put some random guest through to the owner of the hotel chain."

"Call them," Grammy commanded.

Linnie closed the door and did as she was told. "Hi. This is Linnie Bialek in room twenty-six twenty-eight. Is there any way you could get me in touch with Mr. McMillan?" She waited for the operator to explain that Cam was in a meeting or to "accidentally" drop the call.

"Your name again, please?"

"Linnie Bialek."

The operator's inflection never changed. "One moment, please."

Thirty seconds later, Cam's voice came on the line. "Linnie. Good morning."

"Hi." She paused, feeling awkward and adolescent. "I heard you and my grandmother had quite the dialogue."

He cleared his throat. "You're probably wondering why I called."

"Oh, well, I guess. I mean, after last night, I sort of thought . . ." She'd sort of thought he'd called to shower her with compliments and ply her with poetry and beg to see her again, but it seemed rather immodest to come right out and say that.

"I sat in on a very interesting staff meeting this morning," he said. "Evidently there was a spate of vandalism in the back alley the other night."

Linnie sat down on the bed. "Vandalism, you say?"

"Something about typographical errors." His voice deepened with amusement. "Very seedy and sordid. The police got involved."

"Wow." She reclined into the mound of pillows. "This city's really going to hell in a handbasket."

"You're a very complicated woman."

"I'm not complicated, just stubborn." She sighed. "If you give me a bucket and a brush, I'll be happy to go out there and scrub down the wall this afternoon."

"That won't be necessary."

"No, really, it's the least I can do. The good news is, it should be pretty easy to get off, since it's mascara. Waterproof mascara, I grant you, but—"

"Hold on. You defaced my hotel wall with mascara?"

"They didn't mention that part?" She provided an abridged recounting of the night's events. "At least my defacement was spelled correctly. I take no responsibility for the spray paint."

"I see." For a moment, Cam was dumbstruck. "And you were arrested for vandalizing existing vandalism?"

She picked at her cuticles. "Well, at first the officer was going to let me off with a warning. But I sort of forced his hand."

"I see. Do you have a long history of trouble with the law?"

"No, and I can't say I'm in a hurry to revisit the holding cell. Frankly, I found the amenities to be shockingly substandard."

Cam chuckled. "Worse than a twenty-dollar youth hostel?"

"Well, maybe not *that* bad. By the way, thank you for getting the air conditioner fixed."

"Thank your grammy. She provided technical support for our repair crew. Good old Hal. He used to work for NASA, you know."

"Now you're on a first-name basis with Hal, too?"

"I think your grandmother has a little crush on him."

"What else did you discuss with my grandmother?" Linnie's eyes narrowed as suspicions stirred. "Did she tell you why I came to New York?"

"I assumed you were here for vacation. Is that not the case?"

Before answering, Linnie composed a quick mental list of the pros and cons of divulging her participation in the Delicious Duet competition. Given that he now knew about her history of art fraud and vandalism, she could see no possible upside to adding baking fraud to the list of ethics violations. There would be plenty of time to disillusion him *after* at least one more night of steamy sex. Plus, what if she and Amy lost at the finals? The only thing more humiliating than losing was admitting your failure to someone else.

Second place is first loser.

"We're kind of having a girls' weekend," she hedged. "Me, my sister, and Grammy Syl. Now, please, I insist on taking responsibility for my mistake. How much will it cost to have the graffiti removed?"

"It'll cost you one chess rematch. Tonight, my room, at midnight."

She wrapped the phone cord around her index finger. "Same terms as last night?"

"Higher stakes. Double or nothing."

She wasn't entirely sure what that would entail, and she couldn't wait to find out. "You're on."

Then she disconnected the call and used her cell phone to dial the pawnshop in Vegas, the number for which she had now memorized. "Hi, this is Linnie Bialek. Yes, again. I'm calling to make sure that platinum-and-diamond brooch is still there."

When she returned to the sitting room, Amy was tipping the room service waiter while Grammy arranged a trio of plates heaped with carbs, butter, and bacon on the coffee table.

"We're not eating at the dining room table?" she asked. Usually, Grammy was a stickler for napkin-on-your-lap, elbows-off-the-table propriety at mealtimes.

"I'd prefer to eat out here, if it's all the same to you. I want to watch my show."

Linnie glanced at the television screen, where a Rhodesian ridgeback was systematically devouring a dining room set. "What is this, anyway?"

"*Dog Whisperer*," Grammy said. "I watch it every day."

"But you don't have a dog," Linnie said.

"I know, dearest. This way I don't have to deal with shedding or barking or chewed-up chair legs."

"She likes *Supernanny*, too," Amy said, "but I can't watch more than ten minutes of it now that I have kids. All those toddler tantrums and parental breakdowns hit too close to home."

"Oh, pish-tosh. Chloe and Ben are nothing like the brawling hellions on that show."

"Ha. Come over some afternoon when they've missed their nap." Amy folded a strip of bacon into her mouth. "So, how's your boyfriend?"

Linnie refused to take the bait this time. "He's quite well. And while we're on the topic of boyfriends, Grammy, what's the deal with you and Hal?"

"I haven't the foggiest idea what you're referring to."

"You've got a thing for the NASA guy?" Amy clasped her hands together as though this were the cutest thing she'd ever heard. "You should go for it. Grandpa died, what? Twenty years ago? Twenty-five? It's time to move on."

"I have moved on. There's more to life than finding a man, darling." Grammy gasped and raised a hand to her cheek. "Oh goodness."

"What's wrong?" Linnie and Amy both raced to her side.

"This side of my face has gone numb." Grammy announced this with mild annoyance, as though she were remarking on a weather forecast for rain. "I suppose I'd better call my neurologist."

Linnie clicked off the TV and demanded, "Since when do you have a neurologist?"

Grammy pursed her lips, then rolled her eyes and sighed the same way Linnie herself often did. "Well, girls, there's no easy way to say this, so I'll just come right out with it. I've got a brain aneurysm. Three aneurysms, actually."

Amy and Linnie looked at each other, then looked at Grammy, then looked back at each other. Those three short sentences provided so much to process that Linnie couldn't string together a coherent thought, much less a sentence.

Grammy Syl took the stunned silence as a cue to keep on talking. "I've put off telling you because I didn't want you to worry.

Or look at me like a fragile, frail old biddy, the way you are right now."

Linnie's arm was still angled straight out from her body, her hand clutching the TV remote.

"Oh, Grammy." Amy put her arm around the older woman. "How long have you known about this?"

"Only a few months."

"A few *months*?" Linnie finally recovered her voice and, along with it, a spark of anger. "And we're just finding out now? If I had a bunch of brain aneurysms, wouldn't you demand to know about it?"

"Naturally. But I'm an adult and you're a child."

"I'm twenty-eight and she's thirty-one," Linnie pointed out.

Grammy Syl nodded. "Babies. You girls focus on your baking and let me take care of everything else." She gave Amy a kiss on the cheek. "Don't you fret, darlings. I'll be just fine."

" 'Don't fret'?" Linnie flung the remote onto the carpet. "You have *three brain aneurysms.*"

"What does that mean, anyway?" Amy asked.

"It means she needs to get into surgery, stat," Linnie said. "Honestly, Grammy, I can't believe that instead of taking care of yourself, you came to New York to babysit us. Does Dad know about all this?"

"Not yet. And I'm not going to have surgery." Grammy got to her feet with assistance from Amy, then pulled a small floral address book out of her purse. "They can't operate."

"Who's 'they'?" Amy demanded.

"My doctors. They say because of my age and my health and the location of the aneurysms, I probably wouldn't make it through the operation. How did they put it? The risks outweigh the potential benefits."

"But brain aneurysms—can't you *die* from that?" Amy grew more agitated with every passing second.

Grammy gave up. Linnie could see it in the sloping of her shoulders and the sudden weariness in her eyes. She gave up trying to bolster them with cheer and false confidence and gave them a glimpse of her pain and uncertainty. "Well, let's face it: We're all going to die sooner or later."

This just incensed Amy further. Linnie had never seen her mellow, upbeat sister yell at anyone like this. "So you're just going to sit around doing nothing?"

Grammy let her yell. "I'm having brunch with my granddaughters and watching *Dog Whisperer*. I'd hardly call that nothing."

Linnie didn't know how to navigate these dark emotional eddies. All she could do was try to fix the problem. "We'll find a better doctor. We'll get a second opinion."

"Oh, sweetheart." Grammy sat down again. "I've gotten third, fourth, fifth opinions. It is what it is."

"Then what are they doing for you?" Linnie persisted. "What's the prognosis?"

"I'll be fine until I'm not fine. That's all we really know for sure. Now if you'll excuse me for a moment, I really should make that phone call."

"Screw your neurologist." Since everyone else had abdicated their normal roles, Linnie took charge. "Half of your face is numb. We're going to the emergency room." She turned to Amy. "Call down to the front desk and tell them to call an ambulance."

"An ambulance won't be necessary. Dr. Hilman told me that dizziness and numbness are to be expected."

"Fine, then we'll take a cab. But we're going." She collected everyone's coats and made sure Grammy had her insurance card and a complete list of current medications. Amy and Grammy both followed her orders and seemed almost relieved to be bossed. "That elevator had better be working, is all I have to say."

Chapter 22

The elevator worked, and Grammy made it to the hospital without any further complications. She caused a bit of a stir among the emergency room team and the attending neurologists, but after a series of tests and CT scans, she was discharged with a tweaked prescription for her hypertension and a warning to avoid undue stress and exertion.

Seeing her grandmother swathed in the folds of a threadbare blue hospital gown jolted Amy out of her anger and into a deepening sense of dread. Age had settled in so gradually that it had been easy to overlook the increasingly pronounced topography of veins in Grammy's hands and the slackening in her cheeks and jawline. Suddenly, Grammy Syl looked *old*.

"I'll call Dad," she offered, but Grammy stopped her with a single look.

"Don't you dare. I will call him this evening and explain this to him on my own terms. He should hear this from me, not from you."

Linnie kept searching for a loophole in the diagnosis. She wanted to read all the medical charts, scrutinize all the scans, speak directly to Grammy's physicians.

"Don't worry," she kept saying. "We'll figure something out."

And Grammy kept repeating, "It is what it is."

Amy ducked out into the waiting area and called Brandon. "'It is what it is'? She's got three brain aneurysms and she's telling us 'it is what it is'? What does that even mean?"

Brandon didn't say much, but she knew he was just as shaken as she was. "Do you want me to come into the city and drive her home?" he offered. "I can cancel my last two appointments and leave now."

"Would you? Oh, honey, thank you. I keep telling her I'll take her home myself, but she's insisting that she wants us to stay here and win this stupid Delicious Duet thing."

Brandon paused. "You're still going to compete?"

"That's what I said! It's insanity. But you know how she gets when she's made up her mind about something. The woman is impossible." Amy seethed for one more second, then teared up. "I want to come home. I miss you guys. I want to rewind this whole week and start over."

"I'm sorry, sweetie. And I know dealing with your sister isn't helping your stress level."

"I can't believe I'm saying this, but Linnie's been great. She's still a bossy know-it-all, but that comes in handy during a crisis."

Amy nibbled her lower lip. "Ever since she got me arrested, I've really warmed up to her. We're a good team."

After promising to call back frequently with updates, Amy got off the phone and tracked down Linnie, who had cornered a doctor in the hallway.

"There must be something you can do for her." Linnie presented this as a challenge, a double-dog dare to the medical community. "Aren't there any clinical trials she could enroll in? Experimental procedures that show promise?"

The doctor remained empathetic but held his ground. "We have to consider her quality of life. She's in her eighties, with a history of high blood pressure and three large aneurysms clustered near the brain stem."

"Girls." Grammy Syl summoned them from her stretcher. Both sisters immediately reported for duty. "Enough. I've talked to my doctors at length about my outlook and my options, and this is my decision."

Amy opened her mouth to argue, but Grammy Syl shut her down before she could get out a single syllable.

"Must I remind you that I already missed my last chance for an Alaskan cruise? Please don't ruin this trip to New York, as well."

"Wow." Amy was awestruck. "You just earned your black belt in guilt trips."

Grammy looked flattered. "It's a skill that takes a lifetime to master, darling. Keep practicing and you'll have it down before the twins learn to drive." She sat back and sighed. "I know you're upset; believe me, so am I. And I know I should try to be wise and peaceful about this. A better grandmother would probably jot down her memories and reflections in a journal and comfort you with platitudes about the circle of life. But I don't feel old and wise; I still feel like I'm about twenty-two."

"That's why you're the envy of grandmothers everywhere," Linnie said.

"But." Grammy made them wait through a dramatic pause. "I do have one last request. Two last requests, really."

"Anything," Amy said.

"Name it and it's done," vowed Linnie.

"Number one: I want you two to be each other's family after I'm gone. Real sisters who stay in touch and take care of each other."

"So that's why you plotted to bring us together and make us bond." Amy said to Linnie, "It all starts to make sense."

Linnie nodded. "I knew that apple pie smelled like treachery."

Grammy squeezed both of their hands. "It's not treachery if it comes from a place of love."

"Your plan's going to backfire," Linnie threatened. "If you die on us, Amy and I are never going to speak to each other again. We'll be bitter enemies. Way worse than before."

"Crips and Bloods," Amy agreed.

"So you'd better stick around to referee."

Grammy hung on to their hands. "Oh, my darling girls, I wish I could."

Just as Amy was about to reach for the Kleenex again, Grammy brightened. "But that brings us to my second request: I want you to win the championship tomorrow. The whole kit and caboodle. Get one for the Gipper!"

Amy and Linnie stared at her.

"The Gipper," Grammy prompted. "Notre Dame? Knute Rockne?"

Linnie furrowed her brow. "Is that a sports reference of some kind?"

"Oh, never mind. Just bake your hearts out and make me proud."

"We will." Amy rested her hand on top of her grandmother's.

"We'll annihilate the competition." Linnie added her hand to the stack. "I promise you, Grammy. Come tomorrow morning, there will be blood on the blenders."

Grammy beamed. "That's my lamb."

Chapter 23

"It's almost midnight," Amy whispered. "Are you asleep?"

Linnie flipped over to face her sister. They'd been lying back-to-back in the huge bed for hours, each staring out into the darkness. "No."

"What are you thinking about?" Amy asked.

"Nothing, really. Just reciting the periodic table in my mind." Anything to keep her mind off apple pie and aneurysms. "What are you thinking about?"

Amy threw one arm above her head. "Everything. Grammy Syl's sleeping in my guest room right now. Brandon said she insisted on making a huge dinner for everyone in the house, including his mother. She's an octogenarian with a bunch of brain aneurysms who spent the afternoon in the emergency room, and she comes home and whips up a pot roast, mashed potatoes, and gravy from scratch, all because Ben mentioned he likes 'taters.' Who does that?"

"We come from a long line of difficult women," Linnie said. "And getting more difficult with each generation. Try to get some sleep. The finals start at eight, and we have to go over our prep checklist at six thirty sharp."

"You and your checklists. It's not a shuttle launch." Amy shifted position again. "Hey, shouldn't you be slipping out right about now for your late-night rendezvous with your partner in plaid?"

"Are you kidding me? I've never felt less like rendezvousing than I do right now." Her whole body felt as though she'd spent the afternoon boxing and the bruises were just now starting to set in.

"Then don't. Just give him a kiss and say good-bye."

Linnie plucked at the duvet. "What exactly am I supposed to say, though? 'Thanks for the cheap thrills on the chessboard'? 'Whenever I see your name in a celebrity gossip column, I'll reflect fondly on our time together'?"

"Linnie. I'm not going to write you a script every time you interact with this guy. You slept with him; you can speak to him. Figure it out." Two seconds later, Amy relented. "Okay, one tiny scrap of advice and that's it: I know you hate emotional scenes, but sarcasm is not the way to go here. Try sincerity."

Linnie murmured her agreement, but made no move to get out of bed.

"You like this guy, right?" Amy persisted.

"Yes. Very much." *A little too much.*

"Then go."

"I'm not having sex with him."

"Who said you had to? Just be a decent human being and say a proper good-bye."

Linnie swung her bare feet onto the carpet. She stayed that way, half in and half out of bed, for a full minute. "I'm really scared," she admitted. "About the finals and everything after."

"I know." Amy lifted her head and propped herself up on her elbows. "What if we lose? What if we *win*? I don't know which would be more stressful at this point."

"Losing," Linnie said. "Grammy needs her brooch back. We're winning tomorrow. End of story."

"Yeah, but then we'll have to do all the publicity, all those interviews. Do you really want to go on the *Today* show and, like, lie under oath to Meredith Vieira about how we came up with the recipe?"

"If you can handle Grammy Syl, you can handle Meredith Vieira," Linnie assured her. "All right, I'm going. I'll be back in a few minutes. Do you want me to bring you some warm milk to help you sleep?"

"Why don't you recite a line or two of the periodic table? That should put me right out."

This time, Linnie didn't loiter in front of Cam's door before announcing her presence with three quick, businesslike raps. She didn't pinch her cheeks or worry about how pallid and disheveled she looked. And she didn't worry about how to convey her intentions—she figured her outfit would do the talking.

The Bake-Off

Cam opened the door in a matter of seconds, as if he'd been waiting for her in the foyer. He looked like he had just come from a regatta in his starched white shirt, dark trousers, and polished black shoes and belt.

"Whew." He removed his silver cuff links and rolled up his shirtsleeves. "Beat you here by five minutes."

"You just got off work?" Linnie tried to remember what time he'd been on the phone with Grammy that morning. "You worked, what? Fifteen hours? At least?"

"Kind of a long day. But I was highly motivated to get everything done before midnight." He brushed her cheek with the backs of his fingers.

She held out her arms to give him a better look at the saggy, baggy lumberjack pajamas underneath her bathrobe. "Here's the deal: I'm not wearing plaid underwear tonight."

His expression darkened with concern. "Everything all right?"

"No, actually. This afternoon I found out that my grandmother is . . . She's not doing well. And I've lost something very important to her and I'm not sure I can get it back."

He stepped back and held open his door. "Come in."

"I can't. But I'll be leaving tomorrow, and I wanted to say good-bye." She finally summoned up a smile. "I had fun."

"Come in," he ordered. "You look like hell."

Her eyebrows shot up. "That's not very gallant."

"Gallantry doesn't work with you." He reeled her in by her bathrobe belt and locked the door behind her. "How about something to eat?"

"I am a bit peckish, now that you mention it." Actually, she was ravenous. Her stomach felt like it was sucking up against her spine. How had she not noticed?

"Sit down." He guided her into a small but highly stylized kitchen, all done up in polished concrete and gleaming white subway tiles, and pulled out a chair from the table. After a quick inventory of the refrigerator, he reported, "I've got cheese, butter, bread, and beer. And milk that expired two days ago. So unless you're in the mood for grilled cheese, we'll have to order something from downstairs."

"Grilled cheese will be fine."

"Great." He assembled the bread, butter, and cheese along with a knife and a cast-iron frying pan. "Will this work?"

"I guess so." Linnie lifted the heavy pan onto the stove burner and turned on the flame. "Aren't we supposed to toast the bread before we get started?"

"I have no idea. You've never made grilled cheese before?"

"No," she confessed. "You?"

"Nope. Can't say I'm much of a cook." He arranged two slices of bread on the counter and started hacking away at the Havarti. "But it's just a sandwich with cheese, butter, and bread. I'm sure we can figure it out."

Five minutes later the frying pan was smoking, the windows and balcony doors had been opened to prevent the fire alarm from sounding, and the blackened grilled cheese sat in the center of a porcelain plate like a jagged chunk of coal.

"Wow." Linnie poked at the smoldering squiggles of melted cheese that had permanently bonded to the metal. "I guess we should have buttered the pan first."

"Live and learn." Cam grabbed a dish towel and carried the

ruined skillet out to the balcony. "Room service it is. Can I interest you in a dessert? I hear our pastry chef makes a mean apple pie."

"No, thank you," she murmured. "I'm not really one for sweets."

He called down to the kitchen and ordered replacement grilled cheese, along with tomato-basil soup.

"I'm surprised this place doesn't come with a full-time chef," she said, only half joking.

"It does, if you're a guest of the hotel. But as a member of the McMillan family . . . well, let's just say I don't need any extra help maintaining a reputation as an Ivy League prince with no practical skills."

"Skills like making grilled cheese?" Linnie teased.

"Exactly." He grinned. "People can be so prejudiced."

"But you work fifteen-hour days and personally fix leaky faucets for your guests."

"I'm still trying to redeem myself after getting kicked out of college and then joining the Peace Corps when I finally did graduate. I was supposed to go on to business school; instead, I spent two years in Turkmenistan. My brother, on the other hand, has an MBA from Harvard and a flawless résumé."

"The golden child," she said, remembering Amy's words. "Every family has one."

When their food arrived, they ate by candlelight in the little kitchen, Cam still in his shirtsleeves and Linnie in her pajamas.

He kept stealing sidelong glances at her, until Linnie couldn't stand it any longer. "What?" she demanded, dabbing her lips with a napkin. "Do I have something in my teeth? Is my hair on fire?"

"No." He put down his cutlery. "But I have a confession: I know your secret."

Linnie started to ask, *Which one?* Then managed to change her reply to a noncommittal, "Hmm?"

"Your grandmother told me what you're really doing here."

Linnie froze in midchew. "She did?"

"When I called your hotel room this morning, she told me about the photo shoot." He waited for her to jump in and elaborate, and when she didn't, he prompted, "Why didn't you just tell me you were a model?"

"Oh." Words started tumbling out of her. "Well, when you're a model, people assume certain things about you: You're vain, you're vapid, you can't do calculus."

"You can be honest with me," he said. "I'm not going to judge you."

"You keep saying that."

"Because you always seem so defensive."

She ran her finger along the tines of her fork. "Anyway, I'm not a *real* model."

"Define 'real' model."

"The kind of model you typically date."

"I see." He folded up his napkin and sat back in his chair. "And how would you know what sort of woman I date, model or otherwise?"

She realized too late that she had tipped her hand. "From the gossip blogs."

"You don't seem like the gossip-blog type."

"Oh, I am. Absolutely. It's my guilty pleasure."

He inclined his head. "Are you sure those bloggers are referencing me and not my older brother?"

"Um." Damn Amy and her gossip-skimming ways. "No."

"My brother, Mac, is the one who likes to show up at high-profile events with A-list arm candy."

Linnie held up one hand. "Your brother's named Mac McMillan? You're Cam, and he's Mac?"

"His birth certificate says Pertinax, but you only call him that if you want a bloody nose. As I was saying, he likes playing the field. A lot. To the point that it can be a problem, even for the golden child. That's why I'm in charge of the New York properties now. I'm cleaning up a series of messes he made last year." He tapped his index finger on the tabletop. "But now we're veering back into gossip-blog territory, so let's return to the subject at hand. You know what kind of woman I want? I want a fake model who can do calculus. I want a bad cook in flannel pajamas."

Linnie got up from the table. "Cam—"

"I want you."

"Can we please not do this?" She turned and walked toward the balcony. "You want me only because you can't have me."

"Try me," he challenged. "Stay here and try me."

"I can't."

"Why not? You think I'll disappoint you?"

No, but I know *I'll disappoint* you. He'd soon discover that all of her individual attributes—the brains, the body, the infamous "potential"—added up to so much less than anyone hoped for. He stopped arguing with her. Instead, he came up behind her and wrapped his arms around her. They stayed like that for a long time, Cam offering comfort and Linnie letting herself accept it.

Finally, she turned around to face him. She never broke eye contact as she grazed his lips with her own.

This time, the sex wasn't fun at all. It was slow and sweet and sublime.

Linnie opened to her eyes to the faint gray light of early morning. She could hear Cam's slow, steady breathing in her ear and the insistent electric pulse of an alarm clock beeping in the bedroom down the hall.

She was wearing his shirt, and her neck ached from sleeping on the floor. They must have dozed off in the living room after last night's exertions.

The alarm clock kept beeping. Time to get up. Places to go, people to see.

Pies to bake.

She rocketed into a sitting position. "What time is it?"

Cam jolted into consciousness, fumbled on the coffee table for his watch, and squinted at the dial. "Oh shit." There ensued a frantic game of reverse Twister as they struggled to disentangle their bare limbs and get out the door.

Linnie grabbed her robe and peered under the sofa, searching for her cell phone and room key. She had fifteen minutes to grab her ID from her room and hustle through security downstairs. "I'm borrowing your shirt," she hollered to Cam as she tucked the hem into the waistband of her flannel pajama pants.

Cam didn't hear her. He was already in the shower, soaping and rinsing with Olympic speed.

By the time she had located her belongings, he had pulled on jeans and a blue rugby shirt. Together, they raced into the elevator and hit the button for Linnie's floor.

Linnie twisted her hair up into a tangled topknot and did a quick breath check into her cupped hand.

Cam kept glancing at his watch and running his hands through his hair. "Talk later?"

"Later," she agreed.

"I wish I could walk you to your room, but I have to get downstairs. I'm late for a critical work function."

The chime dinged and the elevator doors slid open. "Big summit with the cooling and heating repair union?" she asked as she stepped out.

"No." He looked a little sheepish. "I have to go judge."

"I thought you didn't judge." She smiled. "Isn't that your mantra?"

"I don't judge *you*." He leaned out of the elevator, gave her a quick but very thorough kiss, then ducked back in as the door closed. "Aspiring dessert champions are another matter."

The next five minutes were a blur. Linnie's brain had left the building and her body had gone on autopilot. She dimly noticed Ty Tottenham waiting by the elevator bank across the hall, but today she did not engage. She strode right by him, her hands trembling and her face numb, and headed straight to her suite to gather the equipment she needed for the competition.

From the piles of clothes discarded on the desk chair and the plates stacked on the room service cart outside the door, she gathered that Amy must have had a big breakfast and changed outfits several times before leaving that morning.

She slung her purse over her shoulder and cast a longing look toward her suitcase in the corner. What if she just packed up her stuff and grabbed a taxi to the airport? She could be halfway to Vegas before the Delicious Duet winner was announced, and she'd never have to face Cam, Amy, or szarlotka again.

Then she noticed a note taped to the mirror above the desk:

L—

You better be dead, but if you're not, don't worry—you will be when I finally find you.

xo,

A

P.S. Grammy Syl says she wants to wear her grandmother's brooch to her wake. WHERE ARE YOU???????

Chapter 24

"*What the hell happened to you?*" By the time Linnie finally showed up, Amy had deteriorated into an exposed nerve ending in human form. "We're starting in two minutes."

For the last three hours, Amy's stress had been snowballing while she waited for her sister to show. But now that Linnie had finally scurried in, looking even more frazzled than Amy herself, Amy's anxiety skyrocketed to unprecedented heights.

She hadn't even recognized her sister at first. Between the baggy man's shirt and the shapeless lumberjack pants, Linnie looked like she should be strumming a guitar and begging for change out on a street corner. Her hair was pulled back, her complexion looked sickly, and her brown eyes had gone vacant and dull.

This was not the look of a woman in the Zone.

"Hey." She grabbed Linnie's shoulder and gave it a little shake. "I can't do this without you!"

"It's okay," Linnie murmured, obviously trying to convince herself. "Everything's under control."

"How can you say that?" Amy cried. "Nothing's under control. It's chaos and looting and rioting in the streets! You're late! You're the last person here!"

"Please stop yelling at me. I'm doing the best I can."

Amy complied, but only because her sister's meek, apologetic demeanor was freaking her out.

"I have two minutes to spare, and I'm not the last contestant to show up." Linnie nodded over at Ty, who had just arrived at the adjacent prep station. "He is."

"Those two are so dysfunctional," Amy said. "And by the way, you look like hot death. Are you wearing pajamas?"

Linnie stroked the fine white fabric of her wrinkled shirt. "This is Gucci, I'll have you know."

Since the semifinal round had winnowed down the competition, the baking stations now took up less than half of the ballroom. The extra space had been used to accomodate additional rows of folding chairs in front of the platform stage. Media presence had increased at least tenfold, with journalists roving the aisles and a few radio and TV outlets broadcasting live. "And you never answered my question. Why did you go off the grid last night? I tried to call you a hundred times."

"I had my phone on vibrate." Linnie folded her hands primly. "We must have slept through it."

"Were you hibernating like a bear? Were you drugged?"

"What can I say?" Linnie ducked her head, inhaling Cam's scent on her shirt. "We wore ourselves out."

Snowley Millington made his grand entrance through the double doors at the front of the room. He strode past the rows of prep stations and up to the stage, preening for the cameras all the way. "Good morning, ladies and gentlemen," he said in a booming ringmaster voice. "Welcome to the fiftieth annual Delicious Duet Dessert Championship. Delicious sugar has been bringing friends and family together for over seventy years now, and it is our great pleasure to introduce the contestants who have qualified for the final round this morning. Each year, we select our semifinalists from a pool of thousands of submitted recipes. Our test kitchen in Camarillo, California, reviews these submissions and selects the very best of the best. The finalists hail from all over our great nation, from sea to shining sea, bound together by one common passion."

"Money," Linnie whispered.

"Publicity," Amy threw in.

"Baking. The teams you see here today represent the ne plus ultra of home cooking. Let's give them all a round of applause." With a flourish, he twisted the dial on a giant green oven timer. A single high-pitched ding sounded throughout the ballroom. "The Delicious Duet Dessert Championship has officially begun!"

"Let's do this." Amy first gave their runner the signal to go raid the pantry, then dropped to the floor and pulled stacks of bowls out of the storage cupboard so she could assemble the *mise en place* of dry ingredients. "The secret sisterhood is now in effect. Wonder Twin powers activate!"

But her Wonder Twin didn't activate. Linnie peered into the big clear bowl of the food processor, swaying on her feet.

Amy glanced up, but her hands never stopped moving. "What's with you?"

"I think I need to sit down."

"Are you kidding me? If I'm not allowed to take a bathroom break, you're not allowed to kick back in a recliner." Amy collected the metal measuring spoons, the measuring cups, and the food scale. "I know you're tired, but the adrenaline's going to kick in any second. Suck it up. Isn't that what you always say?"

The runner returned, carrying a large tray stacked with the necessary ingredients, and Linnie deposited the flour on the counter with a thud. "Something happened this morning. With Cam."

"Boy trouble? That's what this is all about?" Amy opened the refrigerator to stash the butter and sour cream. "You need to forget Cam McMillan even exists. Focus like a laser, Linnie. Think about your brooch. Think about Grammy Syl. I wasn't kidding about the wake thing. This morning, while you were passed out in the penthouse, I had a twenty-minute phone conversation with Grammy, who wanted to discuss her elaborate plans for her own funeral. She's already got her outfit picked out, you know, and all the readings she wants everyone to do."

"That's beyond morbid," Linnie said. "Very meticulous, though. The lady knows what she wants."

"I'll tell you what she wants: She wants to wear that diamond brooch for the viewing. She went on and on about it. So I don't care what you do or who you do it with after this pie is in the oven, but until then, buckle down. Right now, the only people who matter are you, me, and the judges."

"I have to tell you something." Linnie held out her palm. "And I'm going to need to take that rolling pin away from you before I do."

"Oh boy." Amy handed it over and folded her arms. "I'm ready. Go."

"I think Cam is one of the judges."

Amy blinked. "Why would you think that?"

Linnie looked like she was about to start hyperventilating. "Because this morning he told me he had to go downstairs and judge a dessert competition."

Amy nodded and started measuring out the sugar. "Okay."

"No, not okay!" Linnie wrung her hands. "This is a disaster. We're going to be disqualified. The rules clearly state that we're not allowed to contact or influence the judges in any way. That includes naked chess and exchanging bodily fluids."

"Well, I'm the only person who knows, and I'm not talking," Amy said. "What did he say when you told him you were a contestant?"

"Nothing, because I didn't get a chance to explain. He kind of sprang it on me at the last possible second."

"How on earth did this happen, anyway?" Amy finished weighing the sugar and moved on to the flour. "I thought all the judges were staying off-site."

"They are, but Cam's family owns this hotel," Linnie pointed out. "He's working fifteen-hour days. He's not going to relocate to the Marriott. That must be why the hotel staff wasn't supposed to let us stay up in the South Tower."

"Well, they sure dropped the ball on that one." Amy shook her head. "Why is he judging this? Is he a pastry chef in addition to being a hotel tycoon?"

"No," Linnie said. "He doesn't even like desserts. But since the McMillan chain is a major corporate sponsor, they get to appoint a guest judge on the panel."

"Well, if he doesn't know that you're a contestant and nobody knows that you two are getting it on, then what's your problem?"

"We're breaking the rules." Linnie started strangling the flour sack again.

"We broke the rules when Grammy entered her recipe as our own," Amy reminded her. "We're low-down, dirty rule breakers. That's just who we are. No point in freaking out about it now."

"But . . ." Linnie swallowed. "He'll be judging me."

"Well, yes, that's pretty much what judges do. But since he'll never know which entry is ours—"

"He's going to be criticizing my work and taking points off for every little thing that's not perfect." Right on cue, the red neck splotches started to materialize. "I cannot do this, Amy. The pressure is—"

Amy reached her capacity for crazy talk. "Zip it. *Cállate la boca. Ferme la bouche.* If I say it in Latin, will you shut up?"

"*Fac taceas,*" Linnie murmured.

"Thank you. Now look at me." She waited until Linnie complied. "You've prepped this crust hundreds of times. All you have to do is churn out some dough, and I will take it from there. But I need those butter striations. So get cracking."

At last, Linnie started moving. She opened the refrigerator and grabbed a stick of butter. "You're so bossy."

"One of us has to be." Amy handed her a knife. "Consider this your engraved invitation to join me in the Zone."

All around them, teams were already whisking and mixing and dicing. The smells of chocolate and fruit and simple syrup commingled in the air.

"Have you consulted my checklist?" Linnie asked. "We're way behind schedule."

"That's more like it. All right, I'm going to peel the apples for the filling. Let me know if you need help with the dough."

Linnie started pouring ingredients into the food processor and was preparing to separate the eggs when the edge of her rolled sleeve caught on the corner of the cutting board and jostled the table. Two eggs fell and cracked open on the carpet. When she knelt to assess the damage, she knocked over the bowl of flour, too.

Both sisters stared at the sticky spatters of yellow and white splashed across the carpet. Miraculously, the bowl of flour had landed right-side up, but a substantial amount had spilled over the side.

There goes a hundred hours of my life I'll never get back, was Amy's first thought. All those evenings she'd spent chopping up fruit and slicing the sides of her fingers with the apple peeler. All the hours she'd banished Brandon and the kids from the house so she could whip up one more batch of szarlotka. All the pep talks from Grammy and lectures from Linnie had finally taken root, and somewhere along the way, she'd invested herself in this competition. She really, really wanted to win. And now she was going to have to settle for second place—again—because of someone else's mistakes.

She sent their runner to go check the pantry for any leftover supplies, but he returned empty-handed.

"Oh no." Linnie clutched her temples. "Oh no oh no oh no *oh no*."

"Hang on." Amy kept her voice calm and controlled. She picked up the bowl, placed it on the food scale, and held her breath while the numbers came up. "We've still got usable flour in here. But we're about two cups short. How much flour is left in the bag?"

"Not enough." Linnie folded in on herself, covering her head as though practicing for a tornado drill. "It's over. I've ruined everything. I should have been here this morning to review the checklist. I should have told the runner to hoard all the dry goods he could smuggle into his pockets. You know other teams are hoarding. The smart teams!"

Amy nibbled her lower lip. "Let's think this through. Maybe Joan and Susan have some flour left over. I'm sure they'll give us some."

"We're their competition. Why would they help us?"

"Because they're our sisters in the muffin tin Mafia."

Linnie remained in her crash position. "But what kind of flour are they using?"

"Does it really matter?"

"Yes!" Linnie looked up. "The all-purpose flour we're using has a ten percent protein content. We need to maintain the integrity of the gluten structure."

Amy took a deep breath, opened her mouth, and closed it again. She left Linnie in a heap on the floor, made a beeline for her fellow Confectionistas, and returned victorious.

"Here's the deal," she told Linnie. "They're happy to give us their leftovers, but unfortunately, they're using cake flour."

Linnie's howl of despair drew startled looks from the neighboring prep stations. "Cake flour only has six to eight percent protein. The gluten strands are going to be totally insufficient. We'd be better off using whole-wheat flour!"

"Well, beggars can't be choosers. We need three batches, right? So we'll do two batches with the regular flour and keep the third batch with the cake flour separate. Let me ask you this: Is the batch with the cake flour going to look any different from the batches with the regular flour?"

Linnie considered this. "I can't be sure, but I'd assume so. The cake flour will probably make the crust look flat and clumpy."

The Bake-Off

"Okay, then we'll use the regular flour for the pies intended for the judges and the visual display," Amy said. "We'll use the cake flour for the crowd sampler."

"Maybe we should just scrape whatever we can off the floor and hope no one notices."

"You'd rather have the crowd eat carpet lint than cake flour? Forget it, Linnie. This is not one of your laboratory-controlled, high-precision speed drills. This is crunch time. We have to improvise, and I need your brain. So get ahold of yourself and *think*!"

Linnie closed her eyes for a moment and modified her breathing. When she opened them, she sounded like her supercilious, sardonic self. "My brain is in working order and at your disposal."

"Good. We need two extra egg yolks, and we need them now. None of the Confectionistas have extra."

"Maybe we could try a substitution," Linnie ventured. "Liquid, flour, butter, and baking powder."

"Will that really work?"

"In theory. We should aim for a high-fat liquid, like cream or whole milk. If I recall correctly, the ratio is four-to-four-to-one-to-one. We'll use that in the same batch we use the cake flour."

Amy dusted off her palms with renewed resolve. "That's going to be one messed-up apple pie."

"It'll be good enough for the rabble." Linnie resumed cracking and separating the eggs.

Amy had to smile. "There's the Linnie I know and love."

One hour later, Amy had assembled the crust and apple filling and was brushing a light layer of cream across the grated dough topping the final batch of szarlotka. "This will help it bake up extra shiny and golden," she told Linnie. "They have a

261

professional photographer shooting each entry, and I'm hoping to use the pictures to start my food styling portfolio."

"You're really going to pursue that?" Linnie sounded amazed.

"If I can." Amy started to feel defensive. "Why? You think it's a pipe dream?"

"No, but you already work full-time, you're raising twins, you have a dog and a house and a husband with whom you're trying to open a dental practice. Many people would consider that a full plate."

"I'm busy," Amy agreed. "But the food styling would be for me. Yes, it'll be hard work, but it will only be a few days a month, and it'll be *my* project. *My* passion."

Linnie hesitated for a second, then offered, "Well, if you need a babysitter, maybe I could come out for a weekend now and then."

"Really?"

Linnie tugged at the strings of her apron. "Sure. Why not?"

"I didn't realize you liked kids."

"They're not 'kids'—they're my niece and nephew. And while I may not have much babysitting experience, I can assure you they'll be in good hands. I know CPR, I can administer basic first aid, and I'm very familiar with the developmental research of Vygotsky and Piaget."

"But can you break up a toddler wrestling match involving biting, hair pulling, and a one-eyed teddy bear used as a weapon?"

"I'll read up on SWAT operational tactics." Linnie glanced at the clock. "Are you done with that cream yet?"

Amy drizzled a few more droplets of cream across the textured topping. "You can't rush an artist at work."

"You can't rush an oven, either. We have to get these in so we can get them out in time to cool. The last thing we need is a judge burning his tongue on our entry. You've got one hundred twenty seconds and counting. One hundred nineteen, one hundred eighteen . . .'"

Amy raised her basting brush and flicked a bit of liquid onto Linnie's apron. "Get out of my workspace and go stalk somebody else for the next hundred and seventeen seconds."

Linnie complied, edging toward Tai and Ty's prep station, where Ty had just returned from a lap around the ballroom to scope out the competition. "The Culinary Channel wants to interview us," he told Tai. "I have to go right now."

Tai spooned sticky caramel filling into fluted chocolate crusts. "Oh, okay, just let me smooth out the top here and we'll—"

"*I'm* going to go talk to them." Ty held up his wristwatch, trying to check his reflection in the crystal. "You stay here and make the chocolate ganache."

"But don't they want to interview me, too?" Tai asked.

"One thing at a time, sweetie. I'm sure everyone will want to talk to you after we win. But for now, I need you to finish up with the chocolate and make sure that nobody"—he glanced accusingly at Linnie—"tries any funny business."

"Fine." Tai leaned away when he went in for a kiss. He either really didn't notice or pretended not to.

"Just mix the chocolate and cream, let it cool for two minutes, and pour it on top of the caramel, okay?" He waited until she nodded in confirmation. "Don't touch the walnuts; I'll put those on when I get back."

"I can handle the walnuts," Tai said.

"No. I want them to look a certain way. Your job is the ganache. No more, no less."

After her husband hurried off to dazzle the cable networks

with his charm and good looks, Tai turned her attention to the saucepan of cream on the stove burner. She poured the simmering liquid into a metal bowl containing chunks of bittersweet chocolate, then stirred the mixture a few times with her spatula and set it aside to cool.

Linnie spied a tiny glass prep bowl perched on the very edge of Tai's cutting board. Hidden behind a stack of used bowls and a canister of Dutch cocoa, the prep bowl held what appeared to be sea salt.

"Excuse me." Linnie cleared her throat. "Is that your salt?"

"Where?" Tai glanced around, but the bowl was out of her sight line.

"Right there." Linnie pointed to the corner of the cutting board. "Is that supposed to go in the ganache?"

"Yes. Oh my God, yes." Tai poured the pinch of salt into the warm chocolate cream and stirred. "I can't believe I did that. Thank you for telling me." She transferred the prep bowl back and forth between her palms. "I'm such an idiot."

"You're not an idiot," Linnie said. "We're all under a lot of pressure today." When she returned to her own prep station, Amy was waiting with flared nostrils and a rolling pin within reach.

"What the hell, Linnie? Why are you helping her?"

Linnie shrugged, unable to explain it even to herself. "She forgot an ingredient, and I pointed it out. It's not like I'm letting her share our oven space."

"Uh-huh. I see what you're doing. This isn't about Tai; this is about Cam. Admit it: You're trying to lose on purpose because you have performance anxiety. You *want* those bastards to beat us."

"They're not going to beat us. We don't need them to screw up their recipe for ours to be better. We can still win, fair and square."

The Bake-Off

Amy leveled her index finger at her sister. "I don't like this side of you."

"I had a momentary flash of human decency—it'll pass; I promise. In the meantime, please hand me the oven mitts and prepare to witness baking perfection. All my calibrations, calculations, and computations are about to pay off."

Chapter 25

"And now, ladies and gentlemen, the moment you've all been waiting for." Snowley Millington consulted the index cards in his hand and waited until absolute silence settled over the assembled crowd.

Linnie held her head high and studied the rotund older man, watching for any nonverbal cues that might hint at what was coming. Mr. Millington wasn't looking at any of the contestants, though—his focus remained on the film crews camped around the stage's periphery.

Next to her, Amy started to melt down. "This is worse than *American Idol.*"

"Our third-place winners, recipients of a full suite of kitchen appliances furnished by DIY Home and Garden Superstores—"

"If we get that, we're selling that crap on eBay," Linnie hissed.

"—are Susan Miller and Joan Whitson of Phoenix, Arizona, for their Razzle Dazzle Rhubarb Upside-down Cake."

Polite applause ensued as Susan and Joan hurried up to the stage to shake Mr. Millington's hand and pose for photos.

Another agonizing pause. Amy started to gnaw on her fingernails.

"Our second-place winners, recipients of a trip to France and a two-week intensive pastry workshop at Le Bernard Culinary Arts Academy in Paris, furnished by McMillan Hotels International—"

"I've already been to France," Amy murmured.

"Screw Paris; I want to get paid."

"—are Tyson and Tai Tottenham of Fulton Falls, Ohio, for their Tempting Turtle Tarts."

People turned their heads and craned their necks as Ty stormed onstage, making no attempt to mask his disappointment. Tai trailed behind him and shook hands with Mr. Millington as if greeting her executioner.

"Wow," Amy said. "No one will ever accuse that guy of being a gracious loser."

Ty stomped down the stage stairs and out of the ballroom, letting the heavy double doors clang shut behind him.

Mr. Millington waited for order to be restored. "And finally, our grand-prize winners, recipients of one hundred thousand dollars, are . . ."

"I'm going to throw up." Linnie moaned.

"Spit it out!" Amy cried.

"Amy Nichols and Vasylina Bialek, with their Secret Sisterhood Szarlotka."

For a moment, all Linnie could hear was Amy's voice shrieking in her ear: "We did it! We won! Oh my God, *we won!*"

Amy started hurtling over the laps of everyone between her and the aisle. Her elation was contagious, and the crowd's cheering swelled as she headed for the stage with her arms held high like Rocky Balboa in a striped apron.

Linnie followed in her wake, quiet and contained, but most of all relieved. Finally, she could stop worrying and pretending and evading. She would cash her check, go get Grammy's brooch, and leave the spotlight behind.

"Congratulations, both of you." Snowley offered them the microphone, but Linnie had nothing to say. Her work here was done.

She posed for a moment alongside Amy, both of them beaming for the cameras while showing off a six-foot-long poster-board check. She turned to the contest official to her right and asked, "Hey, can we actually deposit this thing?"

"Right now?" the woman asked.

"Yeah."

She looked taken aback. "Well, no, this is just for the photo op. In a few days, the corporation will send you and your sister traditional checks, along with some tax forms—"

The double doors clanged again as another Delicious sugar representative loped in from the hallway. He had a cell phone in one hand and a stack of what appeared to be scorecards in the other.

And then Cam walked in. He stopped, locked eyes with Linnie from across the ballroom, and she knew.

The flour bowl was about to hit the floor, and there was nothing she could do but watch it shatter.

While Amy continued to wave and blow kisses, Linnie stepped aside and met the contest rep at the top of the stairs.

"What's going on?" asked the woman who had presented the check to Linnie. "Is everything all right?"

"I'm sorry to interrupt, but I need to speak with Ms. Bialek for a moment." He refused to look Linnie in the face.

Using the enormous check to partially shield them from the audience's view, he introduced himself as Stephen Wexel, one of the contest's chief administrators.

"First, let me congratulate you and your sister on your win." His smile flickered on and off. "I hate to take away from your big moment, but it's my job to investigate any allegation of misconduct." He adjusted his tie. "I'm sorry to embarrass you, but I have to ask this. You didn't have any, uh, *contact* with any of our judges, did you?"

Both of them peered around the edge of the check at Cam, who had been surrounded by a protective posse of men in green. Linnie could tell from the set of his jaw and his impassive expression that he hadn't revealed anything about their relationship. He was leaving it up to her.

"Why would you ask me such a thing?" she asked, trying to buy time while she scrambled to come up with a decent line of defense.

Stephen continued to hem and haw about how he was just doing his duty. "One of the Delicious Duet contestants claims he has a photo of you kissing a judge, but as you can see"—he held up a cell phone, presumably Ty's—"this image is rather blurry, and this particular contestant is known as something of a troublemaker. Still, I would be remiss if I didn't at least ask. Do you or did you have any kind of personal relationship with Mr. McMillan over there?"

Linnie knew she looked shocked—she *was* shocked. Shocked that Ty had caught her, shocked that she hadn't figured it out as soon as she saw him by the elevator this morning. But she could play this off as dismay at being falsely accused. She could deny ever having met Cam, and she knew he'd go along with her.

She could break the rules one more time and get away with it. No one would contradict her.

She stared straight ahead, past the crowds and the cameras, and fixed her gaze on the glowing red exit sign hanging over the main doors. Then she squared her shoulders and uttered a single word:

"Yes."

The microphone picked up her voice and carried it over the loudspeakers.

Everyone in the room immediately quieted down and gave her their full attention. Amy paused in midlaugh, her head thrown back and her eyes sparkling. "Yes, what?" she asked.

Linnie cleared her throat and covered the mic with her hand. "Yes, I know him," she confirmed.

This confession set off a round of gasps and exclamations in the front row of the audience, and word quickly spread back through the aisles.

The contest rep looked even more horrified than Linnie felt.

"You do?" he asked, as if he were hoping she would change her answer.

Linnie nodded. "Yes, sir."

"And you knew he was a judge?"

"Not until this morning."

"A likely story," somebody hissed. "She targeted him."

"And he didn't know I was a Delicious Duet contestant," she emphasized. "Or what I was baking."

There came a snicker of derision. "Riiiight."

"That explains a lot," sniped another voice. "Did you taste the pie they left out for the crowd? B-minus at best."

"So you"—Mr. Millington looked over at Cam, then back at Linnie—"and you . . ."

"Yes," Linnie confirmed. "Yes to everything you are too polite to ask. But again, it's entirely my fault. He was unaware of who I was and why I was staying in the hotel."

Cam started toward her, but a swarm of reporters blocked his path and a pair of security officers hustled him out into the hall while Stephen adjusted his glasses. "I'm going to need a moment to confer with my staff." He stepped back into a cluster of corporate colleagues.

Linnie remained where she stood, bracing for the oncoming tsunami of accusation and hostility.

And then she felt a hand on her back as Amy stepped up beside her. "Don't freak out. I'm right here with you."

"I'm not freaking out," Linnie insisted.

"You're shaking like a bobblehead on a dashboard."

"It's okay." Linnie kept her chin high. "In the words of a very wise woman, 'It's just fucking pie.'"

"Good girl. Hey, if you rip off your shirt and flash the cameras right now, I bet you could parlay this whole fiasco into a reality show."

"Ladies, we've reached a decision." Stephen Wexel returned, looking somber. "I'm afraid you both are disqualified."

Amy nodded and turned to go, but Linnie tried one last appeal. "I know I was wrong, sir, and I absolutely deserve to be disqualified. But please don't disqualify my sister, too. Why should she have to pay for my mistakes?"

The contest rep looked ready to pound back a bottle of bourbon and smoke a carton of cigarettes. "The Delicious Duet championship is a team event. If one team member is out, you're both out."

"But—"

"Forget it." Amy strutted toward the stairs like she was working the runway at Fashion Week. "Begging is beneath you. They can choke on their hundred thousand dollars."

Mr. Millington stepped back up to the microphone and addressed the murmuring crowd. "We apologize for the confusion, ladies and gentlemen. Due to an unforeseen conflict of interest, we have no choice but to revoke the grand prize from Ms. Bialek and Mrs. Nichols. We are delighted to declare Tyson and Tai Tottenham the winners of this year's Delicious Duet Dessert Championship!"

There were a few halfhearted cheers and heckles as Tai and Ty took the stage, but the media throng surged as one toward Amy and Linnie.

"Excuse me! Ms. Bialek!"

"Do you have a comment . . . ?"

"How does it feel . . . ?"

Linnie cringed and huddled against her big sister. "Okay, now I'm freaking out."

Amy threw out a straight arm like an NFL running back and charged through the masses. She used her other arm to shield Linnie's face from the flashbulbs and camera lenses.

"Coming through!" she bellowed. "Step aside." She continued zigging and zagging until they were safely out the door, then collapsed into giggles. "I feel like Angelina Jolie's bodyguard."

Linnie gaped at her in disbelief. "You're enjoying this?"

Amy shrugged. "It's been a long time since I had this much excitement. Now stop talking and run."

The Bake-Off

They hightailed it down the hallway, through the hotel's back exit, and into the alleyway, where all traces of the ANARKY graffito had vanished.

"Cam's people must have been busy." Amy jerked her thumb toward the brick wall.

"His people? He was probably down here with a bucket and a scrubbing brush himself." Linnie sighed. "Speaking of Cam, do you think the CEO of Delicious Sugar is interrogating him right now? Do you think his family will disown him? Do you think he's banning me from all McMillan hotels for the rest of my life?"

"Why don't you give him a call and find out?"

Linnie hung her head. "I don't actually know his cell phone number. Or his exact age or his permanent residence. I never bothered to ask, because I wasn't thinking about anything beyond a week-long fling. You were right. I treated him like a disposable boy toy."

"Cookie nookie." Amy nodded solemnly. She strode toward the sidewalk, raised her hand to summon a cab, and whipped out her cell phone. When a taxi pulled over, she dived into the back-seat. Linnie followed, though with considerably less enthusiasm.

"Who're you calling?"

Amy held up her index finger as she addressed the person on the other end of the line. "Yes, hi. I'd like to book two tickets to Las Vegas, please. The next available flight from JFK. We're on our way to the airport now."

"*What?* But all of our luggage is still up in our room! What about checking out of the hotel? What about your car?"

"Calm down; we'll be back in like fifteen hours." Amy shushed Linnie, then provided the customer service rep with passenger names and her credit card number. Then she clicked her phone shut and buckled her seat belt. "Road trip!"

"But we lost. They're going to shred our giant poster-board check. We'll never bake in this town again."

"Let's get one thing straight," Amy said. "We didn't lose; we won. Yes, we got disqualified on a ticky-tack technicality, but we still won. Now, before we spend five hours trapped in coach eating stale pretzels, call the pawnshop and make sure the brooch is still there."

"We're still short forty grand," Linnie pointed out. She dialed the pawnshop's number from memory.

"I'll work something out with them. Maybe they can put us on a payment plan, layaway, something."

"Don't you think I already asked them about that during our daily phone chats? They don't want to hear about hardship or installment loans or future earnings potential. They only want cash on the barrelhead." Linnie hung up as her call went to voice mail. "They open late on Fridays and Saturdays, and there's a three-hour time difference. But trust me: They're not going to budge on their payment terms."

"Don't be so sure." Amy flashed her big, disarming smile. "I can be very persuasive. And if worse comes to worst, Brandon and I have been saving money for his dental practice."

"Amy, no."

"Hey, if you tutor Chloe and Ben, maybe they won't need college funds."

"Absolutely not," Linnie declared. "I got us into this mess; I'll get us out."

"We're out of options, Linnie. We're also out of time. The most important thing right now is getting our hands on that brooch before Grammy, you know, needs it."

Linnie twisted her head and peered out the rear window as

the cab stopped for a red light. "How much time do we have before the flight?"

Amy checked the time on her cell phone. "If traffic's good, we'll get to the airport with about an hour to spare. Why?"

Linnie leaned forward and rapped on the seat divider with her knuckles. "Turn around, please. We need to go back to the hotel."

Chapter 26

"You don't have to do this right now," Amy said. "You don't have to do it at all."

"Yes, I do." Linnie cracked open the car door. The taxi had stopped in the round portico at the Hotel McMillan's main entrance, and while they were currently surrounded by other cabs, town cars, and vans, Linnie knew that once she got out, she'd be fair game for the media throngs.

"There are journalists and photographers all over the lobby." Amy glanced out the window. "Why not spare yourself the walk of shame and just track down Cam when we get back from Vegas?"

"I can't leave him wondering like that. He deserves better."

"Wow. There's that human decency again."

"I know. Frankly, it's a very disturbing trend." Linnie stepped out onto the curb before she lost her nerve.

"Meter's running," the cabdriver informed her.

"I'll be back in seven minutes or less. Time me."

When she pushed through the revolving door, all conversation stopped. The lobby was packed with contestants, but the only sound was the gurgling of the fountain in the back corner and a phone ringing at the front desk.

Why hadn't she thought to ask Amy if she had sunglasses in her bag? Well, too late. She'd have to do her perp walk sans shades, clad in a wrinkled white button-down shirt, red plaid pajama pants, and no bra.

She glimpsed a few of the Confectionistas by the concierge desk, and when she caught their eye, they turned their backs on her in unison.

"Are we filming?" she heard a reporter whisper to her crew.

"We're filming," the cameraman confirmed.

Great. She was going to be the James Frey of the Culinary Channel.

She forced herself to maintain a slow, stately pace until she reached the elevator bank. With a cheerful *bing*, the polished brass doors opened and Linnie stepped inside. The outbursts began before the doors closed:

"Oh my God! Did you see that?"

"She's got some chutzpah, showing her face after what she tried to pull."

"Who does she think she is?"

Linnie collapsed back against the wall and gulped down air. She had just faced her worst fear—public judgment and humiliation—and survived. Before today, she couldn't have imagined anything more excruciating.

But this morning, everything had changed. And while facing a lobby full of strangers had been bad, she knew that facing Cam would be a thousand times worse.

As the elevator trundled up toward the penthouse, her apprehension mounted. Every time the digital display ticked up another floor, she reached toward the keypad, desperate to disembark.

But she rode all the way to the top of the South Tower, and she didn't allow herself a moment's hesitation before knocking at the penthouse.

When Cam opened the door, his body was impeccably attired in his usual suit and tie, but his face looked haggard. One hand held a glass full of ice cubes and Scotch.

"Let me guess," he drawled, leaning against the doorframe. "You're here to seduce me."

"No." She gazed up him. "I'm here to explain."

He continued to block the doorway and made no move to invite her in. "Why didn't you tell me you were here for Delicious Duet?"

"I'd never been in a baking competition before, and I don't like to fail at things. I don't like to be judged."

"The list of things that you don't like just keeps getting longer." He refused to make eye contact. "Out of idle curiosity, is there anything you *do* like?"

She kept her chin up, undeterred. "I like you. But the more I liked you, the less I wanted you to know about me. I kept thinking that I'd just spend fifteen more minutes with you, and that would be enough."

He rubbed his jawline. "Fifteen minutes. Wow."

"But fifteen minutes was never enough."

The ice cubes clinked as he raised the tumbler to his lips and drained the remaining Scotch. "Here's what I can't figure out: Why did you let me burn the grilled cheese last night? Just so you could feel smug and superior about my incompetence?"

"Of course not. I can't make grilled cheese, either. The truth is, I'm a terrible cook." She sighed and gave a quick rundown of the situation with Grammy Syl, the szarlotka recipe, and the brooch in the Las Vegas pawnshop. "And now she's sick, and I really, really want to get it back for her. She doesn't know I lost it. She gave it to me when I was younger, before we knew how my life was going to turn out. I know that's no excuse, but it's my only explanation." She waited for him to respond, and when he didn't, she said, "Anyway, Amy's waiting downstairs in a cab. I promised her I'd be right back, and I don't want her to have to walk the gauntlet down there, so I have to leave."

"Then leave." He started to shut the door. "That's what you excel at."

She closed her eyes. "Cam, I'm sorry."

"I assume you've heard the gossip about the judge who got blackmailed last year? My brother was that judge. That's why I got named to the panel this year. I was supposed to redeem the family name."

"Oh no." She winced. "Is the fallout going to be really bad?"

He didn't answer her question, instead posing one of his own: "Why did you come up here to tell me all this?"

"Because I still want more than fifteen minutes with you."

"Touching." He threw her a sardonic smile. "But I'll have to think that over and get back to you."

Linnie finally understood how it felt to be on the receiving end of such cold, detached deliberation.

"How'd it go?" Amy demanded as soon as Linnie ducked back into the cab.

"Could've gone worse." She slithered down in her seat until her knees were jammed up against the divider and her head was hidden from view. "He could have actually stabbed me in the eye with a candy thermometer."

"Well, I'm proud of you. That took guts." Amy unzipped the inside pocket of her purse and pulled out a bag of peanut M&M's. "You deserve a special surprise."

"Special surprise?" Linnie tore open the bag and tossed a few candies into her mouth.

"Yeah. I keep an emergency stash of candy at all times. Just in case I'm stuck in line at the post office or something with the kids and I need to break out the heavy artillery. Extra-good behavior merits an extra-special surprise. And PS, I like the red ones."

"They all taste exactly the same," Linnie said as the cab pulled out into the street.

"Not true. The red ones have a little extra something." Amy cupped her palm, and Linnie picked out a few reds. "Thanks. Whew, what a morning. You know, not to get all schmaltzy, but I would hang out with you even if you weren't my sister."

Linnie bit into the sweet spheres of chocolate and gave up trying to mentally prepare for a whirlwind cross-country trip with no set itinerary, no guarantees, and no baggage. The time had come to relinquish her control-freak ways and take life minute by minute. "Hey, I've been thinking. If you still want to get those matching tattoos, I'm in."

Amy's jaw dropped. "Really?"

Linnie laughed. "No. But I had you going, didn't I?"

Chapter 27

From the outside, Longbourne Jewelry and Loan of Las Vegas looked more like a high-end luxury retailer than a pawnshop. There were no iron bars crosshatching the windows, no weeds or crumpled newsprint littering the walkway, no flickering neon sign. Instead, the storefront was tucked away in an upscale outdoor shopping plaza, with bright potted flowers flanking the doorway and a sparkling plate-glass window reflecting the late afternoon sun.

Amy could hardly wait to see what treasures lay inside. "My birthday is coming up. Do you think I could get a good deal on diamond studs or a tennis bracelet?"

Linnie's facial muscles started to twitch as they crossed the threshold. "Probably, but do you think you could really enjoy wearing jewelry that someone had to hock in a fit of desperation?"

"Yes," Amy replied without a moment's hesitation. "The glitter would distract me from the guilt."

While Linnie approached the clerk, Amy scanned the display cases. She saw Rolexes and pendants and even a jewel-studded tiara, but no brooch.

"I'm Linnie Bialek," Linnie said to the guy behind the cash register. "I've been calling every day to check on the status of my grandmother's brooch."

"Oh, sure. You're famous around here." He regarded her with a mixture of awe and apprehension. "Nice to finally meet you."

"Likewise." Linnie opened her wallet and started thumbing through the dollar bills and taxi receipts. "We'd like to buy back the piece. I still have the original claim ticket. Hang on; I know I put it in here."

The clerk shook his head. "Claim ticket doesn't matter. We don't hold anything once the grace period expires."

"We don't have all the cash right now, but these should get us off to a good start." Amy fanned out a trio of credit cards. "And I'm sure you can help us set up a payment plan for the rest. It'll mean so much to our poor grandmother, who's in the hospital. Really, I can't tell you how much we appreciate this."

"Yeah. That's not gonna happen."

"No, it'll be fine," Amy assured him. "I'm talking a very short-term loan, just until I can meet with my bank and get some paperwork started. My credit's excellent—you can check."

The clerk pushed the plastic cards back at her. "I don't know how to tell you this, but you're too late."

"How can we be too late?" Linnie cried. "I called yesterday, and you said you still had it."

"We did have it at that time. I'm sorry, but that's how it goes in this business."

"So you . . . you just sold it?" Linnie said. "And nobody called me?"

Amy returned the credit cards to her handbag and kept dredging through the contents, as if she might find a time machine in there along with all the crumpled tissues and lipsticks and special surprise candy.

"No offense, but we don't have to call you for permission to sell our merchandise," the clerk said to Linnie.

"But you knew I wanted it! That's . . . You . . . How . . . I'll . . . " Linnie sputtered and waved her hands.

Amy moved Linnie aside and took over. "Can you please tell us who the buyer is?" she asked the clerk.

He shook his head. "Our client information is confidential. The state of Nevada takes this stuff seriously."

"I promise we're not going to do anything shady; we're just going to give the new owner a chance to make a really sweet deal." Amy broke out her very sparkliest smile. "Pretty please?"

Another curt head shake.

So she pulled out her wallet and switched tactics. "I'll give you a twenty."

He stared her down, impassive.

"Okay, a fifty. And I'll throw in a free teeth cleaning."

"No."

"Well, there has to be *something* we could do to change your mind."

Now he looked alarmed, as though he suspected them of

trying to catch him breaking the law on hidden camera. "No means no," he said, his eyes darting around. "Don't make me call the cops."

Linnie spun on her heel, caught Amy's hand, and marched toward the exit. "We're outta here."

"Calm down." Amy stumbled behind her as she tried to keep up. "He's just bluffing."

"You might be willing to take that chance, but I am not. Spending the night in a Manhattan precinct is bad enough. I am not going to a Vegas holding cell. I'll die from the filth. I'll literally, physically die."

Amy racked her brain, refusing to give up. "What are we going to do now?"

"Hope Grammy doesn't bring up the brooch again, and if she does, change the subject." Linnie's complexion had taken on a grayish cast from the stress and fatigue, and her oversize white shirt was stained with cinnamon and pie filling. "Come on. Let's find a cab and get you back to the airport."

"You're not flying back to JFK with me?"

"I live here," Linnie reminded her. "My apartment is here, my job. Why would I go back to New York?"

"Because you have no choice. You have unfinished business."

Linnie surprised her by nodding in agreement. "When does our flight leave?"

"Not till midnight. We're on the red-eye, baby."

"So we have a few minutes?"

"And then some. Why?"

Linnie pivoted and ducked back into the pawnshop. "Because I think I may have found the perfect peace offering for the multi-millionaire baking judge who has everything."

Chapter 28

Linnie and Amy straggled back into the hotel lobby the next morning, jet-lagged, discouraged, and sporting pink sequined T-shirts they'd bought from the airport gift shop in a desperate bid for clean clothes: GOOD GIRLS GO TO HEAVEN, BAD GIRLS GO TO VEGAS.

While Amy searched her pockets for their room key, Linnie approached the front desk and placed a package on the counter. "I'd like to leave this for Cam McMillan, please."

The desk clerk picked up the phone, punched a red button on the keypad, and murmured two words into the receiver: "She's here."

Moments later, Linnie heard Cam's voice behind her. "So, you've returned to the scene of the crime."

She turned to face him, bracing for a fresh barrage of bitter accusations. But Cam appeared to have been replaced by a cardboard cutout of a corporate drone, cool and remote in his suit and tie. She had prepared herself for conflict and drama, but she had no idea how to thaw this psychological permafrost.

Fortunately, Amy jumped in to fill the awkward pause. "Hey, thanks for being so understanding about the late checkout."

Cam remained the picture of politeness. "It's our pleasure. I hope you enjoyed your stay."

"Feel free to charge my credit card for the extra night. Oh, and I raided the minibar, too. I owe you guys a bottle of sparkling water and a box of truffles."

"Consider it a gift from the hotel." Cam glanced back at Linnie for a moment. "That's quite a fashion statement."

"I only wear pink under duress." She cleared her throat. "I'll get your shirt dry-cleaned and send it back."

"That won't be necessary." His gaze remained shuttered.

She didn't know what else to say, so she handed him the heavy oblong box, her fingers brushing against his as she did so.

Amy was practically bouncing with anticipation. "Open it!"

As Cam untied the twine and lifted off the lid, his expression softened. He stared at the contents of the box, then finally made eye contact with Linnie. "It's . . ."

"Rosewood and ebony," Linnie supplied. "And antique. I think." The pawnbroker had assured her that the intricately carved chessboard was a collector's set, but she hadn't really been paying attention. She'd been too busy thinking about what Cam would say when he saw it, if he would look at her the way he had when they'd first played by moonlight.

"I know you have to think things over and get back to me, but when you're ready, maybe we could have a rematch." She flipped back her hair with a saucy little smile. "And this time, I'd even let you win."

Amy's eyebrows shot up.

His stony facade finally cracked. "Let me win?"

She shrugged one shoulder. "As an act of contrition."

For a moment, she thought she'd pushed too hard, risked too much. Then he handed the chess set to Amy and reached for Linnie.

"I'm all done thinking it over." He pulled her in for a kiss. "Let's get cracking on that rematch."

She gave herself over to the moment, returning the kiss without a shred of self-consciousness and threading her fingers through his hair. By the time they came up for air, his perfect coif was mussed and his jacket lapels were askew.

"Nice." Amy gave him a thumbs-up. "Rockin' the fauxhawk."

"Particle Man" started blasting away. Linnie and Amy both reached for their bags.

"It's mine." Linnie glanced at her cell phone screen, saw Grammy Syl's name on the screen, and tossed the phone to Amy. "It's for you."

"Oh no." Amy lobbed the phone back. "It's your phone; you talk to her."

"I can't talk to her right now."

"Well, I can't, either!"

"Well, *someone's* got to."

Cam intercepted the phone in midair. "Hello, this is Cam McMillan speaking. How are you, Mrs. Bialek? . . . Yes, Linnie's right here. . . ."

He offered the phone to Linnie, who warded him off with frantic arm waves.

"She's indisposed at the moment. May I take a message? . . . All right . . . All right . . . Yes, Mrs. Bialek . . . Absolutely . . . We'll be there as soon as possible." He turned off the phone and told the two sisters, "We have strict orders to report to your grandmother's doorstep posthaste."

"All three of us?" Amy asked.

"Yes, I'm to report along with the two of you. She was quite clear about that."

"What do you think she's going to do to us?" Linnie asked in a haunted whisper.

"I don't think she's going to *do* anything." Cam looked mystified by her trepidation. "She sounds like she just wants to chat."

"You say that because you don't know Grammy," Amy said.

"Yeah. She's not a chatter. She's a doer." Linnie swallowed hard. "We'd better get out of these T-shirts and back into our regular clothes. Not that it'll do us any good—you know she can sniff out deception from a mile away."

"What are you talking about?" Cam laughed. "She's a sweet, charming, little old lady."

Amy gave a sad head shake. "Poor sucker's never gonna know what hit him."

Chapter 29

"All right, both of you, remember what we talked about and stick to the plan." Linnie stood on the plastic daisies attached to Grammy's woven straw welcome mat and addressed Amy and Cam as though she were a general reviewing battlefield strategy. "Tell her anything you want about Delicious Duet, but nobody mentions the brooch."

"We heard you the first fifty times," Amy said.

"I'm serious. This woman is in her eighties with three brain aneurysms. She doesn't need any extra stress in her life right now."

"Nobody's going to tell her." Cam leaned in to kiss Linnie, but she refused to be distracted.

"If all three of us corroborate each other's stories, she can't break us. Amy and I have already been over this, but there's this classic problem in game theory called the prisoner's dilemma."

Cam sighed. "I'm familiar with the prisoner's dilemma. I won't crack."

"You need to stay focused. The minute she catches you in a lie—"

All three of them jumped as the door swung inward, revealing Grammy in her uniform of pearls, cashmere, and a floral-patterned apron. The enticing, homey scent of apple pie wafted into the hallway as she beckoned them into her lair.

"Darlings! I'm so glad to see you. Come in, come in."

"Something smells delicious," Cam said. He sniffed the air, practically drooling.

"I just took a szarlotka out of the oven."

"At nine o'clock in the morning?" Amy asked, incredulous.

"Baking soothes my shattered nerves, and these last twenty-four hours have been quite disconcerting. You'll stay and have a piece." This was a command, not a request. With a hand signal that looked suspiciously like something she'd learned from Cesar Millan, Grammy indicated that they should stay put while she went into the kitchen.

Amy, Linnie, and Cam milled around the family room in uneasy silence.

"We're doing fine," Linnie murmured. "Just maintain."

Grammy returned carrying a white wooden tray laden with four dainty china mugs containing herbal tea, which no one dared refuse.

"Well." She distributed the tea, perched on the edge of an overstuffed brocade chair, and gazed up at her granddaughters. "You two are the talk of the baking world. The Internet is abuzz."

"It was my fault," Cam said, stepping in front of the sisters. "I never told Linnie I was a judge and a sponsor."

"No, it was my fault." Linnie scootched around Cam. "I should have told him I was a contestant. He asked me flat out why I was in New York, and I didn't tell him the whole truth."

Amy remained at the rear of the pack. "Well, we all agree it wasn't my fault, so may I please be excused?"

"You may not." Grammy's tone was crisp. "Something else is going on with you girls."

Linnie tried to look innocent. "What are you talking about?"

"I've called you a dozen times since yesterday, and you won't pick up. Brandon refuses to breathe a word about your whereabouts. You're hiding something, and I intend to find out what."

Linnie started to sweat. "We've told you everything there is to tell. Cam and I got a little, um, carried away, and I should never have gone ahead with the finals without letting him know who I was, but we baked our hearts out yesterday. Our szarlotka was really good, Grammy."

"Delectable," Amy threw in. "Tai and Ty Tottenham are the real culprits here. Let's figure out what we're going to do to them."

Grammy sipped her chamomile and tightened the net. "It's time to serve the pie. I'm going to take each of you back into the kitchen, one at a time, and have a little chat."

Amy's eyes got huge. "Oh my God."

"Prisoner's dilemma," Cam intoned.

"Linnie, darling, you first." Grammy untied her apron and started toward the kitchen.

Linnie cracked.

"Forgive me, Grammy, for I have sinned." She threw herself down on the carpet and begged for absolution. "I admit it. I admit everything." A detailed confession poured out of her, starting with *The Joy of Cooking* and ending with the last-minute flight to Vegas. "Please, please, you have to forgive me."

There ensued a long pause. Everyone stared at Grammy, waiting for her reaction.

"What happened to maintaining?" Amy whispered.

"So much for the prisoner's dilemma," Cam said.

"The guilt!" Linnie buried her face in the carpet fibers. "The guilt is eating me alive. I just want you to know that I'd do anything to fix this, Grammy."

Grammy still didn't turn around to face them.

"She knows she screwed up, and she's really sorry," Amy said. "Don't worry; I already gave her a good talking-to."

"I should have told you weeks ago." Linnie struggled back into an upright position.

Grammy still didn't turn around, but she finally spoke. "Indeed you should have. And you, Amy. How long have you known about this?"

"Um . . ."

"My grandmother's brooch." Grammy Syl sounded desolate. "Why didn't you tell me about this when there was still a chance to fix your mistake? I would have helped you. I would have figured out a way to get it back. But you knew it was gone and let me keep talking about it like a doddering old fool."

"I should have told you," Linnie murmured. "I know. But I felt so ashamed. I didn't want to disappoint you."

"We didn't want to add to your worries," Amy said.

Grammy nodded. "And do you feel better now that you've unburdened your consciences?"

"No," the sisters chorused.

Grammy dismissed Cam with a wave of her hand. "You may go. Vasylina, come with me. We are going to discuss this further in private."

Linnie shuffled into the kitchen as if she were wearing leg irons and hunched over the table, memorizing the pattern of the wood grain and wishing she'd stayed in Vegas. But Grammy didn't say another word about the brooch. Instead, she presented Linnie with a chair and warm slice of pie.

"Sit."

"Did you just bake this today? Grammy, you need to take it easy. You heard what the doctors said; you shouldn't be—"

Grammy handed her a fork and a napkin. "Eat."

Linnie took a bite and rocked back in her chair. "Holy cow. This is good. Ridiculously good. This puts the szarlotka Amy and I made to shame."

Grammy sat down next to Linnie and tapped her fingers on the tabletop. "Linnie, Linnie, Linnie. What am I going to do with you?"

"I don't know." Linnie couldn't resist another bite of pie. "But listen, you can't blame Amy for any of this. Cam, either. I am the failure here. I am the problem."

"You've always been intense. Even when you were very young, you were so different from other children. I never could connect with you the way I did with Amy." Grammy's eyes welled with regret.

"Don't feel bad about that, Grammy. Amy is easy to love, and I . . . well, I'm not. I know that."

"Darling, I don't love you because you deserve it. I just love you." She covered Linnie's hand with her own. "You always need to win, and it breaks my heart."

Linnie used her fork to push around the crumbs and chunks of apple on her plate.

"Come here, Vasylina." Grammy enfolded Linnie in her small, strong arms. "I don't care that you lost our legacy. I don't care that you got disqualified. None of your mistakes make me love you any less. But, on the flip side, none of your achievements make me love you any more."

Linnie had to laugh a little. "Then why bother doing anything?"

"You're such a smart girl, but so scared." Grammy kissed the top of her head. "Love is terrifying, I know. But love anyway."

Linnie closed her eyes and breathed in the unique scent of her grandmother's hug: talc and perfume mixed with undernotes of sugar and spice. "I'm trying."

"Good girl. And no more secrets between us; do you hear me?"

"All right, but that goes for you, too, then." Linnie went back to devouring her pie. "I know this isn't the recipe you gave us. You're holding out on us. Come on, tell me the secret ingredient."

"I have no idea what you're talking about." Grammy took Linnie's plate and rinsed it off in the sink. "But now that we're finished here, would you go back to the living room and send in your sister, please?"

Chapter 30

"My taste buds are having a rave inside my mouth right now." Amy shoveled another piece of szarlotka into her mouth. "Grammy, seriously, what did you do to this pie?"

Grammy beamed and basked in the praise. "I baked it with extra love."

Amy rolled her eyes. "Don't give me that love crap. Admit it—you laced this with crack."

But Grammy was finished with small talk. She topped off Amy's mug of tea and settled in next to her at the kitchen table. "Well, dear heart, you know I'm disappointed about what happened to the brooch, but in many ways, it's a blessing that it's gone. I wouldn't want you and Linnie to fight over it."

"We wouldn't." Amy paused. "Much. Although, honestly, I

always wondered why you gave it to her instead of me. I mean, I know I'm not the chosen one in the Bialek family, but all the time we spent together, all those weekends and matinee movies . . . I thought we had fun."

"We did have fun." Grammy's smile turned wistful. "And that's why I had to give that brooch to your sister. You got my time and attention. You got the best of me. I've always regretted not having a closer relationship with Linnie."

"Oh."

"Much as I'm sure your parents are sorry that they didn't have a closer relationship with you."

Amy rested her chin on her hand, her elbow on the table in flagrant violation of Grammy's rules. "Hmm."

"Things happen, darling. Time passes. By the time Linnie was old enough to make decisions for herself, it was too late for me to be part of her childhood. So instead I gave her the material possession that was closest to my heart." She tapped Amy's elbow.

Amy straightened up into perfect posture. "Remember when you used to make me walk around with a dictionary on my head?"

"I remember, though I often despair that it did you any good."

"How can you say that? Look at this poise." Amy sipped her tea with exaggerated delicacy. "I make Audrey Hepburn look like a hunchback."

Now Grammy placed her elbows on the table and leaned forward to buss Amy on the cheek. "You're a lady of many talents."

"So will you ever get over your disgrace and disappointment?"

"On the contrary, I've never been prouder. When you entered this contest, you could barely make brownies from a mix. And look at you now—a culinary goddess!"

"Well, let's not get carried away," Amy said. "I can make the apple filling for szarlotka, but that's it."

"You underestimate yourself. Starting this weekend, you and your sister and I are going to bake our way through my greatest hits." Grammy nodded toward the punched-tin recipe box on the shelf above the sink. "Everything you loved growing up: my Christmas bread, my cranberry pudding, my almond mazurka."

"Mmm. Christmas bread." Grammy's swiateczny, a cake made with orange and lemon peel, vodka, and obscene amounts of butter, was the stuff of legends. The finished product was basically a drunken, creamy fruitcake, and Amy couldn't imagine celebrating the holidays without it.

"You can make it for Chloe and Ben when they get older, just like I made it for you. Keep the family traditions alive."

"Well, the traditions might get a few new twists; I'm sure Linnie will find ways to refine the recipe. She'll probably distill the vodka herself from organic potatoes."

"Then it's settled. We'll bake, all three of us. And when the time comes, I expect you girls to make a swiateczny to feed the guests after my memorial service."

"Stop planning your own funeral," Amy pleaded. "It's so creepy and depressing."

"Promise me." Grammy didn't look depressed at all. In fact, she seemed to relish the prospect of directing her own memorial service from beyond the grave. "Promise me you'll bake it together. From scratch." When Amy hesitated, she added, "You can't refuse me, darling. It's my last request."

"You sure have a lot of last requests."

"And I'm so fortunate to have such loving granddaughters to grant them all."

"Fine." Amy threw up her hands. "I promise."

"Excellent. I'll see you and Linnie here Sunday morning at nine. Bring some flour and chopped walnuts and don't be late. But for now, I'm afraid I'm going to have to ask all of you to clear out."

Amy carried her plate to the sink and started to wash the dishes. "Aren't you going to stay at our house? You must be exhausted after this week, and I'm sure you want to sleep in your own bed, but—"

"Bed?" Grammy Syl laughed. "I have to get ready for lunch with Hal, and then I have pinochle night with the girls."

"Grammy. I hate to be the wet blanket here, but you have kind of a dire medical condition. Don't you think you should take it easy?"

"I'll take it easy when I keel over." Grammy gave her a spirited smile. "Until then, I intend to savor every single second."

Chapter 31

Five weeks later

"Auntie Linnie! Auntie Linnie!"

As soon as Amy and Linnie entered the Nicholses' kitchen through the side door, a pair of two-year-olds tackled Linnie's knees and reached up, imploring her to hug them. Though they had met their aunt for the first time only a month ago, the twins had wasted no time declaring her their "fun" aunt. Auntie Linnie could take the dishwasher apart and put it back together again. Auntie Linnie could name every dinosaur and recite entire Dr. Seuss books from memory. Auntie Linnie could play "Particle Man" on the piano.

Amy set down her overstuffed tote bag and observed this

exuberant display of affection with amusement. "Hello? Remember me? The woman who gave you life? I'm home, too."

"Hi, Mama." Ben gave her a quick wave, then went back to slowly cutting off Linnie's air supply with his arms wrapped around her neck. Chloe stroked Linnie's long blond hair with reverence.

Brandon rested his hands on Amy's waist and gave her a kiss. "*I'm* glad you're home. How'd the photo shoot go?"

She kissed him back, then twirled across the kitchen, startling the dog from his nap. "It was long, it was demanding, and it was eighty kinds of awesome because it was *my* project. I learned a ton. We were shooting the package art for a frozen shepherd's pie, which is a pale, gloppy nightmare to work with, but we ended up plating it on retro Fiesta ware and jazzing up the top with yellow and green veggie garnishes. The lead stylist showed me all kinds of tricks. Next weekend, we're prepping organic dog biscuits for a pet-magazine photo spread. The stylist said I might even get a credit in the magazine. You know, the microscopic print alongside the photo."

"Wow." Brandon looked sincerely impressed.

"I know. I never thought I'd be so thrilled to see my name in four-point type. Who needs a front-page headline?"

He peeled the twins off Linnie and tried to herd them into the family room. "All right, guys, Mommy and Auntie Linnie have to bake a cake."

Chloe opened the cabinet in the kitchen island and tried to drag out Amy's bright red electric stand mixer. "Me help."

Ben glanced around hopefully, then asked, "Grammy?"

The adults exchanged a look as silence fell over the kitchen. Grammy Syl had died in her sleep a few days before, quickly and quietly. Though everyone had tried to prepare for her death on an intellectual level, the emotional impact had been devastating, and Amy had deliberately overscheduled herself, trying to stave off the grief. She dreaded sifting and whisking and all the baking activities that reminded her of Grammy, but a promise was a promise.

Linnie started washing her hands in the sink, her face hidden from view. "We'd better get started on the swiateczny," she said, her voice a bit too hearty. "It's supposed to mellow overnight in an airtight container, right?"

"Ben and Chloe, we need you to help us roll out piecrusts." Amy seated the children at the kitchen table with a pair of miniature rolling pins and some metal cookie cutters. "Linnie, did you happen to save any of the play-dough you guys made yesterday?"

"Mooch ate most of it." Linnie pulled a huge, sealed plastic bag out of the refrigerator and scooped out hunks of goo. "But we made slime, too." She glopped some of the substance into a mixing bowl and let the twins stir it with wooden spoons.

Amy looked at the bright green gunk with dismay. "What is that?"

"It's just water, glue, laundry starch, and food coloring. Making our own slime is much more educational than buying some prepackaged crap at the toy store."

"It's educational, but is it machine washable?"

"I guess we'll find out."

"We baking, Mama," Chloe announced with great pride.

Brandon took a seat at the far end of kitchen table so he could keep one eye on the kids and the other on the hockey game on TV in the family room.

Amy opened the refrigerator and pulled out two sticks of

unsalted European butter. "This cake had better be a showstopper. It was Grammy's last request. Her *last* last request."

Linnie nodded and grabbed the egg carton. "Plus, those pinochle players from the senior center are brutal food critics."

"No kidding. I have more performance anxiety about this than I did for the Delicious Duet finals. Speaking of which, have you seen this?" Amy grabbed the newspaper off the counter and flipped to the circular ads, which featured a full-color print ad of Tai and Ty feeding each other bites of turtle tart and laughing like honeymooners. Beneath the photo was the recipe for their "blue-ribbon" dessert.

"Retch." Linnie made a face. "Our modeling shots were far superior."

Amy read the caption aloud: "'All the ingredients for family fun: love, laughter, and Delicious sugar.'"

"They left out blackmail, attempted homicide, and emotional abuse."

"So what are we going to do to them, anyway?"

"What do you mean?"

"Well, I assume you have some diabolical scheme already in motion." Amy crossed over to the pantry and scanned the shelves for flour, sugar, salt, vanilla, and raisins. "What'll it be? Chemical warfare? Shut down their mainframe?"

Linnie plunked herself down on a tall stool and yawned. "Do you even know what 'shut down their mainframe' means?"

"No. That's why this is your department." Amy dumped the pile of dry goods onto the countertop.

"The thing I keep coming back to is that Tai—the female Tai—has her hands full with that guy. Even though she won, she's lost in every way that counts."

"What? The old Linnie would be calling for fire and brimstone and a plague of locusts. Someone's gone soft." The phone rang, and Amy hesitated. Friends and family members had been calling all week with condolences, but she'd let everything go to voice mail. She just wasn't ready to talk about Grammy Syl yet. But when she saw the name on caller ID, she picked up.

Who is it? Linnie mouthed.

Amy held up the receiver, and from across the kitchen, Linnie could hear Rhodes barking.

"Nana!" The twins glanced up from their mixing bowl.

"Hi, Mom," the two sisters said in unison.

Amy wedged the receiver between her shoulder and ear and started drawing horns and fangs on Tai and Ty. "Yes, Linnie's right here, actually. We're making a cake for the memorial service tomorrow." She paused, listening for a moment, then said, "Sure . . . no problem . . . The kids will be thrilled."

Chloe and Ben were clamoring to say hi to their nana, so Brandon took the phone and the children into another room, leaving the sisters alone in the kitchen.

"So what's going on?" Linnie asked.

"Mom and Dad met with Grammy's estate lawyer and checked into their hotel," Amy reported. "They're planning to drop by after dinner. Rhodes is going to be bunking at Chez Nichols for a few days—Mom says the hotel room is not to his liking. I'm guessing that's code for 'the other guests were complaining about the barking.'" She leaned down and gave Mooch a consoling scratch behind the ears. "Brace yourself, little buddy. You're about to get a very high-maintenance roommate."

Linnie nodded. "Good. I haven't seen them in over a year, and it's time I stopped avoiding their calls and cringing every time they bring up my wasted potential. Grammy Syl was right—life is too short for this dysfunctional nonsense."

Amy saw her opening and pounced. "I'm glad to hear you say that, because next week, I'm pricing plane tickets for Rhodes's UDX celebration in May. Want to fly down with us?"

Her sister started flipping through the newspaper on the kitchen island. "I'll have to check my schedule."

"Don't give me that. It's a family celebration in honor of their favorite child."

Linnie rolled her eyes. "It's a dog's graduation party."

"Yeah, and it's going to be a very swanky soiree, so you'd better look sharp. Remind me to take you shopping next time we're in New York. Oh, and Mom asked me if we could come a day early and make a special cake for Rhodes and his bichon frise girlfriend from the dog park."

"What kind of cake?"

"She said she found a recipe online involving dog food and carob." Amy pondered this new culinary challenge. "We could bake a sheet cake and frost it up like a diploma, with a bunch of Snausages where the gold seal should go. It'll be a great addition to my food styling portfolio."

Linnie started to look overwhelmed. "I don't know, Amy. I'm really not a dog person. All the jumping, the slobbering . . ."

"Have no fear." Amy grinned. "We'll give you one glass of champagne at the beginning of the ceremony, and you won't remember a thing. You might even have fun. Besides . . ." She paused for effect. "It's what Grammy Syl would want."

"Oh no. I'm going to get Grammy Syl guilt trips from beyond the grave?"

"It's my job as the older sister to keep the legacy alive."

Linnie yawned again. "Do I have time for a quick nap?"

"You slept all the way here on the train." Amy *tsk-tsk*ed. "Were you and Cam up all night again?"

At the mere mention of Cam, Linnie went misty-eyed and moony. "You know, I never understood the appeal of sweets before, but there's something about whipped cream on washboard abs. I'll never turn away a dessert menu again."

"If you guys don't learn to pace yourselves, you're both going to die of sleep deprivation."

"I'm going have more trouble making it to the eight-thirty lectures than the freshmen who just turned eighteen. Speaking of which, I got my SAT scores on Friday."

"And?"

"Ninety-eighth percentile for my overall score. I screwed up the writing portion."

"Only you would consider scoring in the ninety-eighth percentile 'screwing up.'"

"That's exactly what Cam said. Anyway, I have appointments to talk to admissions counselors at NYU, Barnard, and Columbia next week."

"Good for you." Amy gave her sister a little golf clap. "I knew you'd go back and finish college one day."

"Oh, college is only the beginning. I'm back on the MD track. I'm not stopping until I become a neurosurgeon."

Amy blinked. "But isn't becoming a neurosurgeon going to require a lot of training? Like, a *lot*?"

"Well, I have to finish college, then go through med school, residency, and fellowship." Linnie ticked off the requirements on her fingers. "So about sixteen years total. That's for a normal person, though. I figure between large class loads, summer semesters, and previous credits, I can shave off a few years. But yes, I'll be over forty by the time I'm finished. Turns out, I'm going to be a very late bloomer."

Amy hesitated, not wanting to offend her sister. "Are you sure that's a good idea? Considering what happened the last time you started a premed program?"

Linnie's gaze sharpened with intensity. "Last time I went to college, I did it because everyone else wanted me to. This time, I'm doing it for me. An MD is more than an intellectual status symbol to me now. After what happened to Grammy Syl . . . If *I* had been her surgeon, I would've saved her. Trust and believe."

"Well, you've already got the God complex down, so you're off to a good start." Amy pulled an apron over her head and turned around so Linnie could tie up the back. "And if anyone has the smarts to make it through med school, it's you."

"Just as important as smarts, I've got steady hands. All those years at the blackjack table are going to translate to virtuosity in the OR."

"College and medical school," Amy mused. "You're looking at a whole lot of tuition."

"Yeah, I've been thinking about that, and I can always work weekends at the blackjack tables in Atlantic City." Linnie suddenly sounded too casual, almost cagey. "I could make decent tip money if I act cheerful and friendly and, you know, pretend to be you. Plus, Kyle swears he's going to pay me back a hundred dollars a month for the next thirty-three years."

"Uh-huh." Amy could tell there was a *but* coming.

"But I was doing some research last night, and it turns out there's a gingerbread house competition in Virginia every Christmas, and the winner gets fifty grand."

Amy backed away from the table. "No."

"Then there's the annual chicken cook-off in Chicago every summer for a hundred thousand dollars, and a cookie challenge in Texas worth almost a quarter of a million."

"Linnie. We're pie pariahs. We're the new Tai and Ty."

"So what? We can't go back to Delicious Duet, but we're still legally eligible for other competitions. It's not like the Olympics; there's no International Baking Federation to ban us for life. Let everyone gossip. Let them judge us. You and I both know that our szarlotka was good enough to win. All we have to do is win one big competition a year. I could pay my tuition; you could buy Brandon a dental practice."

Amy kept shaking her head, even though she felt her resolve weakening. "Didn't you learn anything from the fiasco we just went through?"

"Yes, I learned everything I need to know to make sure we win the next one." Linnie's brown eyes sparkled. "Come on, Amy. We can do it. You know we can. Let's look right now—what kind of cookie recipes did Grammy have stashed away?"

"You're a bad influence."

"A bad influence who's going to help you put your kids through college with chocolate-chip cookies."

"Hang on; let me get the box." Grammy had brought over her recipe box when they embarked on their multigenerational baking marathon a few weeks ago. "These are more valuable than any jewelry," Grammy had told them, holding the battered tin box as if it were a gem-studded gold coffer. "All of these recipes have also been passed on from my grandmother and her grandmother."

Amy flipped through the yellowed, dog-eared index cards.

"We need to transcribe these and laminate the originals," she said. "They're going to disintegrate if we keep handling them."

"Didn't she organize these at all?" Linnie peered over Amy's shoulder. "At least she should have alphabetized them, or grouped them by main course versus dessert."

"Wait, we definitely need this one." Amy located the card labeled *Swiateczny*. When she tried to extract it, the card remained lodged in the box. "It's stuck."

"Well, don't rip it," Linnie cautioned. "If we're careful, we can probably separate it from whatever card it's stuck to."

At that moment, the card came loose, along with a small bundle of tissue paper.

"What the hell?" Amy and Linnie unwrapped the tissue to reveal the platinum-and-diamond brooch, along with the claim ticket from the pawnshop and a note in Grammy Syl's feminine script:

L—

Your hands are fast, but my eyes are faster. You can't fool a fooler, darling.

XX, Grammy

P.S. Add two teaspoons of vanilla to the szarlotka filling.

"She knew," Linnie breathed. "She must have seen the claim ticket the morning we came back from the drunk tank."

"She always did love to have the last word." Amy picked up the brooch and held it up for inspection. The intricate grooves carved into the platinum were a bit grimy, but the cognac diamonds glittered with an inner fire. "But how'd she get this back?"

"Who knows? Maybe she wired the pawnbroker the money and had him send it to her. Maybe she had a crony in Vegas to do her bidding. The real question is, If she knew about all this the whole time, and she knew she was getting the brooch back, why did she let us fly to Vegas and then grovel for forgiveness in her kitchen? To torture us? To teach us a lesson?"

"To bring us together," Amy said softly.

"See? I rest my case. She wanted us to keep baking as a team. Her recipes are our inheritance, and this Christmas cake is a masterpiece. It's just selfish not to share it with the world." Linnie picked up the canister of raisins and rolled it between her palms. "Although I've been thinking. I know that Grammy used raisins soaked in hot water, but they might taste even better if we mix in a little bourbon."

"I don't know." Amy nibbled her lip. "Should we really be tampering with perfection?"

"Nothing's so perfect I can't improve it just a little bit."

"Spoken like a future neurosurgeon."

"Hey, people can say a lot of things about the pair of us, but they can no longer claim we can't bake. This cake is going to taste delicious, thanks to me; it's going to look exquisite, thanks to you; and it's going to keep Grammy right here with us while we figure out what comes next." Linnie spooned raisins onto the food scale and did the mental conversion from cups to ounces in her head. "We're Bialek girls. We have a reputation to uphold."

"A reputation for starting scandals, breaking rules, and making scenes." Amy laughed. "At least we're not boring."

"Exactly. We stick together and get things done. And if anyone else has a problem with that . . ."

Amy set the oven to three fifty, affixed Grammy's antique brooch to her apron, and finished Linnie's sentence for her. "Let them eat cake."

Grammy Syl's Christmas Eve Cake

ANNOTATED BY LINNIE BIALEK

SUGGESTED SOUND TRACK: Tchaikovsky's *Nutcracker Suite*,
Bing Crosby's *White Christmas*

Ingredients:

½ cup golden raisins

½ cup dried cranberries

Boiling water

½ cup Granny Smith apple, peeled and diced

½ cup grated orange peel

¾ cup finely chopped walnuts

2 ½ cups flour (set aside 2 tablespoons of this)

2 tablespoons baking powder

¼ teaspoon salt

2 cups powdered sugar

5 eggs

1 cup butter, softened to room temperature

1 tablespoon grated lemon peel

2 teaspoons vanilla

3 tablespoons vodka, plus an extra splash for the hot water

Instructions:

Preheat oven to 350 degrees.

Butter and flour a glass baking pan, 9 x 13 inches.

Prep the fruit filling

Combine the golden raisins and dried cranberries in a bowl. Bring water to a boil and submerge the dried fruit. Spike the hot water with vodka or brandy as desired.

Peel and cut up the apple into quarter-inch cubes, then grate the orange and lemon peel. Better yet, convince your baking partner to do all this while you put on some festive holiday music.

Set aside 2 tablespoons of flour.

After the dried fruit plumps up, drain the mixture.

Combine the raisins, cranberries, chopped walnuts, apple pieces, and grated orange peel with the 2 tablespoons of flour. Set aside the lemon peel for the cake batter.

Make the cake batter

Sift together the remaining flour, salt, and baking powder.

Attempt to stop your baking partner from changing the music to Run-DMC's "Christmas in Hollis."

Using a hand mixer or stand mixer, beat together the eggs and powdered sugar on high speed for 2 minutes.

Using a stand mixer, beat together the butter, lemon peel, and vanilla.

Add the vodka to the butter mixture and resume mixing.

Slow down the mixer to stirring speed and pour in the egg mixture.

Stop the mixer and add the flour mixture at three to four intervals, mixing thoroughly between additions. (Mix just enough to combine all ingredients—do not overmix. Or else.)

Using a silicone spatula or large spoon, fold in the fruit filling, again mixing just enough to combine.

Bake at 350 degrees for 30 minutes, or until sides and top are golden brown and an inserted toothpick comes out clean.

Try to dissuade your niece and nephew from changing music to "I Want a Hippopotamus for Christmas." Give up, give in, and sing along at the top of your lungs.

After removing the cake from the oven, allow it to cool in the pan for 10–12 minutes. Run a knife edge between the cake edge and the pan; then turn the cake onto a wire rack and allow to finish cooling.

Once cake has cooled completely, store in an airtight container for 24–48 hours before serving. This allows the flavors to "muddle and mellow" (Grammy Syl's words, not mine) into rich, buttery perfection.

Serve with whipped cream or ice cream. Happy holidays!

Acknowledgments

Thank you to . . .

Susan Miller, Confectionista extraordinaire, who generously shared tales from the trenches of cooking competitions.

Pastry goddess Carol Blonder, who introduced me to the "Zen sport" of rolling pastry dough and gave me the courage to attempt piecrust from scratch.

Tai Burkholder, who said, "I'd be thrilled if you named a character after me! It could even be a villain!" Um, thank you and I'm sorry. I owe you a Costco-size pallet of Crystal Light.

Police officer Eric Whittington and Superior Court Judge Joseph Heilman, who answered my endless questions about jail, bail, and what a nice suburban girl has to do to get arrested on a school night.

Marc Reid and Ori Brown of the Marc Reid Salon, who dished about what it's really like on a photo shoot. When *Vogue* asks me to pose for the cover, I'll be calling you both to act as my glam squad.

Danielle Perez, my wonderful editor and late-night e-mail

buddy, who shares my love for baked goods and high-maintenance dogs.

Christina Hogrebe and Meg Ruley, my amazing agents, for keeping me sane and gainfully employed. Because of you, my corporate dress code is fuzzy slippers and my coworkers are canine. Who could ask for anything more?

Beth Kendrick is still mastering the Zen art of making piecrust, but she can whip up a decadent chocolate-cranberry cheesecake, and her chocolate-chip cookies have been described as "utopian." Her previous novels include *Second Time Around*, *The Pre-nup*, and *Nearlyweds*. She lives in Arizona with her family and a pair of unruly rescue dogs. Visit her Web site at www.BethKendrick.com.